The Fifth Axis

A STORY OF WITCHKIND

AUTHOR'S PREFERRED EDITION
BOOK THREE

DON JONES

 Created with Vellum

The Fifth Axis

A STORY OF WITCHKIND

After thousands of years, the Fifth Axis—the primal force of Creation and Beginnings—has been Forged. But now Aron, the newly minted Adherent of the Fifth, goes on a spree of destructive and dangerous Creation, starting unstoppable storms, earthquakes, and other disasters.

Daniel Scratch, Adherent of the Sixth Axis of Death and Endings, must stop him. But Daniel's own powers have become erratic and unreliable, leaving him breathlessly traveling the world in an attempt to stop Aron, discover his motivations, and protect the world.

This epic conclusion to the Adherents of the Axes trilogy will have Daniel questioning everything he's ever known about power, responsibility, magic, and even the world in which he lives.

Also by Don Jones

Daniel Scratch, a story of witchkind®

Master of the Tower, a story of witchkind®

Clara Thorn, the witch that was found

Endless Sky®: Truthsayer

The Never: A Tale of Peter and the Fae

Free eBooks!

The Achillios Chronicles trilogy, *The Prime Wave Accounting* duology, and *short stories of witchkind* are all available **for free** by joining the author's newsletter at DonJones.com.

for Meghan Riley

Contents

the world
Bryssi
Greensea
Great Northern Wood
Soloton
Northsea
Chiton
Rushford
Farreach
Lastpointe
Evermore
Landshire
Duocastella's
Tallesin
Westhead
Fyngershire
Spurham
Twynsits
The Tower of Endings
Lakewood
Withring
Cuppton
Little Bay
Carvendam
Meadowside
Disemstoke's
Nworlons
Hook
Baythwaite
Nek
Pease
Harbsmouth
Wisding
Farreach
Thornwaith's
Soysen

CHAPTER 1

The Search

I bolted upright in my bed, drenched coverings falling away from me.

For the first time since I'd come to the Tower, I'd tossed and turned all night, slipping in and out of a dreamless, unsatisfying unconsciousness that couldn't truly be called sleep. Visions of the Great Northern Wood haunted me. The Karal, my rivals, had leashed a power we all thought would go untamed. The Fifth Axis. My brain had been fumbling at deciphering the implications.

Just before dawn, absolute exhaustion had claimed me, dragging me into a welcome numbness. Then came the pain, searing and stabbing, that blasted through my eyes and into the center of my brain.

Aron. The name settled into my mind even as the pain in my head faded. Without knowing how, without knowing why, I knew the pain was connected to the new adherent of the Fifth Axis. My twin. My opposite. The world's new embodiment of Creation, Life, and Beginnings.

With a low moan, I swung out of bed to start my day.

I ached. I'd been going nearly nonstop for days, working to repair the damage I'd done to the Veil, the magic that helped witchkind hide their true nature from the humans we lived among. My legs were sore. My back was stiff. My neck was acutely tender. My head throbbed. I was tired, truly tired, in a way I'd never been before. Even my eyes seemed bruised and beaten.

The flickering shadow servants of the Tower, the *driežai*, seemed to move more silently than usual, staying in the edges of my vision as if worried about bringing me further discomfort. On one of the Tower's open upper levels, peering out at the gray, choppy ocean from the stone crenelations, I slowly ate toasted bread and cheese and sipped steaming hot kavos. To the west, the second moon was setting. To the east, the sun began trudging its way through the cloud-smeared sky. The wind off the sea bore the first bite of winter, far too early for this time of year. The world, it seemed, was as off-kilter as I felt.

Aron. Again, my mind turned to the new adherent. I'd caught only a glimpse of him through the magics that had, after all these centuries, finally Forged the Fifth Axis. The Axis of Beginnings and Creation, of Life. The Axis that had somehow managed to avoid being Forged all those years ago. And now it was invested in Aron, a man of middling-brown skin, plain clothing, close-cut black hair—the perfect model of "average" among human and witchkind alike. He'd been enrobed by magic as the Fifth was chained to him. In that moment, my own power, my Axis, had been temporarily forced from my body. When I'd come to, Aron was gone. And I ached. I still ached. *I need to find him.*

With grim determination and the mug of kavos gripped firmly in my hand, I arrived at the Tower's second level. Each of the structure's upper levels had a specific, singular purpose aligned to one of the Axis's major Forms of Power: communication, judgment, defense, and so forth. The second level was a large, circular, nearly empty space, its sole attraction being the magically powered map table set against an exterior wall.

"Aron," I ordered the map. It could find almost anyone of witchkind, even an entire clan, simply by hearing the name. The map would zoom and slide until it displayed a bright mote of light indicating the target's location. I could zoom in farther, until buildings and even people moving about their day were clearly visible. But some of witchkind could hide from the map —a feat Clan Karal had managed when I'd been an apprentice in this Tower. And Aron was one of them.

The map didn't seem to know what to do. It jittered, slewing back and forth as if searching, but ultimately stopped, zoomed out to a continent-level view, and then . . . sulked. "Aron," I repeated, but the map made no move. I could feel its magic complaining darkly. I looked up to the shadow servant that always lingered here. "Nothing?" Faceless, it shrank into the stone wall, as if apologizing for its inability to obey. I sighed. "Fine." I stalked down the stairs to the main level rather than letting the Axis take me there instantly. Neither my head nor my stomach seemed ready for magically fueled travel.

I stepped off the wide, circular stone stairs when another lance of pain speared me, sending me to one knee. My now-empty mug fell out of my hand, shattering into several rough shards. *Driežai* swarmed instantly, carrying the pieces away and leaving me with a thudding heart and the taste of copper in my mouth. *Aron.* It was an absolute certainty in my mind, although I had no idea how or why. These jolts of pain were somehow his doing.

I leaned into the Axis, pushing my mind into the diffuse, world-spanning awareness that connected it to every Ending, everywhere. Endings of life, yes, but also Endings of everything. Arguments. Relationships. Dinners. Days. The Axis was aware of them all, complicit in them all. But it's awareness eddied and frothed, which was nothing like the smooth surety I'd come to know of it over the past three years. I held my breath, ignoring the throbbing pain that was already starting to fade, and *felt*.

There. A lazily spinning swirl in the Axis's awareness, centered on something . . . different. I gathered the Axis to me, invoking its Form of Travel, and took myself there.

I arrived amid an explosion of vegetation. The lush meadow, obviously far to the west and just brightening under the first touch of sunlight, thrust upward, tall grasses tickling my waist. Enormous clumps of brightly colored flowers blazed with in hues more intense than I'd ever seen: burning crimson, emeralds that all but glowed, ceruleans so deep they rivaled the clearest summer skies. Even under the last of the moon's waning light, the violets, titians, cobalts, and ambers stood out boldly from the blue-green canvas of tall grass.

The meadow pulsed with life. New life. Without question, this was the result of the Fifth—

I gasped as another hot pain seared through me. I forced myself to breathe deeply, to sink back into the Axis's distant awareness, until I found another gentle vortex. I took myself there.

This time, I found myself on a wharf. From the dim rose glow just beginning to lighten the sky, I figured myself somewhere in the southeast. A dozen fishing boats were still tied up, their crews staring in awe at the still-dark seawater beneath them. One shouted, and others began running toward the wharf from the town behind me.

The sea was full of fish.

It was as if these ships had crept out in the night, filled their nets with their catch, and then returned, only to empty their holds. The fish jumped and flipped, seemingly too numerous for the waters of the harbor. All around the ships, fish leaped and frothed, pushing over and past one another in confusion.

"Adherent," said a soft, deep voice at my side. A middle-aged man of witchkind. His blue eyes stood out against the dark skin of his face. "What's happened?"

"You're a fisherwitch?" I guessed. Few others of witchkind would be awake this early in a fishing town. He nodded, still transfixed by the glistening chaos before us. "I suspect," I said slowly, the pain in my head finally receding, "that the new adherent of the Fifth is exercising his powers."

The man looked at me, his eyes growing wide. "Did you say the Fifth?"

I nodded. "Forged at last, it would seem."

"So these fish. . ."

"Created by magic. Or drawn here. Probably the former. I don't know."

"When?"

"Yesterday. Hours ago, I think." I shook my head. "I've not slept in . . . days."

"Was this . . . the trouble with the Veil?"

I chuckled despite myself. "No, that was something else. Dealt with now. The Veil is fine. Provided this kind of thing"—I gestured to the water—"doesn't upset it again. No, we've stepped swiftly from one crisis to"—I indicated to where fish were finally beginning to sort themselves out and disperse—"to whatever this is."

"Will we—"

I gasped and fell to my knees.

"Adherent!" the man cried.

"It's fine," I managed between clenched teeth. The pain had receded more quickly this time, but its intensity had crested. "I need to go." Once again, I leaned into the Axis's distant awareness, found the whirlpool that represented Aron's use of his power, and took myself there.

This continued through the day: a stab of pain would announce Aron empowering a new Beginning. I would seek him out as quickly as I could, then take myself there. Without variation, I was met by a newly Created riot of life: meadows full of flowers, forests with new trees stretching toward the sun, fields of grain grown ready for harvest months early, sea cliffs covered in dense flocks of birds. Each time, no sight of Aron. I returned to the Tower late, exhausted and frustrated.

And it began again the next day. I followed much the same pattern, although the pace slowed throughout the day. Aron's Creations were becoming more deliberate and thoughtful—less extravagant. He was coming to grips with his power. But still, I never saw him, arriving moments too late each time.

And then he stopped.

No energy tugged at me. Not sharp, stabbing pain. It was evening. I waited, letting myself sink into my Axis's broader awareness, but after two hours, I gave up and returned to the Tower for another failed attempt at sleep.

On the third day, Aron's efforts were more noticeable, slicing into my mind like a thin knife. I didn't need the Axis to detect him—it hurt so sharply that I couldn't travel immediately, instead needing several long minutes to recompose myself. And of course, by the time I could investigate where the pain had come from, Aron was gone. Tiny new forests had overtaken what had previously been rolling meadows, each new tree evenly spaced in a perfect, orchard-like grid. The local rabbit population had exploded elsewhere, with so many small, furry gray bodies bounding about that I wondered how they'd manage to feed themselves. The next location was the most worrying: a small seaside village that had collapsed into a conglomeration of petty arguments. These I Ended as quickly as I could, but after questioning a few of the local witchkind, I found no one knew what had set them off. Aron's creations were becoming more abstract.

By evening, I found myself in a meadow where a new mountain had thrust up from the earth and reached toward the sky. Mesla, senior adherent of Earth, arrived moments after me, rising from the ground itself and shaking dirt from her simple brown shift. "What's happening?" she asked as she surveyed the new landmark.

"You don't know?"

"There have been messages. They've been . . . confusing. Something about the Fifth Axis."

"Nothing confusing about it." I sighed. "Clan Karal—or whatever they're calling themselves these days—finally did it. All the magic they stole with their machines, using Mother's identity rune—"

Mesla nodded, her eyebrows climbing to her hairline.

"That's what it was all for. They Forged the Fifth and anchored it to one of their own. A young man named Aron. About my age, I'd guess."

"You've seen him?"

"Briefly. As it was happening. I've been chasing him for days. Every time he does this, every time he Creates, I feel it."

"Through your Axis?"

"I assume so. It's incredibly painful, and I truly wish he'd stop. This is the boldest Creation yet," I added, nodding toward the spire of rock. "I think he's experimenting."

Mesla nodded slowly. "Debesi's people have been spreading messages, trying to figure it out. Have the humans noticed?"

I listened. Not to her, but to my Axis, to the world itself. Before Aron arrived, I'd spent considerable effort trying to heal the Veil, the magical construct that encouraged humans to ignore magic and find mundane explanations for the supernatural. Since then, I'd become more sensitive to the Veil, more aware of its existence. "No," I said slowly. "The Veil, at least, seems intact. And quiet. So far the humans may just see Aron's work as miracles from their gods." Most of their priests were, I suspected, more than happy to take credit for a bounty of fish or an inexplicable early harvest. I much preferred that to their Hunts on witchkind.

"You said you can feel it?"

"I couldn't possibly ignore it. It stabs through my mind like a hot poker. I don't know if he feels me as well, though."

"Why would you feel anything? You don't feel when we use our Axes, do you?"

I shook my head. "I never have. And I don't know. My Axis . . . when I was there, when they Forged the Fifth, my Axis seemed . . . eager. More than that. The magic was so powerful, so intense, it felt like my own Axis separated from me." Her eyes grew wider. "Just for an instant. Maybe my presence there linked Aron and me somehow. I don't know." I yawned.

"You look terrible."

"I *feel* terrible. I haven't slept properly in days."

"There's an inn not far—"

She stopped as I shook my head. "I'd just be drawn back to the Tower anyway. I might as well take myself there."

"A moment." She knelt and put her palm against the ground. It sank in, the earth like water to her. The power of Earth. She withdrew her hand, clutching a smooth sphere of shiny blue granite. "Take this. Lay it under your pillow."

I took the sphere and eyed it curiously. "What will it do?"

"It'll calm you. While you lie there, it'll make it hard to focus on anything. You'll find it soothing, I promise. It won't force you to sleep, but it'll help."

"Honestly, I'd welcome it forcing me at this point. But thank you."

She surveyed the rocky prominence before us. "You think he'll continue?"

"I've been chasing him for three days. He's been slowing down. This is the longest stretch I've had. Maybe he's tired."

"But maybe not tomorrow?"

I shrugged. "Who's to say? Gem—his family, a woman I spoke to, was there. She implied they had plans for him." My jaw clenched as I remembered Gemma's lies and betrayal.

Mesla frowned. "That seems . . . dark."

"I agree. I don't know their motives." I yawned again. "But I have suspicions. He's doing more than Creating rocks and forests. There was a village—I don't even know where I was, to be honest—where every man, woman, and child was engaged in a screaming match. The whole place, a thousand arguments."

Mesla wrinkled her brow. "Why would that be Aron?"

"I can End arguments. Stands to reason he could begin them."

"But why—oh."

I nodded. "If this is what his clan elders are pressing him to do—create strife, turmoil—well, now they know he can."

Her eyes grew wide as she considered the ramifications.

***

Either Mesla had understated the power of her gift, or I'd been so exhausted that I hadn't needed more than a nudge to welcome oblivion. My head still pulsed with a gentle ache, but I felt, if not refreshed, then at least less like a corpse-to-be.

I managed to finish breakfast without incident, washing down the last of the calming tea before an unexpectedly gentle twinge of pain stabbed my temples. I sighed, rubbing my head, before sinking back into the Axis and taking myself to yet another swirling vortex of magic.

"Oh!"

I blinked. Before me was a man around my age, with middling-brown skin, middling-brown hair, and middling-green eyes. He was wearing a crisp white shirt and black trousers, and his eyes were widening as he took me in. "Aron?"

He nodded vigorously. "You're Daniel?"

"You can tell?"

He smiled and touched a cheek.

Of course. My pale skin set me apart from most people, human and witchkind alike. "What have you been doing?"

His eyes sparkled with a sly gleam. "Practicing."

"Experimenting, you mean."

He shrugged. "Maybe that. I'm an Archon now."

I scowled. Is that what they'd told him? That he was an Archon? "You're not. Not really. The Archons Forged the Axes. Your family did this. Did it to you."

He frowned. "I'm still special."

"They told you that?" He nodded. "I suppose you are. Any adherent is."

"I'm the only one of me."

"True," I allowed. "As am I."

"Are you special as well?"

I chuckled, but there was no humor in it. "I guess I am. I doesn't always feel that way."

He frowned. "It hurts, sometimes. Like a headache."

"When you use your power?"

"No, usually just after. I've been taking myself away as fast as possible, but the pain still comes. It's fast, but hard."

"Taking yourself away how?" Every Axis had a Form of Travel, but I obviously knew nothing about his.

He shrugged, still rubbing the sides of his head. "It just does. I tell it, and it takes me." Not unlike my own Form of Travel, then. "But the pain still comes."

"It affects me too," I said slowly, earning a confused look from him. "I think I feel it every time you use your power. Maybe your own headaches come from me using mine."

"You've been . . . Ending people again?"

Again? What had his family been telling him about me? "No, I've been looking for you."

"Why?"

"Because I—" I started. That was an excellent question. Why was I looking for Aron? "The headaches, maybe. You . . . it felt connected to you, I think. Could I ask you to . . . just stop? Just not use your power for a while? I won't either."

His eyebrows lowered slightly, and he nodded. "Will the voices stop as well?"

My eyebrows drew together in confusion. "Voices?"

"In my head. They're loud. Indistinct. Insistent." He fluttered his hands around his head, frowning as he tried to describe something that he clearly didn't understand. "Pushing, proving, suggestion, wooing," he said in quick succession. He was rambling, but he managed to come back to himself after a moment. "I just want them to be quiet."

"I don't know. I've . . . there have never been voices. In my head." Which wasn't strictly true: while my Axis hadn't spoken to me as such, I had certainly felt its awareness. Its intelligence.

"It wants more, you know," he said, lowering his hands and taking a deep breath. "More, more, more."

"More of what?" I kept my voice calm, despite a sudden clenching in my chest.

"*More,*" he said insistently, his eyes suddenly boring into mine. "More of everything. I gave it more fish. More flowers. More birds. More—"

"I saw those things," I interrupted, holding out a hand in what I hoped was a calming gesture. "You don't have to do that all the time. They'll be born on their own, the fish and the birds. The flowers will grow on their own. You don't have to do it all." My Axis quietly attended to all the small Endings in the world without my intervention. I assumed his did the same with Beginnings.

"More grains," he continued more calmly. "Ending the growing season, quickly."

Ending?

"It wanted a mountain. To End all the flatness."

That didn't make sense. Mine was the Axis of—

"I can start arguments, you know," he said casually. "I can End the peace. Give people something to argue about."

As I'd Ended arguments, creating . . .

Oh. I'd Created peace, hadn't I? Kirmin, my mentor, had said Endings are the other face of Beginnings. And so Beginnings were the other side of Endings.

A cold trickle of fear dripped down my spine.

"It wants more," Aron continued, a sob catching in his throat. "To start more. To begin more. To have more. It's . . . anxious. Eager? It's been held back."

"It's been free for centuries," I argued.

"The Axis? I know. They explained it. Not that." His voice trailed off and his eyes seemed to unfocus slightly.

"I don't understand," I said. "What's been held back?"

He flapped his hands more wildly. "I don't know. It just hurts. And it won't stop. More, more, more. Make, make, make. Start new things, stop others." He fell very still and took a small step toward me, his eyes drilling into mine. I forced myself to stand my ground. "I need to make it stop." His voice was suddenly cold and flat.

"I don't—" I began, but he stepped back and waved me to silence.

His head cocked to one side, and his gaze seemed to look

over my shoulder. "They're in there too," he said in a distracted tone.

"Who?"

"Them. The elders." His voice was now that of a child's, one who'd done something wrong and was about to be punished. Small and fearful. Full of a gentle dread.

"Elders? Your clan, you mean?" He nodded, shrinking in on himself. He wrapped his arms around his chest, and a tear ran down one cheek. "What do they want?"

His eyes snapped back to mine, wet and afraid. "*Power.*"

He shook his head, more tears running down his face, and vanished.

CHAPTER 2

Family Ties

The only firm connection I had to Aron's family—my family, if you go back far enough—was Gemma. After she betrayed my trust, I had little desire to speak to her, but I knew of no other way to find Aron's masters. They'd once been called Karal, but they'd done something to End that, leaving me with no way to track them down.

I spent a frustrating few hours of searching in Tower's map room. Asking for Gemma resulted in another skittering, sliding performance that ended with the map zooming out and sitting sullenly still. But then it came to me: like everything else in the Tower, the map table was ultimately powered by my Axis—and my Axis had felt off for days. Even its stable, distant, diffuse awareness—the sense I'd used to chase down Aron—had felt unsteady. Perhaps that same disruption in my Axis's awareness was preventing the map table from working properly.

I tried to still myself as I sank into the world-spanning aspect of the Axis. It tossed me about like a dinghy lost at sea. But rather than fight to stay afloat or sink into it, I tried to exercise some control. I'd never managed to influence this part of the Axis before despite trying to give it orders. Now, I simply tried to give it calm—a calm I didn't entirely feel myself. My current state of exhaustion seemed to lend me a stillness that sufficed. Slowly, ever so slowly, the swirling slowed. I couldn't stop it, but I could at least reduce the Axis's apprehension, transmuting the roiling to gentle swaying.

As I came back to myself, I once again ordered the map table to find Gemma. it complied. Hesitatingly and jerkily, it slewed itself to focus on the town of Withring, where it reluctantly kindled a point of churlish green-gold light. It hovered over an unremarkable building—a human shop of some sort. Gemma was likely in a hidden space attached to it. Traveling their directly would be difficult, so the adjacent alley looked attractive.

I took myself there immediately, nausea suddenly gripping my stomach. *The Axis is still unsettled.* I wondered how bad it would get.

I'd arrived in an alley between two wood-and-stone buildings, and I braced myself against the nearest one until my head stopped spinning and my stomach righted itself. Was this all because of Aron? Was his mere existence enough to do this to me, or had the Forging of the Fifth damaged my connection to the Axis?

I shook my head, putting my questions aside. Time enough for them later. According to the map table, Gemma was in the very building I was leaning against. I pulled myself upright and walked toward the alley's mouth, rapidly scanning the structure for an entry rune. I found it at the very corner of the building, a shallow carving in a granite cornerstone, and tapped it, bracing myself as a swirl of cool magic—much gentler than my own had been that day—swept me inside.

I found myself in an entry foyer, a common-enough arrival point for witchkind residences. A comfortable, worn carpet adorned the center of the small room, covering well-polished wooden floorboards. Clean, plastered white walls surrounded me, and an arched doorway led to the rest of the residence. The witchkind who'd built this space could have filled it with almost anything, used almost any materials available to them. I'd always found it amusing that my people chose finishes and furniture so similar to those of their human neighbors.

The echoes of a gong were just fading, having announced my arrival. A rapid scuffle of footsteps followed.

"Daniel." I blinked as my eyes adjusted to the dim light, provided by unflickering yellow globes of light hanging from the ceiling. Gemma looked a couple of decades older than me, having dropped the glamour that once disguised her appearance. She frowned as she crossed her arms. "I'm surprised to see you here."

"I'm surprised to be here," I admitted. "But I need to find Aron. I need to know his—your—clan name."

"Now, Daniel, any clan that changes its name wants it kept a secret." Her smugness grated at me.

"I'd imagine." So they *had* managed to change their clan identity. Complex, difficult, and often painful, but not impossible. But for so many people? What could have made that worth their while? What was in it for the former Clan Karal?

"How did you even find me?" Gemma asked.

"I have my ways."

"Ah," she said, a mocking grin widening her mouth. "The mighty, mysterious adherent. I'll have to ask Aron if he can do something similar. Match you, so to speak."

"I still need to find him. Where is he? Or just tell me the new clan name so I can track him down myself."

She arched an eyebrow. "Why ever for? You can't undo the Forging."

Why would she think that was my goal? "Maybe. Maybe

not. That's not the point. He's been experimenting with his powers, causing no end of trouble. He'll endanger the Veil again if it continues."

"We'll endeavor to keep him leashed, then." Her tone was cool, confident.

"As you have been, you mean? You seem to have done a poor job at it."

"The elders have their plans, and I'm not privvy to all of them."

"Elders? Who specifically?" She merely tilted her head a bit. I found her arrogance frustrating. "How can you possibly expect this to hold?" I asked, my voice growing louder. "What makes you think you can leash an adherent, especially one of such a primal Axis? Will Aron live forever? Will the Fifth Choose more adherents? What if it doesn't? What if Aron dies? What happens then?" I was all but shouting now, but Gemma showed no response. She simply stood, glaring at me with her arms crossed casually in front of her. "Is he here?" I demanded.

"No," she said coolly. "And why should you care? You're probably just jealous that your power now has a check."

"Is everything all right?" A short, round little man came up behind Gemma, a hesitant smile on his face. "I heard voices."

"It's fine, Quintin," Gemma said evenly, her eyes never leaving mine. "This is Daniel. He's an adherent. *The* adherent, in fact, of the Sixth Axis. He doesn't always tell people that."

I clenched my jaw, but it was a fair point. I suppose there'd been a certain amount of deception on both sides.

"I can get—" Quintin began.

"No need for anything," Gemma interrupted.

"Quintin," I said, careful to keep my tone even. "Are you familiar with Aron? I believe he's from the clan—"

"Say nothing," Gemma snapped, her eyes flashing. "Go

back in the house. Tell everyone else to leave us be. This is a private conversation."

Quintin looked at me uneasily. I forced myself to smile, and that seemed to make him even more uneasy. He backed into the archway behind Gemma before scuttling away.

"I'm quite aware that you hate me," Gemma said easily as the sound of Quintin's footsteps faded away. "But I have to tell you, jealousy of power doesn't look good on you."

"Hate you?" I found myself surprised. "I don't hate you." But what *did* I feel? "You—you lied. I *liked* you—who I thought you were, at least. I'm just . . . your clan has offered nothing but deception. Lies."

"You weren't actually falling in love with me, were you?"

I couldn't tell if she was gloating or genuinely curious. "It was nice not being alone."

She laughed violently. "I'm old enough to be your moth—"

"I had a mother. And I obviously didn't know your true age at the time. Because, as I've said, lies."

"You know, this doesn't need to be a confrontation. We're of the same family, in the end."

"In the *beginning*," I corrected her. "Not the end. And you're right, this doesn't need to be a confrontation. Tell me where Aron is. As you say, he's family. I'd like to meet him."

"Our families shared a goal. You were in the archive. You must have seen that."

"A shared goal to . . . what?" I couldn't decide whether she was trying to distract me from finding Aron or genuinely trying to win me over.

"Control both the Fifth and Sixth Axes, obviously. Your branch did their part, which I have to say was a great deal easier, what with the Sixth already existing. Our side spent generations trying to gather sufficient power. Centuries researching the magic that could Forge an Axis. But don't act as if your family had some kind of noble ambition. They wanted power, plain and simple."

"But *my* family is gone. I'm the last. I'm not leashed. What they wanted or didn't want doesn't matter. No power went to them. *Your* clan killed humans. You used my mother. You almost burned down the Great Northern Wood. But you and your elders have *plan* beyond that, do you? No plan to *handle* Aron. He's one adherent! You have no idea what will happen if he dies. What will happen to the new Axis." I stabbed a finger at her. "I need to know where he is. Right now."

"I'm not telling—"

"I can make you."

"You won't."

I wasn't sure she was wrong. My anger with her betrayal warred with my sheer exhaustion, and my intense desire to go home to my Tower, crawl into my bed, and never come out again. "Your clan is playing with a power they don't understand. And you've invested it in a single person who's completely unprepared. You have to see the danger."

"Perhaps the Fifth will Choose others," she argued. "Perhaps it won't. But the Sixth has always managed, hasn't it? With a single adherent, and sometimes not even that."

My throat tightened. This particular aspect of my Axis was still fresh and raw in my mind. "Precautions were taken," I said softly. "Sacrifices were made. You've done none of that." *Precautions.* I shuddered as I thought about all those souls, the spirit of every former adherent of the Sixth, trapped forever in the Tower's Foundation, acting as anchors for when the Axis had no living adherent. I'd join them one day.

"What sacrifices?"

I bristled. "That's my business. You wouldn't know anything about—"

"About sacrifices?" Gemma snapped. "You mean something like burning out your *identity* because some young upstart ruined plans that had been in place since before he was born? Or do you mean giving up everything you've ever known—your business, your home, your everything— to take on a new identity?"

My ire flared. "None of that would have happened if Karal wasn't draining power from humans!" I shouted. "Using my *mother's* identity rune! They cut off her hands and kept her in an iron cage!"

Gemma fell silent, and I wanted more than anything to believe I'd seen sorrow and regret in her eyes. "I'm sorry," she said softly. "I knew about the rune. I didn't know . . . I'm sorry."

My heart was thudding against my chest, and I inhaled deeply, willing it to slow before I did something rash.

"Wait," Gemma said, her voice even quieter now. "That rune. The one that went missing."

"Mother's identity rune," I said wearily. I suddenly found that I was tired of the rage. Maybe it was the events of the past few days, but I simply no longer had the energy.

"But you . . . did something. It was gone."

"I Ended it." *I'm so tired.*

"But . . ."

I nodded, and it felt as if the muscles of my neck might simply give up. "She died."

Gemma stared at me for a long while. "I'm sorry."

It meant something. I felt my anger waning.

"But we don't have to fight anymore. We don't have to lie. All six Axes are now leashed. You hold one set of reins, and we hold another. It was always meant to be this way. Knowing where Aron is won't change anything."

She wasn't hostile, and I certainly lacked the will to fight.

"If the death of my mother taught me anything, it's that nothing is simple. Not where magic is concerned."

She looked at me for a long moment, assessing me. "What do you mean?"

I felt myself being earnest, not combative. "Aron's not well. His mind. There's . . . something between us, he and I. I don't know if it's our Axes, or if it's because I was there when you chained the Fifth to him. We're . . . affecting each other. He—"

"Affecting each other? How"

I paused for a moment, giving myself a chance to phrase my next words carefully. "He . . . hurts. So do I," I admitted. "But it seems to be worse for him. I found him. Hours ago, at most. He was rambling. He's . . . unfocused."

Her face betrayed her concern. "Aron was the steadiest, most loyal candidate. We were careful," she insisted. "We selected someone your age. Someone quiet. Intense. Not as arrogant as you." I let that go. "But steady."

"I was Chosen when I was thirteen," I reminded her. "Every adherent is. How old is Aron?"

"Twenty-two. But why should that—"

"It took me five years to adjust to my Axis. To learn to use it. Five long, lonely years. You've given him, what, seconds?"

"The Archons were—"

"The Archons knew what they were doing, and even then, they struggled with the power. Trust me."

"You can't possibly know—"

"I *can*. My Tower holds many secrets. Too many." I'd discovered as much when I'd restored the Veil. Galas, the Archon of the Sixth, was forever bound to the Tower, along with all past adherents of the Sixth. The horror of all those trapped souls was still strong in my mind. I'd never fully understood why my Axis was able to hold the memories of my predecessors, and the revelation had been—remained—sobering.

She blinked several times as she processed that, and then shook her head. "Aron is clever," she insisted. "He'll—"

"He'll experiment. And that's what he's been doing. He's raised schools of fish, flocks of birds, forests' worth of trees. Crops are ready for harvest months ahead of time. He's overgrown meadows. He's pulled a mountain out of the ground, for Origin's sake!"

A flash of uncertainty sped across her expression. "You're just—"

Despite my exhaustion, a last ball of anger managed to rekindle itself in my chest. "Just nothing!" I snapped. "This has nothing to do with our family's feud. You've put a sixth of the world's magic power, half of its most primal power, in the hands of someone untrained and unready! And you claim to have him leashed?" How could she persist in this? Was she completely ignorant?

"Where is he now?" I demanded. Almost by reflex, I summoned my Axis's Form of Mind, defined by the rune *to know*:

My stomach cramped as the Axis obeyed, settling itself over Gemma.

"I don't know," she said.

My blood ran cold with magic, and the skin on the back of my neck seemed to shrink. A lie. "Try again." I kept my voice flat and hard.

She frowned. "I don't. They're keeping him—"

"I can tell when you're lying, you know. I can End lies, Gemma. Once I know to look for them." *I can End you* was the unsaid accompaniment.

She blinked, and then a wary craftiness overtook her. Her expression hardened, and she let her hands fall slowly to her sides as she raised her shoulders a bit. I'd danced this dance enough to know she intended to resist me. My feelings for her —for what I'd thought had been her—came crashing back to me, colored by the fact that it had all been a lie, a gambit to keep me distracted from her family's workings. The butterflies I'd felt in my stomach were now shards of glass. The joy I'd felt when she'd simply touched my arm was now a crawling disgust. I'd been wrong: nothing was settled between me and this creature.

She opened her mouth to speak, and with a flick of the Axis's power, I Ended the air around her. Her eyes grew wide for a split second as her lungs struggled to find purchase in the vacuum. I released the magic, and she stepped back, startled, as air rushed to fill the void I'd created. She gasped twice, one hand on her chest, and looked up at me.

Her expression was no longer crafty and clever. I saw fear.

"Don't lie to me again," I warned her.

She stared at me for a moment before softly saying, "I'll tell you. Only please, don't hurt him."

The concern in her voice was genuine, and I felt a twinge of regret at acting so harshly.

"He's my son," she finished.

CHAPTER 3

Elders

A tree smashing into my chest couldn't have taken my breath away more effectively. "Your *son?*" I repeated, incredulous.

Gemma nodded. "It's why—I wanted to be there. When it happened. Even though I wasn't part of the ritual."

The still-unresolved pain over losing my own mother clashed with my dislike for Gemma, and I forced myself to unclench fists I hadn't even realized I'd made. "I don't want to hurt Aron," I assured her. "But he's causing damage. He can't—"

"It's the elders," she interrupted. "They're the ones making him do it. This is all their plan."

Which I knew, but . . . hmm. "Can you tell me where *they* are, then? Your elders?"

Her eyes widened and I imagined I could hear her heartbeat quicken. "I can't," she whispered, shaking her head quicky. "You don't know what they'd do."

"You don't know what *I'll* do," I reminded her, although I wasn't as convinced as I'd been when I Ended her breath.

Her eyes flicked over my shoulder and then back to mine. I turned, examining the wall behind me carefully. What could she possibly—

Ah.

A tiny entry rune had been scratched into the corner of a gilded frame that hung on the wall. "A space *within* this space?" I asked softly. That was powerful magic.

"What are you going to do?" she asked in a low voice as I stepped toward the wall, carefully examining the rune.

"I'm going to ask them what they want," I said easily. "And convince them to stop."

I touched the rune, trickling just a bit of power into it.

The sensation of being drawn into the space-within-a-space was unlike any I'd ever felt. Usually, the sensation of flying or flowing accompanied one's entering a hidden space. This was like being squeezed and forced through a narrow opening. I emerged in the new space with a *pop*, air rushing away from me as I appeared.

The walls around me were plain, smooth stone. The ceiling was low, easily within reach of my outstretched fingers, and the passageway was tight, scarcely wider than my shoulders. Illumination came from spheres mounted to the walls, each glowing a soft, steady orange-yellow. With a blank stone wall behind me, the passageway stretching forward seemed my only path. I followed it for a dozen or so steps before it opened into a room, though the walls were only a few paces more apart than the passageway. Portraits covered those walls, and a heavy, over-stuffed chair dominated the center of the room. Sitting in it was the oldest living person of witchkind I had ever seen.

He glared at me with small brown eyes set deeply into a dark, heavily lined face. His bald pate dully reflected the light globes, and his wrinkled hands clenched the arms of his chair.

"Found us out at last, boy?"

"You know who I am."

He let out something halfway between a wheezy laugh and a raspy bark. "Know who you are? Whelp. I knew your great-great-grandmother. Knew her daughter. Knew *her* daughter. I arranged your mother's marriage with one of my own grandsons. Yes, I know you, boy."

My fists clenched at my sides. "Where are the rest of you?"

"Rest? Oh, the elders." He waved one wizened hand toward the portraits. "They're there. Visionless wretches the lot, and I'm well quit of them."

My eyes grew wide. "You mean *you're* the only clan elder?"

"The only one as matters. One of the only ones who ever has! The others, *pah*. Assistants. Faces. *I* lead the clan. *I* have brought us our victory."

"So you're the one giving Aron his orders."

The old man sneered. "He is ours. *Mine.* My plan, the whole thing. All the hoarding, all the planning. All the details so cleverly conceived. You slowed us down for a bit," he acknowledged with a slight nod of his wizened head, "but we got what we needed, didn't we? Forged an Axis! Not so many as can say that." He coughed heavily before pulling himself more upright in his seat. "Can't stop it now, can you? Can't just magic away a rune this time."

My anger began boiling inside me, but I forced myself to focus. "Aron is damaged."

He nodded slowly, a smile stretching his furrowed, withered features. "But he minds his elders still."

"His *mind* is the problem," I said flatly. "He's not prepared to be an adherent. He wasn't Chosen, wasn't trained. His mind is breaking. And when it does, do you know what will happen to his Axis?"

He shrugged. "Choose another. We've plenty of candidates."

"Or it may break free."

Another shrug. "Not a concern."

"Why are you doing this? What's your game?"

"Game?" he snapped, his eyes glinting coldly. "This is no game, child. For centuries we've schemed to take the two most powerful Axes. Your side of the family beat us to it—bred you to be attractive to the Sixth. But we had the harder role." He leered at me. "We had to *make* our Axis. Forge the Fifth. Couldn't simply dangle a tasty treat in front of it. No, we had to *make it!*"

"But why?" I demanded.

"Same reason all the Axes were Forged. Power. With the Fifth chained, we can counter even you. Take our place on the Taryba. *Replace* the damn Taryba. But more importantly," he started, but dissolved into a fit of coughing. I made no move to help as he convulsed over and over, finally wiping his mouth with the back of one hand, panting slightly and glaring at me.

Replace the highest governing council of witchkind? He was insane. "More importantly what?"

"Not yours to know," he whispered roughly. "But you can join us. Beginnings and Endings, as it was meant to be."

"Meant to be?" What was he talking about?

"Oh, did old Pranasa not discuss it? I know she was set to watch over you. She was the one who accepted your father into the family, you know."

I hadn't, but it was hardly surprising. Pranasa, my great-great-grandmother, had ruled the family home from her attic domain. She'd been well past life but hadn't moved on to death. It made me wonder for a moment if the man in front of me was truly alive, but he didn't have any of the dense, dank smells I'd associated with Great-Great-Grandmother. "Discuss what?"

"The *prophecy*, fool child! The one that's ruled our families since we, since witchkind, came to this forsaken world!"

He glared at me for a moment, took a deep, hesitant breath, and recited:

Sky and Earth, Flame and Sea
Cast adrift, their center lost
Until a Sixth might come to be
To join them all, or pay the cost

My eyes widened. Great-Great-Grandmother *had* told me that. I'd even shared it with Kirmin. My mentor had called it a prophecy as well, although she'd dismissed it, calling it one of the Axis's great mysteries. But she'd said it had come *after* Galas. This old man had implied it was much older.

"Oh, she did mention it." He smirked. "Didn't tell you what it meant, did she?" "Well, not my job to educate you." His mouth set into a stubborn line.

The Sixth was obviously a reference to the Axis they'd just Forged. In the original plan, Beginnings had been the Fifth, of course, but—I shook myself. This was off topic. "So you want to rule witchkind?" I asked. "That's what this is all about?"

"Witchkind?" He laughed again, then hacked a noise that turned my stomach. "Everyone, stupid child. Humans and witchkind. The lot. Something *you* could have done, if you'd have had the fortitude. The proper guidance. But no, your family was always shortsighted. Wanted an adherent, never thought what they'd do with it if they got one. But *we* are meant to rule. Not these petty councils. Not the Taryba. *We,* the ones with all the power, must wield it."

"Who do you mean? All of the adherents?" Now I was confused.

He laughed until it turned into another hacking cough.

"Not all, of course. Only the most senior. But they won't get involved, will they? Never have. Never truly understood." He shook his head. "So we will. Through Aron."

This old man's ambitions apparently knew no bounds. "Aron is disrupting the world. It may seem innocent now, but he's sowing a great deal of chaos." Much like the chaos I'd created—the recent incident with nearly destroying the Veil, for example, or when I'd tried to help clear an obstructing rock formation from a river.

"Course he is. It's what he was told to do. And he'll do more. This is all just practice. Soon they'll all be begging him to stop. And for the right price, for the right incentives, we will."

"I can't let you do that," I said. I pulled my Axis around me, mentally grasping its tattered edges and bringing it to focus on the old man.

"You can't stop me, fool," the old man wheezed. He smacked the arm of his chair, and I was spat out of the hidden space, suddenly lying on the floor. I quickly looked up at the gilt frame and saw the rune there curling with smoke as it burned away.

"You spoke to them?" Gemma asked.

I pulled myself to my feet, my head spinning. "Him. Your 'clan elders' are an ancient old man." Gemma's eyes widened. I pushed the Axis out and around me but couldn't find any trace of the space I'd just been in. He'd collapsed the entrance I'd used, but that didn't mean there weren't others. "How else can I get to him?"

"One man?"

"One," I repeated grimly. "He implied that everyone else you may have seen was just a front. How do I find him again?"

"I don't know." I glared at her. "Truly, I don't. Aron's the only one who's even used that entry rune. Nobody else is permitted."

"He's putting everyone in danger," I muttered, my eyes still casting around the room. "Aron wasn't down there. Do you know where he would be? At least tell me—"

A crash of magic slammed down upon me, driving me to my knees so fast, so hard, that I cried out in pain. It wasn't a Summons, but it carried much of the same sensations. Urgency. Need. Danger. "All right!" I shouted through it, leaning forward under the physically palpable weight of it. "All right!" I repeated. I hauled the Axis back to myself, fed it the torrent of power smashing into my brain, and let it take us there.

CHAPTER 4

Magestorm

I arrived flat on my face, with gritty, sharp-edged sand pressing into one cheek. The crushing sense of urgency had faded but was replaced by the searing, howling pain of magic being misused. Freezing, wet, roaring wind sent more sand blasting through the air. I could barely tell which way was up, only that down was clearly the dirt that my face was pressed into.

I levered myself to my feet, squinting against the biting air and sleeting dirt, and tried to get my bearings.

The sun was setting. That was west, then. It cast an angry red light across the sky, sitting like a swollen tick on the horizon. The wind was sharp and bitter—so I was in the north. Westhead, maybe. No, there was more heaving gray ocean than land. Bryssi? Or—the sight of black, lichen-encrusted rocks cinched it. I was at Lastpointe.

"Adherent!" I turned in toward the call, holding my hands over my eyes to filter out some of the blowing grit. "Adherent!" a man's voice repeated, shouting through the sound of this most unnatural storm.

A dark shape pushed through the wind, leaning this way and that as the gale shifted directions. That shape resolved into a stout man of witchkind, who leaned in close to be heard. "My name is Ander, adherent of Sea! How did you know to come?"

"I could hardly ignore it," I shouted despite us being just inches apart. "You didn't send the Summons?"

"We've had no time!" he replied. "But whatever the reason, praise the Origin you're here. This hurricane blew up out of nowhere—in seconds, I tell you! We've lost at least two boats, crews and all. Marten and I have been fighting it, but it resists us!"

"Marten is also of Sea?"

"Aye!"

"Take me to him!"

Ander didn't answer and instead grabbed my forearm in a viselike grip. "We can't sense an eye to the storm," he shouted as he pulled me along the shore. "Normally we'd try to move the eye over us, give ourselves room to work. But this doesn't seem to have a locus—no place of calm!"

Aron's work, I thought grimly. The elder's work. Inflict damage on the world and demand ransom. That was their game. A return to the days before the Forging—but with them in control of the chaos. No current adherent but Aron would have acted this way, although he hadn't had the benefit of being brought up as an adherent, and his clan certainly didn't care. They didn't have the lessons Kirmin taught me or the do-nothing attitude cultivated by the other senior adherents.

"This is Marten!" Ander hollered as we approached another dark shape. This one turned out to be an equally stout, heavily weathered man who somehow found the strength to stand perfectly upright in the storm, as if it were nothing more than a gentle breeze.

"What have you tried?" I yelled as Ander and I huddled against Marten.

"Cooling the sea," Marten shouted back. "We've pulled energy from the water—more than we ought—which should have killed it instantly. Storms can't live without warm water. But this one can."

"Something else is feeding it energy," Ander agreed.

Aron. I cast about with the Axis, but I couldn't sense any of the eddying magic that I'd used before to find Aron. Could he be feeding this from farther away? The choppy water and the waves in the Axis's diffuse awareness seemed to move as one. There was no finding him. "It's fueled by magic," I shouted. "How else can we break it?"

"Can you End it entirely?" Ander asked.

I stood up a bit more, my eyes nearly shut against the wind. "I can try!" This shouldn't be an abstract exercise of the Axis's power: storms were real phenomena, they were local, and they always ended of their own accord, at some point. I just needed to hurry that along. I focused on the Axis's local presence, pointed it out to the ocean, and *pushed*. I held the simple, directive rune for Ending firmly in my mind, as I had done a hundred times before:

The power of Ending pounded down all around us as the Axis almost gleefully lashed out. *At last*, I thought with relief. *Something is going ri—*

Even as I thought it, I felt the Axis *shatter*. Its power spun back to me—too fast. My legs collapsed beneath me as Marten and Ander grabbed my arms to keep me upright. I gagged as my insides seemed to churn. The Axis moaned in my mind, whimpering and sore, as if it had been thrashed.

A wooden *crack* pierced the air. I could just make out the murky, dark shape of a small ship fetching up against the nearby docks. Ship, docks—it all smashed into the rocky shore, splintering into thousands of sodden shards.

"I guess not," Marten shouted. Even he was hunched over as the wind seemed to pick up strength.

"We need to do it together!" I shouted, shaking an arm loose long enough to wipe my face clean of vile fluid and wet sand. "I can't End the storm, but maybe I can counter the magic in it! If I do that, if I take its energy away, can you break the storm itself?"

The two looked at each other before nodding in agreement. "Aye!" Ander hollered. "We'll need to pull a spout of water from the sea!"

Marten nodded again and seemed to brace himself. "Say the word, Adherent!"

I gathered myself and my Axis. I lowered myself to my knees, figuring it would give me a shorter fall if I collapsed again. The Axis rallied, and I forced it through the storm, seeking out whatever unearthly power was feeding this monster. *There*, I thought grimly as I found a bright, golden, swirling loop of magic. This thread wasn't being fed externally; the immense amount of energy had managed to reinforce itself in a perpetual loop. I recalled the runes at the base of the Tower's Foundation. The rune construct looped the Axis's magic over and over, maintaining both the Tower and reminding the Veil to conceal witchkind from humans. I didn't know what had set this particular loop in motion—although I obviously had a very good guess—but I saw at once how to break it.

I pulled the Axis together, holding a different rune in my mind:

Sustabdykite ciklą. It had come from the last pages of the Book of Endings. It unlocked the means to nullify magic. To nullify life. I'd never thought I'd need it—and would never have dared consider it. But in this very moment, I *knew* this was its purpose.

"Now!" I cried as I forced the Axis to obey. It jerked the rune out of my mind and hurtled forward, crashing into the loop of golden power. In the same instant, an enormous pillar of freezing-cold seawater erupted from the ocean, forcing itself high into the sky. The air around us was instantly fueled with freezing mist, just as my Axis arrowed into the opposing magic.

A thunderclap a thousand times louder than any I'd ever heard buffeted us, shoving the air ruthlessly out of its way, knocking us to the ground.My Axis roared in triumph, but it hadn't won without a price: my entire spine seared with pain, and my head felt as if it was full of molten brass. Deafened, I couldn't hear my screams of agony, but I imagined them harmonizing with the deeper cry of the Axis in my mind.

Everything went still.

Time itself seemed to freeze, the grit in the air becoming motionless. It lasted less than an eyeblink but felt like an eternity, an endless stretch of time in which I couldn't inhale, couldn't even feel my own heartbeat. The world sounded dull and distant.

Then everything collapsed.

A thousand barrels of cold seawater rained down on us, carrying with it the dirt and sand that the winds had swept into the air. Out of habit, I tried to reach out with the Axis's power and End the wetness and freezing cold around me. The Axis didn't even respond, instead choosing to curl around my belly, licking its wounds. The burning sensation in my body was replaced with a shaking, shuddering cold. I leaned forward on my knees, resting my elbows on the ground, and vomited whatever was left inside of me.

"Up with you, Adherent," Ander said gently as he and Marten carefully pulled me up by my arms. I strained to hear him. "Still with us?"

I nodded wretchedly.

"That's done it." Marten sighed, relaxing his grip on me to see if I could stand. I stumbled, caught myself, and then nodded again as my legs managed to find some strength.

"Here then," Ander said. A wave of warm magic poured over me, pushing the seawater off my skin, out of my clothes, and out of my hair. My hearing returned in full.

"Thank you," I gasped. My heart seemed to relax to a steady pace, although I still felt as if I might need to sleep for a week.

"I've never seen the like of that," Marten said quietly.

"Nor I," Ander agreed.

My ears had stopped ringing so loudly. "That's all three of us, then," I added.

I took stock of our surroundings. The nearby docks were utterly shattered, and the hulks of a half dozen ships had been pummeled into the shoreline. Beyond that, building after building had been smashed in. People were emerging from the wreckage of ships and buildings, shaking themselves off as they stumbled around to look for other survivors.

Martin and Ander looked like the fisherwitches I'd seen everywhere, despite being obviously skilled adherents. They were stocky, with muscular builds and thick, powerful hands. Their faces were weathered, their hair cropped short. Their clothes—now as dry as mine—were simple and sturdy but designed to stand up to hard use.

They looked as exhausted as I felt.

"Are there any . . . you mentioned ships . . . " I asked, not sure how to phrase it.

"No point," Marten said with a sigh, shaking his head. "Not in a storm like that. They all had fisherwitches with them. If any survived, they'll have made it back. Those without fisher-witches . . ."

"Too sudden," Ander agreed. "When waves like those come down on you, heave you over and send you down . . ." He shook his head. "Too sudden."

"I'm sorry," I said quietly.

"I'm too late," a voice called from the shore.

"Gilioj!" Marten called, lifting a hand in greeting. The old senior adherent of Sea strode toward us, his boots splashing in the now-gentle surf, shedding water almost instantly as he strode toward us.

"I felt the disturbance," he said as he drew closer. "But the sea itself fought me." He shook his head. "I've never felt anything like it."

"It was Aron," I said, earning three quizzical looks. "Gilioj, have you heard? About the Fifth?"

"The Fifth . . . Axis?" Ander asked, frowning as Gilioj nodded slowly.

"The Fifth was Forged yesterday," I said. "Wait, yesterday?" It seemed so long ago. "No. It's been a few days. I've lost track already. I haven't slept much."

"The Fifth," Marten breathed.

"And you think this is the Fifth's storm?" Gilioj asked.

"I do. There was a loop of magic feeding it. Golden in my mind's eye. It . . . resisted my own Axis. I couldn't simply End it."

"Creation," Marten whispered.

"It was the energy Clan Karal stole. Stole and hoarded," I explained. "They used it all to Forge the Fifth and chain it to one of their own. A man named Aron, about my age. He's been experimenting with his new power."

"This," Gilioj said wearily, looking past us to the shore, "was an *experiment*?"

"Possibly. Their elder apparently contrived a way to leash the new adherent. Or they'd planned to. I'm not certain it's working, whatever they intended. If Aron did this, he may have been directed to."

"Directed?" Ander said with a frown. "Who would—" He stopped himself, his face turning a dull gray. "Control."

"Possibly," I repeated, nodding slowly. "They mean to use his power to cause problems, to extract things from others. Money. Power. Position. Aron on his own didn't seem inimical." *Dangerously unbalanced,* perhaps, but he hadn't struck me as evil. "But the clan and their influence . . ."

"It felt as if the sea itself fought us," Martin said, echoing Gilioj's words. "As if our own Axis was against us."

"Creation would be powerful," I said. "My own Axis

would, under normal conditions, be able to End anything you contrived with Sea. Stands to reason the Fifth would be able to . . . Begin something. And keep it going."

"Which is why your Tower was built," Gilioj muttered. Heat flushed my face. We were not meant to be caged! I opened my mouth for a sharp retort, but he just sighed and waved me down. "Peace, Daniel. You did well here. I meant only that this new Fifth Axis has no fetters. None we understand, at least." He looked over the wreckage, thinking. "It's good that you were here," he said, turning to Marten and Ander. "Are you the only ones of us?"

"On the island, yes," Marten confirmed. "There are fisher-witches, of course. Two dozen here, more in Bryssi. A few in the smaller hamlets along the western coast."

"They wouldn't have had the power to affect this," Ander noted.

"No, of course not." Gilioj rubbed his bald pate. "Of course not." He paused for a moment. "Walk with me, Daniel?"

"Of course."

We left Marten and Ander behind as they moved toward the demolished docks and those in need of aid. I followed Gilioj along the shoreline but far from where the water could lap at our boots.

"You don't think much of us, do you?"

"Us?"

"Adherents. Any of us. We four seniors especially."

"You could do more good in the world than you do."

"We helped break this storm."

"You did," I admitted.

"You think we waste our power. Normally."

"On your little charms, yes. On standing by and doing nothing, yes."

"Adherents of Sea always respond to a storm. But we don't

always break them. Storms serve a need. They're natural. They'd occur without us. And so yes . . . we often stand idle."

"If all of witchkind had even a piece of your power, would they all stand idle as well?" I challenged him.

He sighed. "No. Of course not. And I take your point. Our lack of action is an action of its own."

"Why do I think you won't change?"

"I'm too old. I've been an adherent for a hundred years, at this point. More. This is all I know."

"And the others? Your juniors?"

He snorted. "Marten is only a dozen years younger than I. Seems disingenuous to call him *junior*." We crunched through the gravelly beach. "He would intervene more. Many of them would."

"Maybe it's time for one of them to set the rules."

Gilioj gave me a sharp look, but then his expression fell. He looked resigned. "It may be."

His response surprised me. "What are you saying?"

"I'm saying that the rest of the Adherents of Sea will turn to Marten when I'm gone. We've always taken our cues from the eldest of us, just as the other Axes do. All but yours, obviously. Perhaps it is time for me to do so as well."

I swallowed hard. "You're . . . stepping down. It won't change life for the rest of witchkind."

"No? I wonder. We can't give them our magic, you're right. But perhaps Marten will be the protector, and not the hoarder. Perhaps..." He paused. "Hmm. Perhaps I can at least let him try."

I stopped and turned to him. He took another short step before stopping as well. "I don't . . ." I began. "You can't just step down, can you?"

"No more than you." The old adherent sighed. "The Axis will let me go, but that'll be my end."

"Do you . . . is there a—" I stopped, flustered. "I don't know what to do."

"As you've been told before, young Daniel," Gilioj said sternly, "not everything is for you to do."

He turned to look me square in the eye and held my gaze for many long moments. Then he turned and strode steadily into the sea.

My Axis, attuned even in its exhaustion to great Endings, keened a resonating tone in my mind, mirroring the gentle crashing of the low waves on the shore.

I stood for . . . I don't know how long. Several minutes at least, just watching the sea softly slap in against the sand and then slide back out again. Gilioj was—had been—the oldest of the senior adherents. The oldest adherent in the world.

"Adherent?"

"Hmm?" I turned to see Marten walking toward me.

"Where's Gilioj?"

I looked back out to the sea. "I'm told you're senior adherent of Sea now."

Marten stopped, and I could feel his eyes on me. Then I heard him turn toward the sea, his boots churning the gravely sand of the beach.

"I think I'll go," I said at last.

"Don't say . . . " he said. "Please. Let me tell them."

"Of course."

I crunched inland, eventually finding the remains of a foot-path that had once been hard-packed earth. Now it was a muddy mess covered with broken branches and torn vegeta-tion. I followed it into the village proper.

The damage here was extensive, but nowhere near the total destruction of the waterfront. Windows had been broken, and plenty of roofs would need re-covering. The streets—cobbled here instead of dirt—were slick with blown-in mud, and full of debris. The village's humans were moving slowly about, picking up belongings and trash in equal measure. I spotted a few people of witchkind, surreptitiously moving from building to building, from lamppost to lamppost, quietly reinforcing the magics that had helped hold everything together through the storm. A small café had already reopened, and servers were passing out mugs of steaming beverages to anyone who wanted one. An old man, a human, sat crouched next to what must have been a food stall before the storm. It was little more than a pile of broken sticks now, and he simply stared at it, shaking his head slowly in disappointment.

"Thank you," a middle-aged woman of witchkind whispered as she passed me.

"For what?" I asked softly, turning toward her.

"We all felt it," was all she said before she moved on.

Half the world might have felt it, I thought.

A wagon rattled past, heading for the waterfront and carrying boxes of supplies. Two older men, clad in the long gray coats of human physickers, hurried after it, obviously intent on helping whomever they could at the worst scene of destruction.

I followed the street around a corner, passing another couple nailing a heavy oil canvas over the hole where shutters had once kept out the weather. Past that, two small children were making a halfhearted attempt at playing in the street, pouncing in small puddles and chasing each other around a battered stone bench. As I moved through the center of town, and toward its inland edge, I came across a building that, sitting aside those along the docks, had suffered the worst damage I'd seen yet.

One entire wall of the boxy building had caved in. The cause was apparent: an enormous tree, likely a hundred years old or more, had finally been ripped from the ground by the storm and sent crashing into the side of the building. The roof had almost completely collapsed, and I wouldn't have trusted what remained to keep out a stiff breeze. In fact, I was almost ready to reach out with the Axis and just finish it off before it could fall in on someone. Then I realized what the building was.

Lastpointe's human church.

Walking slowly from around the back of the building, looking disheveled and beaten, was Dedicant Ormand.

CHAPTER 5

Dedicant

"**D**edicant Ormand," I said quietly as I stepped toward him.

He looked up, taking only a moment to recognize me. "You're back," he said with a small, sad smile. "I'm afraid I can't offer you a comfortable place to sit, this time."

"I know. I'm sorry."

"It happened so quickly," he said, shaking his head and looking back at the demolished church. "I've never known a storm to come up so hard, so fast." He turned back to me.

Something passed between us, in our eyes, and I nodded slowly. I'd asked him about magic once. Now he seemed to be asking me. "What will you do now?"

"Rebuild, of course. It's what we'll all do."

"It will take a lot of effort."

He shrugged and stepped a bit closer to me. "None of this existed before people came to this island. We built all this. We can build it again."

"That storm was . . . unintended," I said carefully, keeping my eyes on his. "Some people took something. Something they shouldn't have. Much is out of sorts, and I'm afraid this storm is but the first."

He nodded in thoughtful acknowledgment. When I'd last spoken to him—was it just a couple of days ago?—he'd suggested that believing in magic did not contradict the views of the church he served, even if other priests insisted that magic was evil and that its practitioners must be put to death. "And this . . . thing? That was taken?"

I sighed. "Power. A power was taken. It was something that used to be freely available. To everyone. It's now been gathered into one person's control. They seem to be experimenting with it."

"So this was a . . . would you call it a natural power?"

"Very much so."

He sighed and quickly glanced back at the ruin of his church. "People gathering up nature's gifts and hoarding them for themselves. It's an ancient story."

It's pretty much the story of the Forging of the Axes, I thought to myself. His words struck a chord with me: I'd long felt that the adherents of the other four Axes should do more with their power, use more of it to help the rest of witchkind, to help the world. But their unbending policy was to stay out of it—to keep their power bottled up, used only for small, trifling things.

"What do they intend to do with it, those who took this power?" Ormand asked.

"I don't know. I think they feel slighted. Left out. Like they were promised something that never materialized." *That they want to go back to whatever world we all came from*, I added to myself. "I think in a way, they just want it for what it is. Power. This," I added with a gesture to the demolished church, "came from them wanting to prove they have it. To prove nobody can stop them."

He nodded slowly. "Power can make people do funny

things. People often seek power for its own sake. Just to have it, with no idea what they'll even use it for. Even in our church."

"Oh?"

"When we last spoke, I mentioned how my peers see the church as a way to control people. They don't often do anything with that power, but they seem to enjoy having it."

"You don't?"

He chuckled and started brushing dust from his robes. "That's part of why they sent me here. I see the church's power as something to serve its people. My congregation. People believe in the church, and that gives the church power. I would turn that toward the good of the people who believe in it. A virtuous circle, if you will."

A curious idea, and not unlike what I felt adherents should be doing with our power: using it to benefit ordinary witchkind, who'd been left with little power after the Axes had been Forged. "And how would you do that?"

"The church wields power by telling people what to do. Because worshippers believe those instructions are sanctified, if you will, they follow them. I instruct my congregation to do good for each other. To help each other when needs arise. To respect each other. Our books teach exactly that, after all, do they not?" His eyes teased me, as if he was quite sure I'd never read those books. "That's what the Words of Law are, after all: rules to be followed for the betterment of everyone. Do not murder. Do not lie. Love one another. Lift a hand in aid. Four simple rules that keep our communities in harmony."

"They *seem* simple," I agreed.

"They are. But many of my colleagues find other words in the books and craft them into their own laws. Give money to the church. Obey those with wealth. Remain obedient. Marry within your clan. Those are all modern notions, ones that aren't —at least in my view—supported by the texts." He shrugged.

"But perhaps I'm wrong. I'm the one out on this island, after all."

"Would you take that power from the other priests—the ones who misuse it—if you could?"

He thought for a moment before replying. "It saddens me to see something misused that could be put to so much good. I might."

"I'd take the power away as well, if I could. The one that was stolen."

"Would you? Can you?"

"I would. Whether or not I can . . . I don't know. I may need to try."

"Can you convince those who took it to do good with it? To use it for the benefit of everyone?"

I frowned. "I have grave doubts on that front. They wronged a great many people in order to gain this power. I don't think the welfare of others is foremost in their minds."

"So if you take it from them, what would you do with it?"

I hadn't thought that far ahead. If I Ended Aron, if such a thing were even possible now, would the Fifth Axis simply dissolve? Go back to being whatever it had been before? Or would it remain an Axis and Choose another adherent? "I'm not sure."

"Would you keep it?"

If, as I was beginning to suspect, the Fifth and Sixth were somehow linked, would that be an option? "It would be less dangerous if I did. If I even could."

"Are you certain?"

No. Wasn't it time for me to admit that I'd done plenty of damage with one Axis? I'd already damaged the Veil, called attention to witchkind, and let the priests—the ones who used the church to control people—resume the Hunts. "I suppose not."

"Then what will you do?"

"I . . . don't know." Aron's actions would surely threaten the Veil too, and who knows what other damage he might cause before then.

"Dealing with power is always a difficult question. Filled with difficult choices."

"Agreed."

"It's easy to imagine that you'd be the beneficent one. The one who could hold power and believe you were doing so for everyone's good. I know many priests who feel exactly that way, even as they're preaching ideas that mainly benefit themselves."

I nodded slowly, my heart heavy. I'd certainly been guilty of thinking that way.

"Are there . . . others?" Ormand raised an eyebrow, and in my heart I knew he knew I wasn't like him. That I wasn't human. "Someone you could go to for advice? Who could help you?"

I sighed. "There are. Maybe. I'm not sure. Like your colleagues, we differ in our opinions on power." The adherents would rather not use it, a position I realized I was slowly coming to share. Aron was a stark example of why our vast powers should possibly sit unused. "Or maybe we don't. Differ, I mean." I looked past him to the rubble of his church. "Do you have somewhere to stay, until you rebuild? Is there anything I can do?"

"Can you create a new building?" he asked with a smile.

Aron could. Probably as easily as he'd Created the storm that had destroyed it. An Ending disguised as a Beginning. Two faces of the same coin. "Nothing so . . . useful, no."

"I was joking." He chuckled. "No, I'll be fine. I'll put up with someone, help out where I can. We'll get to the church after everyone's homes are sound again. We can speak to our creator from the waterfront as easily as in a building. I imagine we'll have far more important tasks ahead of us for some time."

"The ships." I doubted he knew the amount of damage their little fleet had suffered.

He nodded. "Ships. Docks. Whatever was damaged, we'll repair. Anything can be repaired, given time and effort."

Anything can be repaired. "I hope that's true."

He looked deeply into my eyes, stepping forward to clap a firm hand on my shoulder. "It is. Believe it."

"I will," I said quietly. I meant it.

"May I offer you a piece of advice?" I nodded. "Don't cling too hard to power. It's often best not wielded at all."

"I'm starting to see the wisdom of that."

"Or if it must be used, let it be used by those who most need whatever it can provide."

So all of witchkind. I found myself wondering anew at the motives of the Archons. The Forging of the Axes had taken power from witchkind, left them to live on the leftover dregs of magic. If the dozens of witchkind here in Lastpointe had possessed even a fraction of the power invested solely in the adherents, would that storm have been brought to heel more quickly? Would it have been possible to even create it in the first place? "I'm starting to see the wisdom of that as well."

"Good." His hand dropped and he turned to walk into the village. "I hope you'll visit us again in happier times," he said over one shoulder.

"I will." I hoped I'd be able to, at least.

I watched him disappear around the curving street. *Anything can be repaired.*

I tugged my weary Axis to myself. I needed respite and a place to think. The Tower. But someone called to me.

"Daniel!"

I let go of the Axis. It was Marten.

CHAPTER 6

Demands

"What is it?" I asked.

Marten looked just as spent as I felt. He was walking toward me from the waterfront, and I began trudging toward him. He held out a piece of parchment. "This was delivered to the local headman."

I took it, squinting to make out the writing on it. "*Šiek tiek šviesos*," I muttered. The parchment began to glow slightly, throwing the writing into sharp contrast—but then the light sputtered and died.

Marten frowned. "*Apšviesti*," he said in a firm voice. A suffuse, soft glow surrounded us at once, but then it, too, flickered and faded.

"What's happening?" I asked.

He shook his head. "I don't know. Some of the fisher-witches said their weather magics and protections were faltering during the storm. I didn't know what they meant."

"But the storm's over."

"There was a lot of magic," he suggested. "It may take some time to settle."

"I suppose. In the meantime, I can't read whatever this is."

"It's a warning," he said with a heavy sigh.

My shoulders tensed. "From who?"

"It doesn't say. It only says—here, let me try one more. *Skaitymo lemputė.*" A bright pinpoint of light flared to life at the top edge of the parchment. The light seemed to hold steady. "Well, that works."

The words on the page had been made with a strong hand, the strokes of the letters bold and black. They were oversized, taking up most of the page despite their brevity.

As you can now see, the adherents cannot reliably protect you. We command the Sea and its fury. We can command it to aid, or we can command it to harm. Tell all you know, and await our next sign.

I forced my jaw to unclench. "This is Aron. Or his clan, at least."

Marten nodded as if he'd expected as much. "What do they want?"

"As near as I can tell? To rule."

"Rule?"

"Witchkind. Humans. Everyone." I handed the parchment back, shaking my head. "I don't know. Tell everyone to . . . I don't know. Rebuild. Hunker down. Keep their eyes open. This isn't the last of this."

Marten's face filled with concern. Then he nodded and, without a further word, began walking slowly back toward the wharves.

"It will be easier to give in," a soft voice said behind me.

I whirled, expecting to see Dedicant Ormond, but the

human priest hadn't returned. Instead, Aron had appeared. "You did this," I said coldly.

He nodded. His face looked a bit sad. "They said I needed to. Said nobody would pay attention, nobody would take us seriously, unless they could see the extent of what we can do."

"You've killed people."

He looked genuinely sad at that. "I know. I didn't want to. I've . . . spoken with one of the elders. Let him know I don't want to do that again. He said I might not have to."

"Might not—you don't *have* to do anything! You're an adherent, the adherent of Beginnings!" I said, my voice rising with my emotions. "You're not part of them now! Adherents *leave* their clans, leave their families! We're supposed to *help* people!"

He cocked his head to one side. "Is that true? That adherents help people?"

"Of—" I stopped myself. It wasn't, not as a rule. "I try to," I replied, lowering my voice.

"Do you help your family?"

"My family is gone."

He nodded slightly. "Mine isn't, and this our clan's destiny. They said I could ask you to join us. To help." He paused for a moment and then smiled. "You'd have family again if you did."

"I'm no—" I stopped myself. *No, I am a killer. I've killed.* "This isn't what the Axes were meant for." It sounded unconvincing even to me.

"The elders say the Axes were always about consolidating power. About creating order from chaos."

That's certainly the story we've all been told. "The other adherents don't seek to rule people."

"Mmm," he said, nodding but obviously not agreeing.

"What are they going to make you do next?"

He shrugged. "I don't know. I just know that it's all designed to help us fulfill our destiny as a family. As a clan."

The look on his face was one of absolute, perfect, unwavering conviction. I realized now why they'd chosen him to be their adherent: He'd been fully indoctrinated in their plans. He was their unquestioning tool, their weapon. With him, they stood a reasonable chance of achieving their aims. "I'll oppose you," I said firmly.

His expression fell. "I know," he whispered. "They told me you would. But I wish you wouldn't."

He vanished in a gust of wind, leaving a sharp prickling sensation in my mind.

I felt the last of my energy draining away as the moons rose into the sky. At this rate, I'd pass out, and the Tower's magic would pull me home.

I decided to save it the trouble.

CHAPTER 7

Sunrise

I slept poorly that night, my head throbbing with pain and too fogged to assemble a credible dream. I rolled out of bed well before the Tower's lights brightened to their daytime levels, and wandered into my little dining room. The *driežai* scampered in, laying out a light breakfast of bread and fruit, accompanied by a calming *ramunėlių* tea.

I munched slowly, wondering what to do.

Without Aron's new clan name, I couldn't easily find their elder again. I'd taken Gemma at her word that she had no other means of reaching him—I might revisit that, use the Axis to compel her to tell the truth. As far as I knew, it was impossible to force yourself into a hidden space—an entry rune was an absolute requirement. And that was for a hidden space I was familiar with; for one that was hidden *within* another, I wouldn't even know where to begin.

I could try tracking Aron down again. Perhaps he could be convinced. If I couldn't stop the clan's elder, I could remove his tool. Without Aron, he'd be powerless again.

I leaned back into my chair, swallowing a bite of fruit. I felt the Axis swirling around me, its lethargy matching my own. I eased into its awareness, letting my consciousness spread itself over the world.

Everything was eddied and pooled, now, as if magic itself had been forcefully disrupted. I felt nothing of the particular kind of disturbance I associated with Aron using his power. Either the world itself was in too much disarray for Aron to stand out, or he wasn't using his power at the moment.

I returned to myself. The former Clan Karal seemed out of reach—still. I couldn't find Aron until he used his Axis, at which point it'd probably be too late to stop him. The so-called prophecy still lingered in my mind—but what of it? If the old elder and Great-Great-Grandmother had truly been contemporaries—it still boggled my mind that he'd survived for so long—then it stood to reason they'd both heard the same thing. He'd implied that the two sides of the family were closer, back then. Kirmin hadn't thought much of the little verse, and I'd already broken it down a hundred times to try and make sense of it.

I decided to walk down to the shore to clear my head. Sea air—when it wasn't whipped into a frenzy, of course—had always felt calming, a means of—

A Summons struck.

CHAPTER 8

Magequake

This was a proper Summons, one cast using the proper magic and carrying all the proper signals of need and intent. The need was urgent and came from adherents. Earth, I felt, but the nuance of their request was hard to grasp through the throbbing in my skull. The main feeling transmitted was . . . panic. Sheer, unadulterated panic.

Without even standing, I gathered the tattered remnants of my focus, twisted my Axis about myself, and aimed it toward the Summons.

It deposited me unceremoniously face-down on the loamy soil of a forest. My entire body was thrumming, resonating with some unheard minor chord, a tingling sensation stinging my extremities. But the Summons continued unabated. My Axis should have ended it, followed it, and—

I retched. The nausea had come on suddenly, as it had when I'd traveled before during this time of unwinding magic.

And then I realized it. I wasn't where I was supposed to be.

I managed to push myself upright and wiped my mouth on

my sleeve. I was alone, surrounded by trees. The Summons pounded. I pulled the Axis arou—

Wait.

The Axis wasn't here.

My mind began unhelpfully running around in circles, gibbering in confusion, instead of trying to help me make sense of the feeling. The Axis was gone. I was stuck here, wherever here was. But the Summons continued. How could the Summons continue if the Axis was gone? Was I still an adherent? Where was I? The Axis was gone—

Stop. I forced my inner monologue to shut up, took a deep breath, and waited for my trembling limbs to stabilize. I spent a bit of my personal power, power I'd only recently learned to properly Gather, to warm my limbs and help them still. With another deep breath, I tried to sink into the Axis's distant awareness.

It was still there.

As I continued forcing myself to breathe deeply and slowly, as my frantic heartbeat returned to something closer to normal, I could feel the Axis's local presence more strongly. It was there, just . . . distracted. As I focused on it, that presence strengthened, renewing itself and its connection to me. Gently, I directed it to the Summons that was still pricking my mind. It sniffed warily, then seized that thread of magic. It brought itself around me and took me there.

My arrival this time was less dramatic and—given that the Summons immediately relaxed—on target. Once again, I stood on the edge of the Great Northern Wood, a stretch of scenery I was becoming all too accustomed to. Just days ago, unhinged, uncontrolled magic had set a portion of the Wood afire, and I'd been Summoned to help put it out. That had been a trial run for the actual Forging of the Fifth Axis, which had taken place just a few minutes' walk from here.

My limbs were wobbling again, and I felt dizzy. I sent one foot out sideways as I attempted to maintain my balance. I spread my arms and hunched a bit, worried that I would fall. Why were my—

No, wait. My limbs were fine. It was the earth that was shaking. It was . . . rolling. I'd once spent a day on a fishing ship, fascinated with the work the fisherwitches did, and the deck of the ship had rolled in exactly this fashion. Except this was the ground. The ground was meant to be still.

"Adherent!"

Two Earth adherents were running toward me, their dun-colored robes flapping. "What's happening?" I shouted as they closed the gap between us.

"Earthquakes!" one replied as they pounded to a halt next to me. I'd never heard the term, but it was marvelously self-explanatory—especially in the midst of it.

"It's happening everywhere—the worst is at Evermore!" the other adherent said, still breathing heavily from his run to me.

"Can't you stop it?" I asked.

"We've tried!" the first insisted. "And it shouldn't be happening here anyway. The Wood is one of the most strongly anchored places on the continent. Nothing interesting is supposed to happen here, that's the whole point of it." *Anchored.* An interesting word to describe it.

"Evermore lies near an underground fault," the other added, "and it's bad there. They're going to lose some buildings, we think. Mesla is there now, but we can't get this to stop. It's as if something is fighting our Axis."

"No, not fighting it," the other one insisted. "Suborning it. Hijacking it. It's working against us somehow."

Aron, I thought at once. That's exactly how the storm in Lastpointe had felt to the Sea adherents there. "What do you want me to do?"

"End it!" the first adherent snapped. "Sorry," he added immediately. "This is just . . . we've never seen anything like this. It's . . . bad for this to be happening anywhere, but here especially."

Again, the special situation of the Great Northern Wood that I still didn't understand. "What, exactly, am I Ending? I'll need to give the Axis a command."

They both stared at me as if I was mad. "The earthquake," one of them said somewhat slowly, as if to a small child.

I frowned. A clearer explanation of the cause would have been better. The Axis struggled with abstract or nonspecific requests. But that was all I had to work with. *End this earthquake*, I ordered the Axis. I didn't even know what rune to hold in my mind. But the Axis was paying attention, and I felt it cast its attention to the earth below us, but at that exact moment there was no rumbling. Nothing to End. Its attention wandered elsewhere.

Had the earthquake stopped of its own—

No. A particularly large rumble thudded through the meadow, vibrating my very bones. With a *crack* louder than a peal of thunder, two long sections of earth seemed to separate, creating a narrow chasm between them. This chasm zigzagged away from us, reaching into the Wood and throwing up a cloud of dust.

"End *that!*" the first adherent shouted, pointing to the crack in the earth.

I obeyed, sending the Axis into the ground and instructing it to End the rumbling. I didn't hold a rune in my mind, couldn't imagine which one I'd have used anyway, and hoped that my desperate intent was sufficient.

It wasn't. Perhaps I was too focused on the foot-wide gap in the earth, a geological feature that the Axis didn't understand how to End. The rumbling did pause for a moment, but then another wave rolled below us.

"No?" the second adherent asked.

I shook my head. "I don't know what I'm Ending. What's the actual mechanism, here? What's actually causing this?"

The first adherent took a deep breath. "In most of the world, the earth consists of numerous overlapping layers, each with a slightly different composition." He was speaking quickly, obviously repeating some lecture he'd once been given. Another *boom* rolled the ground beneath us as we adjusted our stances to stay upright. "Those layers aren't evenly distributed—layers end and begin everywhere. Wherever there's a big change in their configuration, you can get faults—sections of earth that are only loosely held together."

"You're really murdering this," the other adherent muttered.

"No!" I said. "This is good. Keep going!"

"Some of these layers are soft," said the first adherent, "and they're constantly in motion. They're also impacted by the deep magma beneath the—wait, do you know what magma is?"

I nodded furiously. I'd become quite acquainted with it these past few days. I'd recently engaged with several junior adherents who shaped glowing-hot magma into a dragon that spewed fire at stacks of iron rails the humans had made. My carelessness during the whole debacle contributed to the near-destruction of the Veil that helped conceal witchkind's magic from humans.

"So the magma is always in motion, and it can push the layers around. Get the right things all going on in the same place at the same time, and the layers shift dramatically—an earthquake."

"Which can't happen here," I noted.

"No!" the second yelled. "The layers here are extraordinarily consistent and stable. The magma reservoir is deeper here than anyplace else in the world! Earthquakes are rare enough as it is, but they *can't* happen here!"

Another wave shook us from beneath, putting the lie to his assertion.

"So it's all layers shifting," I said, earning confirming nods from both of them. "Fine, maybe I can—"

"What is it?" the first adherent asked, noting my change in expression.

Something was pricking at the back of my neck. My spine tingled slightly. "I don't know," I said slowly. "Something's—"

My sentence cut off in a scream as claws of white-hot pain pierced my brain behind my eyes. I fell to my knees—something that had become all too common recently—and clutched my head. The most intense part of the pain vanished in an instant, leaving a pulsing ache behind.

"Daniel?"

I looked up. "Aron." The first Earth adherent offered me his hand, and I accepted his assistance in getting back on my feet. "Is this your doing?"

"What?" Aron's expression was one of genuine confusion.

Another rumble shuddered the ground. "That."

"Oh. Maybe?" He looked around as if he'd never been here before, even though wasn't far from where he'd become an adherent just a few days prior. "They had me do something in Evermore."

"What?" the two Earth adherents demanded.

"They wanted to Create something dramatic in Evermore," he said sadly. "Something the Taryba would pay attention to."

"He's after ransom," I muttered.

"Who *is* this?" the second Earth adherent demanded, pointing at Aron.

"Aron, formerly of Clan Karal, formerly of a clan I don't know the name of, now adherent of the Fifth Axis."

Their eyes went wide.

"Pergalės," Aron said softly.

My eyebrows climbed to my hairline. "What did you say?"

"Pergalės. That's my clan name now. It . . . hurt when they did it. I remember that." His voice was low and soft, and I struggled to hear him over the crunching, booming sounds that were still coming from the crack in the earth.

Now I know their clan name, I thought grimly. *They were right to keep it from me.* But first things first. "Aron, what did you do? What did you tell your Axis to do?"

He looked at me distractedly. "In Evermore?" I nodded. "They said to make the earth beneath the city slide around."

I seized my Axis, and once again sent it arrowing into the earth below us. This time, I gave it a rune, the one for Ending movement. This would be an odd use of that rune, as it was intended to freeze large crowds in place, but I knew of no other to try. *End the movement in the earth*, I ordered. *Here, in this place, End its motion.*

My power blasted downward, and this time I felt the Axis do its work. This was the kind of straightforward, transactional Ending it understood well: this is a thing that is happening, and you're to make it stop happening.

Aron screamed and fell to his knees.

The earth stilled midrumble.

"No, no, no, no, no, no," Aron moaned, holding his head and rocking to and fro.

"Aron," I said quietly, crouching next to him and drawing him into an embrace. "What's the matter?"

"The hurt." He sobbed. "And the earth has stopped. They'll be angry with me."

"The elder?"

He nodded, still sobbing.

"How is he *making* you do this? Your—someone, that is, mentioned a leash. What do they have over you?"

He shook his head. "This is my duty!" he cried. "My destiny! All our destinies! I have to do what they tell me. I can't fail!" A twinge of pain shot up my spine. Aron moaned softly. "It's not working!"

"Aron, you don't *have* to do anything! Everything they've told you, it's lies! Exaggerations! The Axes weren't meant to *rule* people!" *Although they probably were, but it's not what's happened so far.*

"I know that," he said softly, although he sounded unconvinced. "I tried to tell them to stop. That I wouldn't do it anymore, wouldn't hurt people anymore." He sniffed. "We're not supposed to rule. You said that. Adherents aren't supposed to rule. I'm an adherent now, right? So I told them I wanted to stop."

"Then why keep doing it?"

Aron looked up at me, his eyes bloodshot and full of tears. "They told me they'd hurt Mother if I didn't obey."

My world turned red.

My heart hammered against the inside of my chest. My vision tightened to two small circles, each hazed with crimson. My blood pounded in my ears. This clan, Karal, Pergalės, whatever—they were evil. My last memories of Mother swam through my brain, and I again saw her damaged hand, felt her shattered magic, felt her fade as I Ended the rune that Karal had perverted. And now they'd threatened to harm Gemma? I had no love for the woman, but—

"I have to go back," Aron said with another gulping sob.

"Wait—"

I was too late. I felt my Axis *blink.* Every so briefly. Another dagger of white pain pierced my brain as Aron vanished, leaving me to catch myself on my elbows as I fell over.

"Adherent?"

"I'm fine," once again accepting a hand up. "The immediate danger—"

"BY ALL THE GODS OLD AND NEW, WHAT ARE YOU FOOLS PLAYING AT HERE?"

A brace of woodwitches was marching out of the wood, their expressions twisted in anger. At their lead was a short, dark-featured old woman.

"Aunt," I said tiredly. "We—"

"*You* may address me as Ikwity," she snapped, stabbing a finger at me. "What is the meaning of *this*?" she shouted, her finger turning to point at the crevice in the earth. "This is no place to be summoning such magic! You—"

"We didn't do this," one of the Earth adherents protested.

Ikwity whirled around to face him. "You think Ikwity can't tell Earth magic when she smells it? Hmm? Bad enough your petty ancestors chained such powers. Now you go flinging them about with no care for anyone's safety?"

"We—" the other adherent attempted.

"Two creatures, we've put down already this morning! Two! Creatures changed by whatever you've thrown around! They were broken, displaced, wrong! Sensitive, this place is! Sacred! A refuge, the Last Bastion, not . . . not some zoo! Not some sandbox for children to test their stolen magic!"

Stolen? "Ikwity, we had nothing to do with this," I tried, forcing my voice to stay reasonable even as my heart was still thudding away. "We—"

"And *you*," she snapped, whirling back to me. "*Smelled* your power on this, I did! Rip the whole world off its base, you will! We—"

"I didn't do this!" I shouted back, venting some of the

anger that was roiling inside me. "Just days ago, you remember? They Forged the Fifth! He did this at the bidding of his masters. They meant to threaten Evermore, not here. This was . . ." I struggled to find a word.

"Aftershocks," one of the Earth adherents offered.

"That," I said, nodding to him. "I Ended them."

Ikwity stared at me, suspicion written all over her face. "Smelled of Endings," she insisted, although she'd stopped shouting.

"I'm not sure there's a difference."

"Still, boy, you keep your magic *away* from the Wood, you understand?" She was back to shouting now, and my fury quickly rekindled. "Take your Earth, take your Endings, take your Axes, take your—"

"WE DID NOTHING!" I roared. My Axis mantled my emotions, its power flaring out around me. The two Earth adherents fell backward, landing on their asses. Three of the woodwitches who'd accompanied Ikwity fell to their knees, their eyes wide. The others took several steps backward. Even the old woman stopped midrant, snapping her jaw shut. "We did nothing!" I repeated, wrestling down my temper.

"You have no idea," she said in a cold, menacing voice, "what you will unleash. None of you do." She treated each of us to a long, penetrating glare. "Keep all of your upset away from the Wood."

With that, she spun round and marched back into the forest, the woodwitches scrambling to accompany her.

I sighed and helped the two adherents to their feet. "What was that all about?"

The first sighed, brushing himself off and extending his hand. "Jakub." We shook. "You know much about the Wood?"

"Apparently not," I replied. "Daniel," I said, offering my hand to the other.

"Timot," he replied as we shook.

"Magic is taboo here," Jakub said. "It's why nobody witchkind lives in Greensea, and the few who live in Rushford temper their magic. No hidden spaces even. They live in the open. The woodwitches keep basically everyone out of the Wood itself, and they only use the smallest, personal magics."

"But why?"

They both shrugged. "I don't know that anyone's ever gotten the right answer," Timot said. "I grew up in Evermore, and as kids you hear stories. Stay away from the Great Northern Wood. The Wood is full of monsters. Obey your parents or the woodwitches will carry you away. That kind of thing."

I looked into the trees, but the dense canopy made it so dark I couldn't see more than a few strides in. I sent the Axis to sniff about. There was *something*. Something odd. *Old.* "She mentioned creatures. Have you met her before?"

Both adherents shook their heads. "No," Jakub said, "but did you notice?"

I turned back to him. "Notice what?"

"She's not witchkind."

My eyes widened.

"Now that you mention it, she didn't have the smell," Tomit agreed slowly.

"Smell?" I asked.

"Adherent thing," Tomit replied. "Earth smells magic. Sky hears it. Sea says they can feel it on their skin. Flame . . . what was it?"

"Tastes it," Jakub supplied. "You can sense it too, right?"

"When I look for it," I replied, thinking about it. "It's not a sense, though, it's . . . I just can tell. I guess even if I'm thinking about it, but I just didn't notice. Interesting."

"We should get back to the others," Jakub said after a moment of silence.

"It'll take forever if the earth is still churned," Timot groused.

"Before you go," I said, "I need to talk to Mesla. Did you say she was in Evermore?"

"She's here," a voice said from behind us. I turned to see her rising from the ground, brushing dirt from her robes. "Evermore is under control. A few minutes ago, the quakes seemed to lose their will. Your doing?"

"I believe so," I replied.

"Our thanks," she said with a sigh. Her shoulders slumped. "Evermore is . . . damaged. We can repair and rebuild. But many were injured. A few killed." She peered at me. "You don't look well."

"I don't feel well. Something is . . . wrong. Aron started the quakes."

Her eyes flew open. "Why?"

"Remember Clan Karal?" She nodded. "They're Pergalés, now. Burned away their identities to hide from me and crafted new ones. They chained the Fifth, made Aron their adherent. They've indoctrinated him, made him believe he's fulfilling their destiny. And they've threatened him, on top of it, if he doesn't comply. That storm off Lastpointe yesterday—that was him."

"I'm told Gilioj is gone," she said quietly.

"I saw him go. Yes."

Mesla's expression grew sad and lonely, her soft eyes glistening with unshed tears. "What could possibly threaten an adherent?"

"They've promised to harm his mother."

Mesla's eyes grew wide. She'd been with me when I'd attempted to free Mother— when I'd realized Ending her identity rune, Ending her, was my only choice. "They would do that to one of their own?"

"They want power, and they are already ransoming lives en masse. What's one of their own to them if it means they succeed?"

"Despicable."

I nodded. "My Axis . . . it's tied to the Fifth, somehow. I think . . . I think the Fifth and the Sixth might be the same thing." Her brow wrinkled in confusion. "Whenever Aron uses his power, I feel it. Painfully. When I use it, I think he hurts too. My Axis seems to weaken when he draws on the Fifth as well. I think only one of us can use our power at once."

Her eyes widened again, and I saw comprehension in her face. "The Archons—"

"Yes. I think they lied. Or misunderstood. I don't think the Fifth escaped. I think they just couldn't Forge whatever it was, into two separate things. Not all at once."

"But now it's done."

"It's incomplete. *I'm* incomplete." A bit of my pain surfaced in my voice, and Mesla winced.

"Our own powers have been . . . diminished," Jakub said quietly.

Mesla looked at him for a long moment, then nodded. "I think we're all feeling it." She looked back to me. "Daniel, is it possible that Forging the Fifth has damaged the Origin, somehow?"

The mythical source of magic, the thing that all witchkind revered. Our version of the human deity. I shrugged. "I don't know. Maybe there just isn't enough magic of Beginnings left free in the world, and you're feeling the effects of that. Maybe it's what everyone felt when they Forged the Axes originally. Maybe it will settle down." I shrugged again. "I just don't know."

"We need to do something," she said firmly.

"I know."

"Where will you go first?"

"It turns out I know Aron's mother. And now I know their clan name. I'm going to go find her if I can. If they have nothing over him, maybe we can talk. Figure this out. Maybe I can get to their elder and . . . do something." *End him*, my eyes said.

Mesla nodded her understanding. "How can we help?"

"Can I call on you?" I had no idea what was ahead of me, but the strong steadiness of an Earth adherent could be useful, if not reassuring.

"Can you take me with you?" she countered. "Our Form of Travel isn't as swift and limited to undisturbed earth."

"Normally I'd say yes. Right now, it may be risky. The Axis dumped me in a forest somewhere, on the way here. If you don't mind taking a chance . . ."

She nodded firmly, her expression resolved. "We all do what must be done. Where do we go first?"

"Evermore, if you don't mind going back."

"Why?"

"I suspect the Taryba may be able to give us some news."

She looked confused but nodded assent. I took her arm and called on my Axis.

CHAPTER 9

Evermore

Every member of witchkind's highest governing body was present in their council chamber when Mesla and I arrived—an arm's length above the granite floor. She and I fell into an ungainly pile, and by the time we'd untangled ourselves and stood, we'd gained the attention of the entire room.

"The earthquake," I said. "Was there a demand?" A dozen confused gazes met mine. "A demand," I repeated, growing frustrated. "Requests. Warnings. Something someone delivered after the earthquake abated. Or during it—I don't know."

One of the counselors, Trisian, an even-tempered woman who'd often taken my side in arguments with the council, pointed behind me.

Mesla and I turned to see an upright slab of granite, tall as me, leaning against the chamber's grand doors. Into its flat, glossy surface was carved the demand:

. . .

Earth and well as Sky. All of Evermore must bend the knee. Prepare to step down and be governed by your betters. We will be in touch.

"What do you know of this?" one of the counselors asked.

I turned back to them. "The same clan that caused the storm at Lastpointe, the same clan that was draining humans for power—they used that power to Forge the Fifth Axis on the edge of the Great Northern Wood. When was that?" I asked, turning to Mesla. "A week ago, now?"

"Almost," she nodded with a sigh. "It feels like much longer. Do you need me to move it?" she asked the counselors.

"If you can," an elderly man said. "We've tried, but our magic is . . . uneven."

"That's been going around," I said grimly as Mesla used her Axis to decompose the slab into a pile of tiny fragments.

"Can the adherents not stop them?" another counselor asked.

"The power of Beginnings is . . . difficult to counter," Mesla said slowly. "Working with Daniel, yes, we were able to stop the earthquake."

"And the storm," I added. "But it was difficult. Far from a sure thing."

"And even the Axes have been responding . . . unevenly, as you say," Mesla finished, nodding at the older counselor.

"So they mean to make themselves kings?" It was a hard word to hear. In the True Language of magic, *king* was *karal*.

"Singular, I believe," I replied flatly. "I'm given to understand their entire clan has but one elder."

Eyes rose. "To maintain a clan identity with but one elder —" someone whispered.

"He's positively ancient, if that helps," I added.

A few heads nodded. "It might." Lina, the Taryba's senior counselor and its official spokesperson. "Age confers a certain . . . gravity. Stability. But still, to hold an entire clan . . ."

"He claims he knew my great-great-grandmother," I said. "Assuming he was young when she was fairly old"—I did some quick math in my head—"he'd have to be at least two hundred." The women in my family tended to give birth fairly early for witchkind, as early as forty.

"Not unheard of, and that might be sufficient to anchor an entire clan's identity," Lina mused. "So now he means to rule all of witchkind?"

"Apparently," I said, shaking my head. "There's a whole story about destiny, about them having been meant to control an Axis for hundreds of years, about how the adherents should be in charge of the entire world."

"Well, at least we're included," Mesla muttered.

I gave her a reproaching side-eye. "He didn't expect us to participate, but he's willing to take it all on himself."

"How kind."

"How can we help stop this?" asked Acantha, the sharpest of the counselors. "If there have been attacks on Sea and Earth, can we presume Flame and Sky are next?"

I nodded tiredly. "You should assume so, yes, although I have no idea when and where. Get the word out. Tell people to be prepared. Their magic may not be enough to protect them. It may not be reliable. Evacuate hidden spaces in case they collapse. Seek physical shelters."

"That will set off a panic," a counselor pointed out.

"We have nothing else to tell you," Mesla said sharply. "I will help Daniel as best I can. We all will. In the meantime, take what precautions you can." She turned to me. "You believe speaking with the boy's mother may help?"

"Rescuing her might," I said.

"Then let us go to her now."

"I think it might actually be wiser to try and find their clan elder. He's at the root of this."

"Do you think you can?"

I sighed. "I'm not sure. But I want to try."

Mesla nodded, her mouth set in a line as she took my forearm.

Gently, I begged the Axis.

CHAPTER 10

Gemma

The Axis managed to comply, depositing us gently in the Tower's map room.

"This is interesting," Mesla said, holding her hands behind her back as she leaned over the map table, peering at the detailed depiction of the continent.

"Hopefully this will work." I cleared my throat to announce my command. "The elder of Clan Pergalès."

The map shuddered briefly before steadying but otherwise didn't move.

"I was afraid of that."

"What?"

"They've gotten skilled at hiding themselves from me. From this map. Maybe if I knew the elder's given name . . . I don't know. He's likely moved his hidden space. I would if I was hiding from me."

"So we go to the mother?"

I nodded. "Gemma. Of Clan Pergalès."

"Oh!" Mesla exclaimed as the map began sliding and zooming. "Oh, that's clever, I've never seen anything quite— Is it supposed to do that?"

"No," I said with a sigh as the map stopped, spun through a complete circle, and then zoomed back out to the continent-wide view. "It's Aron. All of this is powered by the Sixth Axis, and it's been in a mood since the Fifth's Forging." I frowned. "Give me a minute."

Once again, I calmed myself and sank into the Axis. It was less turbulent than it had been, but it still wasn't the smooth steadiness I'd grown accustomed to. I focused, willing it to slow its churn, to even its awareness across the continent, and to find Gemma.

"It's doing something."

I ignored her, focusing intently on keeping the Axis evenly dispersed as best I could. I'd never been able to fully control this aspect of it, and it still had vortices here and there—the largest of which was probably Aron—but I was able to calm it enough for the map table to do its work.

"Oh, there's a light."

My eyes snapped open, scanning the map before it could fade. "Landshire?" It was a tiny village in the far east, north of the Great Northern Range and just south of the river that separated it from the larger Chiton. "They're really making an effort."

"How does this work?" she asked curiously.

"Endings are everywhere. The Sixth Axis attends to them, and so does the map."

Her forehead wrinkled. "Attend? Are you saying the Axis is somehow responsible for every death in the world?"

I shrugged. "It's always felt that way. And I know I can withhold it."

Now here eyebrows rose. "You mean prevent deaths from happening?"

"For a short time. It's an effort. Are you saying your Axis isn't responsible for every little thing that goes on with the earth? Surely its power is at work when you're not asking it for something."

She was quiet for a moment. "I never thought about it. Hmm. But what's next?"

I tapped the map where the glowing point of light was just starting to fade. "We go there."

I started to pull my Axis around us, but she stopped me. "Do you mind if I try something?"

"What?"

"The Axis of Earth is steadying. Strong. If you don't mind my saying so, your Form of Travel feels a bit . . . rough. Even when you brought us here."

"I did warn you."

"I know. I'm just wondering if I can lend a hand, so to speak."

"I don't see why not."

"Give me a moment." She closed her eyes, and I could feel Earth magic moving around her. It was a slow, implacable force, not entirely unlike my own Axis, but less flighty. The earth wasn't a transactional power, it was a *forever* power. Earth magic preserved and maintained. "Okay."

I pointed my Axis to the last wisp of light on the map table, and ordered it to take us there. It wrapped around us in a ragged flurry, but something about Mesla's Axis seemed to steady it. What had started to feel like another rough ride became smoother, surer. The map room blinked out, and a near-freezing cold settled onto us as we appeared in Landshire.

"I've got it," Mesla said, laying a hand on my arm. The cold immediately backed off, and I again sensed her Axis at work.

"How does that work for you?"

"The earth is hot, far below, and incredibly stable just a few feet down. I just pull on that difference a bit. Can't you do something similar?"

I shrugged. "I just End the cold."

"Fascinating. Is this our destination?"

We'd appeared on the outskirts of town, with the cloud-topped mountains of the Great Northern Range far off behind us. Before us stood storehouses and stables designed to support the brave—or possibly mad—trade caravans that trekked through the lone pass connecting Landshire to Taliesin on the other side of the range. Most of the structures here were made of wood, carved from the hard, durable local evergreens. But our target was a low building of local stone, stacked and mortared together. I pointed to it. "It's that one. But—"

"No, I can feel it."

Iron. A fury began rising in me. Karal—Pergalės, whatever—had used a similar structure, also crowned with the magic-sapping metal, to imprison Mother. If I had to guess, the inside would have upright bars forming a cage.

Mesla and I stepped as close as we could to it. "It's starting to pull at my magic," she said, stopping a dozen paces away.

"It's odd," I said as I took another step or two further. "I've heard others describe it that way. But mine isn't. It's more like it's repelled."

"Pushed back, do you mean?"

"No," I said slowly, tasting the Axis's reaction to the iron. "More like being repelled by something distasteful. It doesn't want to go forward. I'm even finding it hard to lift a foot to take another step. Gemma!" I called out.

The building had two small ventilation slots near its roofline. "Who's there?" a woman's voice floated out.

"Daniel. And a friend."

I imagined her weighing her options: engage with the

enemy of her son or rot in a cell. "You can see what they've done."

"Are you okay?"

"My magic is gone."

"That's the iron. Have they hurt you?"

"They haven't even told me why I'm in here!" Her tone was angry now.

"It's Aron. You're his leash." Behind me, I could sense Mesla bristling. I hadn't fully explained the situation before we'd left.

"That's ridiculous," Gemma yelled back, although she didn't sound entirely convinced. "They've used magic to leash him, they said."

"What magic could leash an adherent?" Mesla called.

I could almost feel her simmering. "Who's that?"

"Mesla, senior Adherent of Earth."

Another silence. "I don't understand."

"You can't leash an adherent with magic, Gemma," I called back. "We're too powerful. There's no bond I couldn't End and therefore no bond Aron couldn't Begin a new life without."

"Begin a new life?"

"Beginnings and Endings are two sides of the same coin. I had to move past my own Ending to become adherent of the Sixth. Chances are Aron can . . . Begin himself. Whenever he wants to. He's been told that your safety, probably your life, is forfeit if he doesn't obey."

"He set off an earthquake under Evermore," Mesla said loudly.

Nearby, a couple of human hostlers had looked toward us, pausing from their work at hitching horses to wagons. I idly Ended their attention and created a bubble of silence around myself, Mesla, and Gemma's prison.

"Buildings have fallen," Mesla continued. "People were injured. Killed."

"The Great Northern Wood was threatened. Again," I added.

Another silence. "What do you want me to do?" Gemma asked, her voice a bit softer.

"If we can get you out of there, will you speak to Aron? We need to him stop listening to your elder. This bid for power is killing people."

"They told me they were taking me to keep me safe from you."

I barked a laugh. "From me? And so they put you in a cage where you couldn't use magic? Come on, Gemma. I'm the one letting you out. Are you ready to quit trusting them? Quit obeying them?"

She was silent for a long time now, and I looked back at Mesla, who simply shrugged. "I'd be ready to burn their rune out of my soul again," Gemma said at last, her voice hard.

"We can arrange that," Mesla murmured. "And it might be a good idea. They likely have a means of tracking their members."

"They won't track her to where I'm going to take her," I said softly.

"How will you get me out?" Gemma asked. "There are iron bars surrounding me and across the ceiling."

Mesla chuckled. "No need to worry about that."

"What?" I asked.

"Nobody ever thinks of the floor." She sank quickly into the earth, a sight that never failed to unnerve me.

"Hold on Gemma," I said. "I think we may have—"

"Oh!" Gemma cried out.

"—a plan," I finished with a chuckle.

"This is a lot, Daniel." Mesla's voice came from inside the

cell. I could hear the strain in her tone. "Even with an Axis, I'm—"

Gemma screamed, sending a shiver of fear down my spine. What happens when iron stymies an Earth adherent? What happens when their magic is incomp—

"Never mind, that's better," Mesla finished, her voice oddly muffled now. A moment later, the earth began collapsing in front of me, somehow falling in on itself in a long shoulder-wide trough nearby me. I peered into it. The bottom had been fashioned into a ramp.

Before long, Mesla and Gemma came walking up that ramp, turning slightly sideways as they squeezed through the tight space. Gemma looked washed out and perturbed.

"All okay?" I asked.

"She dropped us into a pit," Gemma muttered, brushing dirt from her dress.

"Our Form of Travel doesn't accommodate passengers," Mesla said with a shrug. "It seemed the easiest way to get you out of the iron's influence." With a gesture, she commanded the trough to refill itself, and within seconds a wide patch of roughened dirt was the only sign it had ever existed. "Not perfect, but I could get some grass to grow on—"

"It's fine," I said. "Gemma, I'm taking you to the Tower of Endings. My home. I have some questions I need you to answer, and we're going to try to call to Aron. You'll need to stay there, no matter what. Do you understand?" She nodded, her eyes wide. "The Tower can keep you safe from the clan." For as long as I'd been adherent of the Sixth, I'd kept an open-island policy, permitting anyone to alight on the island and walk up the path to the Tower. That permissiveness Ends now. None without an explicit invite will be allowed on the island. "Mesla?"

"I have things to attend to. Evermore needs our help." With that, she sank back into the earth.

"That is unnerving in the extreme," Gemma muttered.

"I couldn't agree more. But you may find this less comfortable than last time." My Axis whirled around us and spirited us to the Tower.

"Oof," Gemma gasped, bending over and resting her hands on her thighs as we appeared in the Tower's foyer. "That was rough."

"I warned you. It's Aron. His existence. The Fifth Axis. It wasn't meant to be Forged, and it's disrupting the Sixth now. The others as well, to some degree. Possibly magic everywhere."

She exhaled deeply and stood upright. "How?"

"I don't know. But what's more important is learning why. Come in here. Have a seat." I led her into the Tower's library, its magically expanded space soaring high overhead, and showed her to a comfortable chair. "Do you need anything? Tea? Something to eat?"

"Watercress would be wonderful, if you have it. And tea, yes."

"Tea. Watercress sandwich."

"Yes, that would be—oh!" she exclaimed, as a flickering, shadowy *driežai* delivered her request. "Ah, thank you."

"You're welcome," I said coolly. "Now, I need to know why your elder is doing this. I know he wants power. Position. But more specifically. Why? What was the plan from the outset?"

"You said *he*. I still can't believe . . ."

"There was only one man in the hidden space. One old man. I told you that, after he ejected me."

"I'm sure they wouldn't all congregate in the same place all at once."

"He implied he was the only living elder."

"That's . . . not possible."

"Have you seen others?"

"Of course," she said, but I could see her confidence waver. "They've explained the plans, the Great Work, the—"

"Yes, there have been *people*. But are you certain they were your *elders*? The ones actually making decisions? Not just people playing a role?"

"I—" she started, but fell silent. "How can there have been only one?"

"I'm starting to get the impression that the people of your clan have been ill-used."

Gemma looked at me for a long time, sipping her tea gently before she answered. "They spoke so passionately about the Great Work. About finally bringing the Fifth Axis under control, making it available to everyone."

"The power of Creation was never unavailable," I pointed out. "That's the downside of the Axes, the thing the stories don't discuss. The thing the Archons seemed to have glossed over. Forging these powers *restricted* them to the adherents."

She blinked. "I guess I never thought of it that way." She shook her head more slowly this time. "They . . . it was our clan against the world, they told us. We were very tight, very close, you know. Just four families in the clan, maybe three hundred of us total. We were in a race, they said, to finally Forge the Fifth. You were our main opposition six years back. They said you'd be jealous of having balance, of there being an equal Axis in the world. When you disrupted our plans and stopped us from gathering power, we took it as proof."

"You were killing the humans you Gathered from. You know that right?"

She took another sip of tea. "I think I didn't want to know. They'd already said Aron was a candidate, the right age and all. After what I found in your family archive—well, our family archive—that seemed to confirm it."

"But why? What did they get out of it all?"

She sighed and set the teacup back on the table beside her. "The two families, Statybininkas and Laikytojas."

"Builders and Keepers," I translated. Those names in the archive."

She nodded. "Clan history is that they were the ones who helped build the bridge to this world from wherever we all came from. The Exodus. But they weren't politically astute. They'd expected to be leaders in the new world, but they were overshadowed. Pushed aside. They weren't allowed to put up a candidate to be Archon. Instead that honor fell to Jura, Leipsna, Zeme, Vejas, Galas, and Gyvenima, rest her spirit."

I smiled at Gemma's effortless recitation of the Archons' names

"They were from the big families—the ones too large and too powerful to care about being on the Taryba. They saw us, our predecessors, as menials. Workers. No way were they going to give us a seat at the table. And so after the Axes were Forged, the two families made plans to seize two of them. The big ones."

"Endings and Beginnings."

"With the latter being decidedly more difficult."

"So this was all . . . just to be in the mix?"

She sighed. "Originally, but not anymore. My clan holds grudges. I can admit that. They want power, and they want to rub everyone's noses in it. After having been locked in an iron cell, I can see it. Setting an earthquake on Evermore—they won't ask for money to make it stop. They just want everyone to know they can do it again. They want the bowing and scraping." She gave me a hard look. "Like you get."

"I don't—"

"Oh, you do. I don't know if you enjoy it, but the whole world, all of witchkind at least, lives in fear of you. What other

Axis can cast down a Judgment and enforce it the way you can? Not just common witchkind, but other adherents call for your aid through Summons. And you could simply ignore them, never minding how much magic an ordinary person has to Gather to cast it."

"I never meant—"

"I know you didn't, Daniel." She gave an exasperated sigh and picked a pinch of watercress out of her sandwich, munching it slowly before continuing. "You seem . . . very kind, actually. You remind me a bit of Aron, when he was younger." Her eyes were a little misty, now. "But you know the history of your predecessors."

I slowly nodded acknowledgment. "There have been many bad ones. And perhaps very few great ones."

"And so our clan wanted that. The respect. The power. I think your ascension vexed them greatly."

"They knew I was related?"

"We have genealogists. We were never meant to mingle, once the plans began. Keeping apart felt like the only way to stay safe. But your family clearly lost track of us. Marrying your mother to one of ours? What were they thinking?"

"I don't know," I said softly.

"And this whole tradition of burning out the husband's clan identity? It's just cruel."

"They were very . . . focused," I admitted. I knew so little about them, really, but everything I did know pointed to single-mindedness. They'd been just as determined in their quest to own an Axis. If any of them had survived alongside me, would they have directed me in the way Aron was being directed now? Would I have been their tool, their pawn? Would I have gone along with it, just to make my family happy?

I was very afraid I might have.

Gemma picked up her sandwich and finished it in several

large bites. "Thank you for that. They'd given me nothing in there. Do you have a way to find Aron? As you found me?"

"It's easy enough. He disrupts my Axis—and I his, I think. If he's using his power at all, I can tell. He hasn't since the earthquake." *I'm not sure if I should be glad of that or afraid.* "If I can find him, if I tell him you're here, will he listen? Will he come here and ignore your elder?"

"I believe so. Yes," she said, sounding sure of herself. "Do you—adherents, I mean . . . Do you still have clan runes?"

I shook my head. "We're Chosen when we're thirteen. Clan runes aren't fully set by then. Whatever we do have fades—and I never had one. Others, I hear, keep in touch with their families, support them, send them money"—something that still grated on my nerves, but this wasn't the time or place. "But no."

"Will Aron still have his, then?"

I blinked. "I hadn't considered it," I said slowly. "I honestly don't know. Apart from the Archons, no adult has ever become an adherent. I don't know whether his Axis would have purged his clan rune or not."

"Then there's something you need to know," she said in a very small voice. "After Shura. After you stopped her . . . excesses." Gemma took a deep breath. Shura had shown no remorse when draining energy from humans. How many lives had she taken? "They carved a new rune into us, making us a new clan."

"Pergalės."

Her eyes widened. "Ah. So you know."

"I know I wasn't meant to."

"We knew you had some means of tracking us. We had to hide. But that's not what I'm trying to tell you. The rune they crafted—it was more than our name. They added something."

My skin crawled, and my stomach clenched. Given what the elder had already done . . . "What?"

"They called it *Mirties Spąstai.*"

I translated in my head. "Death trap."

She nodded. "Any of us can be killed from afar if we disobey. I think they'd hesitate to use it on Aron, but if they believe he's forever beyond their reach . . . "

"Then why the iron cage?"

She shrugged. "They can't monitor me all the time. That was to ensure I was fully under their control. That I couldn't use my magic. I couldn't even call to Aron."

My heart started pounding. "Gemma," I said calmly, "what if they discover you're gone?"

Her eyes flew open, and her skin went gray. "They . . . need me. For Aron. They wouldn't—"

"I wouldn't be so sure," I said grimly. I held out a hand and summoned the Book of Endings. It dropped easily into my hand, appearing out of thin air. Despite its size, it had little heft to it, making it easy to catch. I took it to a nearby bookrest and opened it, flipping quickly through the thick vellum leaves.

"What are you doing?"

"I End things, Gemma. Better than anyone."

There: *Narystės klane pabaiga.* "Were you serious about no longer wanting to belong to your clan?" I asked quietly, turning to look at her.

"You . . . you can do that?"

"I suspect it will hurt a lot less than whatever they did to burn Karal out of you." The Axis's Endings had always been swift, painless, and effortless.

Fear resolved into acceptance on her face. "Do it."

Without another thought, I sent the Axis lancing toward her, holding the rune in my mind:

She inhaled sharply as it hit her, her shoulders tensing for a moment. But then she exhaled slowly and seemed to relax. "You were right. That was . . . odd. But not painful. Thank you."

"You can feel it?"

"Oh, yes. It's gone. There's a piece of me missing, again. Where they used to be. But it's fine." She paused, and her expression gentled. "You've been kinder than I expected. Than I deserved."

It took me a moment to reply. What could I even say? She'd deceived me. I'd lied to her. She was twice my age. I was never going to have time for a relationship anyway. I'm trying not to be the monster some of my predecessors were. "You're welcome."

"Can you do that for Aron? Remove his rune?"

I had no idea. "Maybe," I prevaricated. "If it's still even in him. I may need his cooperation. If you urge him . . ."

"I will."

"All right. I'm going to go find him, then. Stay here. Bring her food and drink at her request," I ordered the Tower. "And admit no one without my express consent. And in my presence." The atmosphere of the Tower seemed to harden at that. Gemma would be safe from her clan here.

"Where will you start?" she asked.

At that moment, a jab of pain spiked into my skull.

"What?" Gemma asked, seeing my grimace.

"Aron." I gasped as the pain faded. "He's using his power."

"Can you tell where?"

A Summons hit me between the eyes. "Pretty sure I can, yes."

CHAPTER 11

Magefire

I arrived poorly, literally rolling head over heels on a slick, cold, stone floor in near-darkness.

"Daniel!"

I'd recognize Zmogus's rough shout in any circumstance. I swore I could hear his scowl. He thudded over to me, grabbed an arm, and hauled me to my feet. While helpful, my body protested the treatment, complaining mightily in my stomach and muscles. "You were quick," he said, quickly bowing his head in what I belatedly realized was a show of thanks.

"What's happening? Where am I?" I forced myself to breathe slowly, to stand upright even as my head spun and my vision swam. I was standing in a long, wide corridor, stone walls rising twice my height on either side. Everything was slick stone. Torches were set into the walls at regular intervals, lit with actual, orange-yellow flames, not the steady lights preferred by most of witchkind.

"You're inside Flamefast," he said. I stifled a laugh, the name a little too on the nose. "Have you been here before?" I shook my head as my eyes adjusted to the dim, flickering light. "Thought not. Not many visit the home of Flame adherents."

"Is Aron . . . please don't tell me he's attacking you."

Zmogus nodded grimly. "He's not out there right now. But he was. Fortunately we're well-defended here within the hill. Flamefast has long been a worthy fortress."

"A fortress." This was unbelievable. Nobody else had fortresses. Even my Tower wasn't a *fortress*.

"Built by humans, centuries ago. Small factions warred with one another almost continually back then. Whoever built this clearly wanted to be left alone."

"And so they built a fortress. In a hillside." I knew I needed to just move on, but my befuddled wits wouldn't let me.

"Yes, and that's the problem," Zmogus growled. "We're in the inner chambers, the living areas. That's surrounded by an outer wall that goes all around and over the inner portion. There's a gap about three times your height between the two. Fortified outer door, fortified inner door."

My head was spinning. "Please explain why this is important."

"It is. As a defensive measure, the gap between the inner and outer walls can be filled with fire."

Filled with fire. Because of course it could.

"If someone breaches the outer wall, they have an inferno to contend with. One we can obviously keep going for a long, long time." His gravelly, coarse voice sounded smug.

"So . . . you get attacked often?"

"Never in living memory, no."

"But still." A fortress filled with fire.

"Whoever originally built this must have had enemies," he said with a shrug. "But today *we* were attacked."

"By Aron."

"The adherent of the Fifth, yes."

"What did he do?"

"The outer doors are usually only opened a small amount. Plenty of room to get in and out. But the doors are heavy, and we're no Earth adherents. Aron closed them. I don't know how —it takes six of us to move them at all unless we use personal magic to push them."

"I'm sure there's a roundabout way in which closed doors represent a Beginning," I said, rubbing the bridge of my nose. "He's actually really good at that, it seems." I was starting to feel I needed to speak with him—not just to stop him, but to take instruction on getting an Axis to obey abstract directions. "Then what? I assume a set of closed doors don't pose that serious a challenge to you all."

"Of course not. We could push the doors back open. But he also closed the inner doors." Zmogus's voice seemed to be accusing me of being a simpleton, which in my current condition seemed quite fair.

"And the inner doors are . . . harder to open?"

He scowled at me. "Of course not. They push open just as easily. It's just that he's filled the defensive space with water."

"What? Water? How?"

Zmogus shrugged.

"He probably Began a spring or something. Is it leaking in?"

"The doors seal completely. The defenses originally relied on burning oil, and so the doors would need to seal tightly enough to keep that out. Otherwise the defenders would have burned themselves alive in here."

"So you can get out."

"Not easily, no," he said, his scowl deepening. "Traveling through earth is . . . difficult for us. Open air is easier with our Form of Travel. But water? Impossible. There's no way we can pass through it."

Unbelievable. "So you and how many other adherents of Flame are trapped in here?"

"Almost all of us. Sixty."

"Wait, there's only sixty of you?" I'd somehow imagined there must be hundreds.

"I said almost. There are seventy-two of us. Flame has never Chosen as many as the others—excepting your Axis, of course."

"Of course. Fine. If this inner portion is completely surrounded—"

"It is."

"—and the doors are completely watertight—"

"They are." He pointed behind me. "You can see for yourself, just down the corridor."

"Stop interrupting me. How much air is in here?"

"Air?" he asked with a puzzled expression. "Why would air—"

"To breathe, you great idiot!" I snapped. He was struck dumb at that, and his face slowly indicated his comprehension. "Have you ever kept all the doors closed?"

"Of course not."

Of course— "Fine. So there's some degree of urgency, here."

"The inner sanctum is huge, it holds plenty of air."

Sanctum? He was really too much. "Fine. Let's think this through. Did Aron say anything? What he wanted?"

"No. Dmitri saw him, though, and described him to me. That's how I know it was him. Why wouldn't he just attack us in here?"

"He probably can't get in here, having never seen it. That's assuming his Form of Travel works like mine, which I'm pretty sure it does. I had your Summons to anchor to; without that, I'd have had to walk here." I wouldn't mention that my map table could have pinpointed him and led me here, if it were working reliably. This was a cordial enough conversation, but I didn't yet trust Zmogus enough to reveal all of the Tower's secrets and abilities.

"So can you . . . End the water?" Zmogus asked, finally coming to the point.

"I doubt it. I can't believe he managed to fill it so fast, to be honest. What you're describing sounds like an immense volume of— Did you hear that?"

It sounded like two enormous boulders being pushed against one another, a grinding, cracking noise amplified a hundredfold. It filled the enormous chamber, the low grumbling setting my bones to vibrating in sympathy.

Zmogus nodded grimly. "That's the stone overhead creaking under the weight of all that water. Someone Summoned you as soon as they saw Aron; we've been all over the continent fighting fires he's been setting, so I've trained them all on the Summons—for emergencies. By—"

"Wait, all over the continent?" I hadn't sensed a thing.

"Yes, tiny fires everywhere. But they grow easily once started." Perhaps that was why I hadn't sensed Aron doing this. As frazzled as I was, brief, small uses of his power might not have registered.

"But they Summoned me here?"

"They'd have realized immediately something was wrong. But by the time you received the word, he was gone, the chamber filled." His frustration and annoyance flared with the recounting. "Why can't you just End it? The water?" Zmogus insisted.

"I'm thinking about it!" I snapped. "But I can't just End water. Water doesn't have an End. It's always there. It changes form, moves from place to place, but it doesn't just stop existing."

Wait, that was it. *Water moves from place to place.* I didn't need to End it, did I? I just needed to let it out. "I'll be right back."

Gingerly, I had the Axis take me outside to the front door of Zmogus's personal citadel.

Seriously . . . a fortress? Before Aron, who even needed a fortress? And all it had done was get Zmogus and his fellows trapped.

The front doors were indeed fortified. And huge. They were triple my height across and four or five times my height high. They seemed to fit together tightly indeed; I couldn't make out where the two massive slabs of rock came together.

Words had been carved into the doors, the grooves deeper than my thumb and the letters taller than my forearm.

Bend the knee. Rule with us, or be ruled by us.

Bold statement. Clearly, the elder hadn't met Zmogus.

I looked around. This hill—a minor mountain, really—sat on the edge of a flat meadow, the ground sloping gently away in every direction. Letting the water pour out here would be messy, but it would eventually spread out, wouldn't it? I was hesitant to create a pit or trough; Mesla's comments on the earth's behavior, since Aron's ascension, made me want to avoid messing with things I didn't fully understand. But all I needed to do was give most of the water a place to go. It didn't matter if the surrounding area became waterlogged for a while.

And I had the perfect means. I imagined it would irritate Zmogus to no end, and honestly, as tired as I was, that seemed like nothing but a bonus.

Water didn't End, but stone and rock certainly did. It took centuries, millennia, but eventually the environment—wind, rain, baking sun—wore all rock down to dust. Just as I'd done to the rock formation in the river near Twynsits, I could hurry that process along.

I stood well to the side of Flamefast's gigantic front doors, pulled my Axis to me, and Ended them.

Stone crumbled into gritty dust as a truly overwhelming, unimaginable amount of water came crashing forth. It flooded the meadow as I'd expected, ripping up grass and flowers and leaving thick, wet mud in its place. The rush of water even managed to dig a deep, muddy furrow directly in front of Flamefast's entrance. Zmogus would be delighted.

The deluge took several minutes to subside, a testament to the sheer volume of water Aron had managed to direct. I waited and was relieved when the flow eventually slowed to a trickle. I'd been half-afraid that whatever Aron had done to bring all that water here in the first place—Creating several new springs was still my best guess—would still be gushing water. But whatever he'd done didn't seem to offer a perpetual supply of water.

A spike of pain shot through my skin.

"I knew you would do that," came a singsong voice behind me.

I didn't even turn around. "So now you're attacking the adherents directly?"

Aron was quiet for a moment. "The elders were angry," he said in a small, childlike voice.

"Your little fires weren't impressive enough?" I turned to face him. His expression was drawn and troubled, and his eyes were darting back and forth, refusing to meet mine.

"*Have* to show the adherents, *have* to show everyone, *nobody* is safe, *only* Beginnings, *have* to overwhelm them," he recited, his voice taking on a worryingly mad cadence.

"You don't have to," I said, careful to keep my tone even. "You—"

"THEY'LL HURT MOTHER!" he screamed, his eyes suddenly locking onto mine as they widened in anger. His brown skin flushed almost purple, veins standing out in his neck and on his forehead.

"Gemma is safe," I said quietly.

As quickly as it came, his anger fled. "Safe?" he asked hopefully. "Safe as in home, safe as in bed, safe as in a box?" There was a madness in his eyes. This was the damage I'd been worried about and had tried to get his elder to understand. I felt it in my own mind, the twisting and wrenching of my Axis. Only my long familiarity with it, the discipline Kirmin had drilled into me for five years, was keeping me sane.

"I can take you to—" I started.

"They're calling me," Aron interrupted, his expression tight. "Calling for dinner! Time to come in!" His mouth puckered in a tight frown. "Or not. Time to go blow. Gusts and gales." He shook his head. "Or no dinner at all."

"You don't have to—"

But he was gone.

I sighed and took myself back inside.

"Water's gone," I said cheerfully, even though my stomach

felt queasy from all the traveling in quick succession. "Your front doors may need some work, though."

Zmogus frowned. "How much work?"

I shrugged with feigned guilt.

"You Ended the doors?" There was the Zmogus I knew so well, scowl and all.

"As I said, this seemed urgent. I didn't want you all suffocating in here, and I don't know enough about the structures involved in boring a hole through the hillside. I'm sure Mesla or someone could help you build new ones." I tilted my head. "Out of curiosity, why me? Why not call an Earth adherent? They could have made a hole just as quickly."

The man had the courtesy to look slightly embarrassed. "I didn't think of that." Then he straightened and looked more composed. "But there's no Summoning magic for anyone but you. All of our communications charms rely on Sky magic."

"Which were obviously blocked."

"Yes. Open the doors!" he shouted, and several Flame adherents ran to the interior doors, leaning into the doors and beginning to push them outward. As soon as the doors split open, leftover water began gently lapping inward. Zmogus looked at it with a disdain deeper than he'd ever leveled at me.

But I wasn't quite done with him. "Do you mind if I ask you some questions? About Aron, I mean. I think I have a plan to stop him, but I want to get as much information as I can before I try to find him." I kept my voice as level as possible, even though I was laughing madly inside as the water continued to trickle inward.

"Of course," Zmogus growled. "Come inside. No, don't turn it to steam, you fools. We'll bake in here!" he shouted. Two of his adherents looked sheepish and walked slowly toward the now-gaping exit. "This way," he told me, stalking down the corridor deeper into Flamefast—no, I just couldn't keep thinking that name. I'd end up laughing in his face.

"Why do you need a fortress?" I asked as we walked. "If you're not normally being attacked, that is."

He was quiet for a moment, although I imagined I could hear him grinding his molars. "Adherents of Flame are put under much pressure to . . . perform. More so than adherents of the other Axes."

"Really?"

His shoulders looked too tense to shrug. "Apart from Sea, people see as us the most useful Axis. Sea adherents have a well-defined place in the fishing villages. Us? Everyone believes they can find a 'use' for us. It's easier for us to be here. Where we can't be . . . forced." His voice hardened on that last word, and I suddenly realized that even Zmogus must have a . . . past.

"How long have you been an adherent?"

He snorted. "Do I look so old to you, boy?"

"No, I just—"

"A hundred and thirty years."

My mouth fell open, and I closed it quickly before he could see it. He might well be one of the oldest adherents in the world, and he absolutely didn't look it.

The long entry corridor opened into a vast domed space. The center of the ceiling must have been a dozen times my own height overhead, and I could scarcely believe that all this fit within the hillside. Normal-sized doorways were spaced evenly along the walls, and there must have been seventy or eighty of them in total. Sleeping rooms, I realized, for the adherents of Flame, if not entire suites for each one. Between each pair of doors was a sturdy worktable. More worktables formed concentric rings in the middle of the space, which must have been three hundred feet across. The inner rings of circles were interrupted here and there by large wooden crates, bins, and other containers.

"What is this place?" I asked as Zmogus came to a stop at the outermost ring of tables.

"Our home," he said roughly. "Our workshop."

Workshop. I realized what I was looking at, and confirmed my suspicion by glancing into a nearby crate, which was full of small, uniformly made wooden charms. I stepped closer and picked one up. It was well-polished, and a single rune had been carefully carved into one side, the deep lines filled with some sort of matte-black substance. "Fire starters," I said, shaking my head.

"Oh, your famous disapproval," Zmogus mocked. "Yes, they're fire starters. Yes, we sell them—for a pittance. And yes, they help ordinary witchkind save a bit of their own personal power, providing a reliable way of safely lighting cookstoves and hearths."

I'd made no secret of my disdain for the other adherents' businesses. They made money from the power of their Axes, constructing magical charms that performed simple tasks. But the desperateness of recent events had made my dislike of these charm workshops even more intense. "You realize that if our Axes didn't exist, ordinary witchkind would have more than enough power to light their own fires?"

He turned to me and stood very, very close, almost nose to nose. It took an act of will not to take a step back.

"Do you know what happens to a family whose child is taken for an Axis?" he asked. His voice was low, almost dangerous. "They lose that child. Lose their magic. Lose the work they might have done. I left a sister behind, and without me, my family struggled. And so yes. We try to earn some money and send it back to help. These charms?" he said, pointing to the crate without taking his face away from mine. "The magic in the coins we receive for them is a fraction of the magic that goes into them. Witchkind who buy these from us exchange a pittance of their power for far, far more. We do use our power to help others. But you," and here he stabbed a thick finger into my chest, "choose to see things through only one set of eyes."

"I—"

Zmogus's face twisted into a sneer as he stepped back. "Always *you*. Now, ask me what you will do about the adherent of the Fifth before I throw you out of here, boy."

I'd like to see you try, I thought at once, and even the Axis bristled around me. But fighting with Zmogus wouldn't solve anything, and he'd made a good point. "You said you'd been running around, putting out fires. You suspect he started them?"

"We don't ordinarily see three dozen fires flair up in a single day, no," he said. Why did nearly every phrase he uttered seem to imply that I was stupid? "And we've seen him start at least a couple."

"You never spoke to him?"

"He left quickly."

It bothered me that I hadn't been feeling Aron using his Axis so much. "Were these fires . . . big?"

"A tree or two. Left alone, they'd have spread far and wide."

"And you can you tell when that happens?"

"We're Adherents of Flame, boy. Of course we can. Can you not feel every death in the world? The end of every argument?"

"Definitely not."

He gave me an odd look. "Truly?"

"Of course not. Origin defend, how horrific would that be? You're saying you—all of you—can feel every new fire that's kindled in the world? All the time?"

He nodded. "And every one that gutters and dies. You learn

to ignore the smaller ones, but when a couple of trees are suddenly ablaze, where there'd previously been not even a spark, we notice it."

"That seems . . . useful." And by that, I meant horrible. All the time? "What do you normally do about it?"

"Do?" he scoffed. "We put them out. It's not unusual for a lightning storm to start a fire or two once or twice a year. But there have been dozens—today alone. We've been working like mad to keep them under control."

"Aron's clan—they've been trying to show that the adherents can't counter him. They're demanding all the other Axes bend the knee, just as they've demanded of you. They're intending to replace the Taryba."

"And they see the Axis of Flame as a threat." Zmogus sounded oddly pleased at the possibility.

"They're trying to show they can counter each of the Axes," I said. "The hurricane in Lastepointe—Sea. Two adherents struggled to hold it. Mesla and her people fought back the earthquakes, and their Axis was pushing against them, they said. How big of a fire could you contain with less than a hundred of you?"

"No limit," he growled, a satisfied smirk on this face. "Set half the continent aflame, and a dozen of us could quench it instantly."

"And has your Axis been as obedient as you're accustomed to?"

He frowned. "What? How did you—"

I kept my gaze firmly on him.

"No. It hasn't. I've stayed here. To coordinate. The others, the ones who've returned, said it took them longer to bring the fires under control."

"How long does it usually take?"

"Seconds."

"So I assume it took longer."

He nodded grimly. "Some of them are lazy. I just assumed—"

"All of the Axes seem to be off their game."

"So we're not—" He clenched his jaw. "We're all weakened," he spat through clenched teeth.

I nodded. "They may not know that your Axis is struggling. Their main goal is simply to show some kind of dominance over you: lure you out, distract you, trap you here." Zmogus's eyes flashed in anger. "I do have a favor to ask."

His expression grew even darker. "What?"

"Do something. With your Axis. Something big. Tell me how it feels."

He considered for a moment, then called to one of the other adherents. "Moze! Tell everyone to clear the entry. Make sure they're out of the gap."

A young man ran down the entry corridor. He returned a few minutes later, accompanied by a handful of other adherents. "All clear, Zmogus!" he shouted.

Zmogus looked up at the center of the domed ceiling above us, and I could feel him concentrating. Wafts of steam began floating in from the entry corridor, and I realized he must be flashing the remaining water into steam. While most of it was blasted outside, anyone in that hallway would have been scorched.

A sudden commotion came from the worktables. Adherents were converging on one table, shouting for help.

Zmogus's attention snapped to them. "What's happened?"

"Tory and Anel collapsed!" someone shouted.

I followed Zmogus as he strode quickly to the fallen adherents. They were both young, possibly still apprentices. Both were sitting upright now, blinking slowly. Their faces were ashen. "What happened?" Zmogus repeated.

"I just . . . felt woozy," one said, rubbing his eyes with one hand.

"Drained," the other added. "Just for a second. I think I'm okay now."

Zmogus looked at me, concern softening his features.

"Regular magic has been acting strangely as well," I said quietly. "My own Axis. . ."

"What now?" he growled.

"I need to find Aron."

"Will stopping him fix this? Can you do it?"

"I don't know. I'm hoping I won't have to find out." Gemma was the key.

I couldn't wait to wrap my Axis about myself and leave Zmogus's fortress of fire.

CHAPTER 12

Taliesin

I didn't feel any evidence of Aron using his powers. He'd likely target Debesi and the Air adherents next, but surely he needed to rest as much as I did. Now that I knew his name, I could track him with the map table, at least in theory, but my need to take a break, to not chase Aron across the continent, won out.

When I'd left Zmogus's fortress, I hadn't actually given my Axis a destination. But it must have felt my mood, for it took me straight to the Tower library.

"Oh!"

Gemma bolted from the chair she'd been sitting in, and the book she'd been holding tumbled to the floor. A shadow caught it before it landed, whisking it back to its place on the shelves that soared high overhead.

"Sorry," I apologized, rubbing my eyes. "It's been a day."

"Is everything all right now? Have you seen Aron?"

"Kavos. Some cheese. Oat bread. Yes, but he didn't stay long." Shadows flickered over a table as the *driežai* deposited my food, along with a steaming mug of dark, energizing kavos. "He's been setting examples, I guess you would call it."

"How so?" She looked worried.

"The storm, the earthquake. You know about those." She nodded. "They came with demands, telling witchkind—telling the Taryba—to bend the knee. Then he started setting fires all over the continent, but Zmogus's people—the adherents of Flame, I mean—were too quick. So Aron sealed them in their fortress."

Gemma's brow wrinkled in confusion. "Fortress? How would we seal someone—"

"Trust me, he did. Using water, which is obviously not their Axis' strong suit. I got them out. Aron appeared and remained just long enough for me to tell him you are free."

"It might not help," she said with a sigh, sinking back into her chair. "Actually, are you hungrier than bread and cheese?"

As I looked at the food sitting on the table, my stomach growled. "I guess I am."

"Have you ever been to Taliesin?"

"Several times. It's the closest village to here."

"There's a lovely little restaurant. Human."

"Let's go." I wrapped the Axis around us without thinking, directing it to the village square in Taliesin.

"Oof," Gemma said, wrapping her arms around her stomach and bending over slightly as we arrived.

"Sorry." My own stomach was cramping. "I keep forgetting it's not exactly reliable, right now."

"Nothing has been," she muttered, straightening. She looked around, taking her bearings, and marched down one of the main roads that met at the square.

"What do you mean?" I asked as I hurried after her.

"I can barely summon light," she said as we walked. "Your . . . what do you call them? The shadows?"

"*Driežai.*"

"They would only bring me kavos, bread, and cheese. Like they're stuck. Do you order that a lot?" I nodded. "And look, there."

She stopped short, and I had to take a step back to rejoin her. She was staring at a man—of witchkind, I realized—who was, in turn, staring at a street lamp. The flame inside the lamp was flickering erratically. "What?"

"He's a lamplighter," she whispered. "But look, you can tell he's struggling. The flame shouldn't be flickering at all."

We watched for several minutes as the man clenched and unclenched his fists, his face furrowed in concentration. Finally, he exhaled sharply, shook his head, and walked away, the lamp still flickering madly.

"Adherent," a woman's voice said softly behind us. We both turned to find an older woman of witchkind, nodding respectfully. "Are you here about the . . . troubles?"

I looked around quickly, ensuring no humans were within earshot. "We'd actually come for a meal. What's wrong?"

"There's an inn," she said, nodding toward a jeweler's shop that had closed for the night. "You can eat there and see for yourself."

"Not one of my clan's," Gemma whispered. "And it's a good inn, I don't mind."

"Thank you," I said. She led us to an alley next to the jeweler's and touched the entry rune that was carved into the building's wood-slat wall. I took Gemma's arm and touched the rune myself, letting it carry us inside.

The journey was smooth but took a bit longer than I was used to. We emerged in a respectable-looking inn. The main room held about two dozen trestle tables, about half of which were occupied. The old woman slid onto an empty bench, and Gemma and I sat on the bench opposite her. "Food's simple but wholesome," she said, catching the eye of a server and holding up three fingers. Within moments, mugs of cool water and hot tea were placed before us, followed quickly by bowls of white stew and a plate heaped with thick, hearty bread.

"We've heard of the demands on the Taryba," the woman said as Gemma and I dug in. She made no attempt to keep her voice low, and everyone else in the room seemed to turn to listen. "And that the adherents can't protect us."

"I believe that danger has passed," I said carefully. "The clan making the threats, they—"

"Is it true the Fifth Axis was Forged?" someone across the room asked.

I nodded, seeing no reason to lie. "It is."

"It's upset magic," someone muttered.

"It's hard to Gather," someone else put in.

"I've noticed that as well," Gemma said softly.

"Is the new adherent doing this? The one of Beginnings? We heard about the earthquake in Evermore." Low muttering followed the statement. An attack on Evermore felt like an attack on all of witchkind.

"I hear he still clings to his clan," another said.

"He and his clan were involved," I admitted. "But I believe the danger has passed."

"Dismantle the Taryba and be done with it, I say," someone behind me grumbled. "Not like they've ever done us any good."

"Word is they've got Beginnings *and* Endings under their thumb. They're going after the other four Axes," someone said.

My blood rushed in my ears at the comments. I wasn't under *anyone's* thumb. "Enough," I said, standing. "Look at me. Truly *look*. Unsettled as magic is right now, at least some of you should see who I am. *What* I am."

The room was quiet for a heartbeat before a quiet murmur took over.

"Let me assure you, plainly and simply, that the Sixth Axis is not under anyone's thumb but *mine*. And I am under nobody's control. I have been countering the Fifth, Ending the storm and the quake. Yes, the Fifth and a rogue clan have been seeking to intimidate you, to intimidate all the adherents. But that clan has failed. I have removed their remaining weapon." I stole a look at Gemma, who didn't seem convinced. "Dismantle the Taryba, if you want, I don't care. But you will not be *forced* to bow to this clan who would rule you."

All eyes were on me, and I slowly raked my gaze over the room, letting them feel the weight of my Axis. "Come on," I told Gemma in a low voice. "I've lost my appetite."

I took us directly to the Tower's library and wolfed down the cheese and bread that remained. I gave Gemma a hard look. "When I told them Aron wasn't a threat anymore, you didn't look sure."

"I'm not," she admitted, sinking into a chair. "Aron has always been . . . impressionable. The elders took an interest in him five or six years ago. Coddled him. Filled him with stories of our great destiny." She paused, biting her lip before continuing. "I don't know if he'll stop obeying them just because I'm safe."

"His mind is damaged."

"Exactly. Maybe that means he'll care more about them, about the future they've promised him."

"You continue to say *they*. There's only one elder in your clan."

"So you've said. I still struggle to grasp that. But regardless, I don't know if Aron— What's the matter?"

I felt the blood drain from my face, and I put my hand on the back of a chair to steady myself. "It's Aron," I said with a grimace. "He's using his power again."

"Can you tell where?"

"I'm pretty sure I know."

"I'm pretty sure I know."

CHAPTER 13

Magewinds

I took myself directly to Debesi's home. I'd been there once before to ask something of her, so it was, in theory, an easy enough destination to reach. The current condition of my Axis made it less comfortable: I arrived with a knotted stomach and had to stand still and breathe slowly for over a minute before I could walk again.

Debesi's home, the Aerie, was located on a low peak in the Great Northern Range. It was a large home, one she shared with a handful of other adherents, although nothing as enormous as Zmogus's citadel. Most adherents of Sky, she once told me, preferred to live alone or in small groups, rather than bunching up as those of Flame did.

At least she hadn't named it Skykeep or something similarly grandiose. I grinned despite my roiling stomach.

"Daniel." Debesi stood on the wide front porch of the house, clad in nothing but her usual gossamer robes despite the freezing air.

She looked vaguely distracted, her eyes meeting mine for a moment but then drifting up to stare at the gray sky.

"I've come about Aron. He—"

"He's out there now," she said curtly. "He's been prodding us, off and on, for about an hour now."

"He attacked Zmogus earlier today," I said.

"Attacked?" Her attention was on me now, a frown on her face, her eyes hard and intense.

"He's been probing each Axis in turn. The storm in Last-pointe, the earthquakes. He managed to barricade Zmogus in their . . . fortress."

Debesi's lips quirked at that, the start of a quickly suppressed smile. "And how did he manage that?"

"A lot of well-placed water. He, or someone else, carved a warning into the fortress's outer door, basically telling the adherents to submit."

"You know, I always warned Zmogus that it was better to be free to move than backed into that hillside of his." She shrugged. "Different Axis, different approach, I suppose. But submit? They've obviously never met Zmogus. I'm guessing you let the water out?"

"He's missing a front door now, yes."

"Oh my." She chuckled. "I should have enjoyed seeing that." Her amusement faded almost instantly, the same distracted expression slipping back into place.

"If Aron's been here about an hour, then he must have come directly here. He may have even been going back and forth. But he's hardly *my* Aron. He—"

"I was teasing. He's been prodding us more gently, though. Nothing so bold as a face-on attack, although we're a lot harder to tie down than Zmogus's people. He started with a blast of air pushed up the mountainside. Easily gentled, as it was too warm and didn't want to be up this high anyway. He managed a vortex for a moment, but we've more experience with the sky than he does. He doesn't understand how it works, and so his efforts are little more than irritating. I've put a handful of younger adherents on it, and they're monitoring him closely. What is his game?"

"Not his. His clan elders. Elder, I should say. He's trying to establish the clan as a power, using Aron. They had his mother prisoner and threatened to harm her. This is the same elder who once ran Karal, Debesi."

Her eyes widened. She'd been there, along with Mesla, when I'd attempted to rescue Mother from the iron cage the Karal had kept her in. "You said *had* his mother?"

"Mesla helped me pull her out. She's in my Tower. I need to find Aron, get him to stop."

"I can take you to him now," she said confidently, and I felt the air grow denser around me as she summoned her magic.

"Wait a moment." I could feel a gentle pricking in my skin, telling me Aron wasn't too far off. Debesi raised an eyebrow, and the air around me loosened. "Aron and I are affecting one another. The Fifth and Sixth weren't meant to be separated like this. That's my theory, at least. My powers are . . . compromised. If he's not harming anything right now—"

The pricking sensation briefly crescendoed as the gentle mountain breezes suddenly grew into a howling gale. Debesi rolled her eyes, and with the barest flick of one hand, the wind died down again. "He doesn't understand temperature and pressure," she said disdainfully. "He's trying to start something, but he doesn't know what fuels a proper windstorm. They're much more nuanced than a storm fueled by moisture. But you said you're affecting one another? His power seems intact enough."

"Neither of us is what I'd call reliable. If one of us is doing something significant enough, the other feels pain. Our Axes . . . they're not opposites, exactly."

"You once said something." She paused for a moment, thinking. "Every Ending is a Beginning?"

"And every Beginning an End, yes. Two sides of the same coin, not two distinct powers."

She nodded slowly. "So you're saying you may not be able to stop him if he's not reasonable. If he doesn't listen."

"I don't know. Maybe not."

"I can bring a handful of older adherents with me. We can help counter him with you."

"I appreciate it. We can—"

"Another moment," she said, stepping off the porch and coming closer to me. "This irregularity in your magic. It has been happening elsewhere. Is Aron the cause?"

I nodded slowly. "He may be. But I didn't know about the widespread instability of magic until today. But I was just in Taliesin, and witchkind there have noticed."

She chuckled. "An advantage of being an adherent of Sky. We spread ourselves out across the world, some of us living in the towns and villages, others in small cottages scattered here and there. We can hear each other anytime we need to. The Axis carries our voices to the corners of the world. Magic has been irregular everywhere. Ordinary witchkind have found their powers scattered. I've an adherent to the south, in Nworlons, and she says the locals describe their magic as *pulsing*. Some have been unable to Gather."

Someone in Taliesin had said as much. "Why would that be true?"

"I haven't had a moment to investigate myself. But I've heard said that magic has lost some of its flavor. That it was . . . the word they used was *grynas*. Do you know it? In the True Language?"

"*Pure*. Roughly. But I don't understand. Why would pure

magic be harder to Gather?" This was the first I'd ever heard of magic being flavored.

"All magic is flavored of the elements. Sky and Sea, Earth and Flame. Each person of witchkind has their own . . . mmm, not preference, exactly. *Lygiavimas*, it's called. My sister used to teach at Duocastella's; she could explain it better."

"That means . . . orientation?" I asked.

"Close. *Affinity*. A person with Sky affinity would Gather magic that was touched with Sky. Earth to Earth, and so on. If magic is losing its *lygiavimas*, it would be more difficult for them to Gather. Might even be less stable. If magic used to bind the hulls of ships no longer tasted of Sea—"

"The bindings might fail," I finished. "I understand. It's been happening to everyone, then. But I'm not sure why that would be the case now. I mean, I had assumed it was just magic being unsettled after the Forging of the Fifth. But that shouldn't have changed the fundamental nature of magic. Would it?"

"Most bindings are about Creation, more so than Endings. Perhaps the power of Beginnings being bound up in an Axis has taken the tint from magic?"

I nodded slowly. "It could be. We don't really understand where our magic comes from, but—"

"Magic comes from the Origin," Debesi said instantly. "That's never been a question."

It's never been a fact, either, I thought. More akin to the humans' religious beliefs than anything anyone had proven. "Yes, but what is the Origin? What if it is, or is at least partly, the power of Creation? Of Beginnings? What if the Fifth Axis is . . . I don't know. A part of the Origin?"

Her eyes widened fractionally. "That would imply that your own Axis is as well. Or was."

That had never occurred to me. But if the Fifth and Sixth

were indeed two sides of the same coin . . . "I've realized, over the past few days, how little I understand about the true nature of magic. Of the Axes, even. But what if . . ."

"If what?" Debesi prompted me when I paused.

"What if chaining the Fifth has somehow compromised the Origin?"

She looked at me for a moment and sighed. "Since you ascended, you've railed against us for how we use our powers. The charms, the little favors we sell."

I raised my eyebrows at the sudden change in topic, but Zmogus's tirade came back to me. "I may have been hasty in that assessment," I admitted.

"You were. But perhaps you were also not wholly wrong. Consider: if leashing the Fifth is indeed what has now begun to diminish all of witchkind, then what were we like before any of the Axes existed? If the power of the Axes were not chained, would that give ordinary witchkind the magic they need, right now?"

Don't cling too hard to power. It's often best not wielded at all. Ormand's words came back to me.

"Debesi, why were the Axes formed?"

Her brow creased. "Surely you know the histories."

"I know the stories. That magic was raw and wild, damaging the world. That the Axes were formed to bring magic under control."

"Correct."

"Is it, though? Is it correct? The power of Beginnings certainly wasn't out of control. It wasn't Creating storms and earthquakes. I didn't even know what an earthquake was until this morning!"

The crease deepened. "What are you suggesting?"

"That the Archons' motives were less . . . selfless. That they simply wanted the power for themselves. Just as Aron's clan does."

She thought about it for a moment and then sighed. "I don't know how it matters, all these centuries later. We are where we are."

"Yes, but now even ordinary magic is failing."

Debesi took on a grave countenance. "Daniel, without magic being reliable, even the humans will begin to suffer. Their buildings, their ships—"

"Will fail. They need our magic as much as we do, even if they don't know it."

She chewed her lip for a moment, an uncharacteristically vulnerable tic. "You bring me to my point, then. Daniel . . . my own Axis has become unreliable too." Her voice was soft now, and I wondered if she was using her magic to carry it to me through the gusting breezes. "We lost a young adherent. Just now, on her way to assist us. The Axis simply . . . stopped. When she was traveling, high in the air." I could see the muscles of Debesi's jaw clenching and releasing.

That explained the vague look she'd had when I arrived. "Debesi—" I gasped as a stab of pain pierced my skull. "Debesi," I got out. "It's Aron."

And it was. Whether his previous attempts at summoning a windstorm had been experiments he'd learned from, or whether he'd found an altogether new approach for his Axis, what was coming was serious. I could feel the air around me stiffening, the pressure increasing even at this altitude. The temperature dropped, and I began shivering. Debesi's eyes widened in panic, and she stepped down from her porch and grabbed my arm. "Inside. Quickly."

She led me up the short set of steps and into the relative comfort of her home. A fire flickered merrily in the fireplace, but it began to gutter as the winds outside picked up, drawing air away.

Debesi was muttering under her breath, and I caught snatches of what must have been instructions, given in the True Language, to her Axis. *Tawelwch. Dal. Rhyddhau.* Be calm. Be still. Let go.

It wasn't working. Through one of the Aerie's expansive windows, the world had darkened. The winds were picking up grit and dust, pelting them against the building with a hissing sound.

"This will need to get worse before it gets better," she said grimly. "Lina! Angelika!" she called. "Are you still here?" Two women scurried into the room from a hallway, one younger and one closer to Debesi's age. "This is the new adherent," Debesi said quickly. "He's driving this wind through sheer force. Can you feel it?" Both nodded. "We need to pull the reins from him. Lina, you will steer." The younger woman nodded. "Angelika, you and I will pull. You understand?"

"Move it even faster?" Lina asked. "Will the building hold?"

"The Aerie will hold through far worse," Debesi assured her.

"I can—" I started.

"Do nothing," Debesi said sharply. Which was just as well, since my head continued to pulse with a hot, angry pain. "Lina, are you ready?"

"The Axis's hands are slippery," Lina said, her face tight with concentration. Her hands twitched at her side. "There will be no precision in this."

"We need none," Debesi said. "Up the mountainside and over. Keep it low as you can. Make it work against the terrain. Angelika?"

The older adherent nodded grimly. "Ready."

"We begin."

All three closed their eyes, and I could feel their magic harden around us. Outside, the winds picked up speed. It sounded as if they'd doubled in power, and as I listened, they doubled again. The building shook around us, and I took a step back from the large windows as they began rattling and flexing in their frames.

"More," Debesi whispered. All three adherents' hands were at their sides, twitching in odd, syncopated gestures. *More.* They began swaying slightly, in time with one another, slowly leaning a bit to the left, then a bit to the right. "MORE," Debesi insisted softly.

"It's drawing away from me," Lina said, panic in her voice. "The Axis."

"Tory and Anel collapsed!" someone shouted.

"Debesi, pull back a bit," I said quickly.

"This is no time to—" she began, her tone irritated.

"Trust me!" I said. "There's only so much Axis to go around!"

Her eyes snapped open and she glared at me.

"It's coming back to me," Lina said with relief.

Debesi's eyes widened and the irritation vanished from her face. "We pull together, then," she said, giving me a brief nod before closing her eyes.

The winds were howling now, the Aerie's doors pushed shut so tightly by the force of it that I doubted I could force my way out, had I been foolish enough to try. Small pebbles rattled against the outside walls and pinged against the windows. I pulled the irritated, smoldering presence of my Axis close to me, unsure of what I could contribute should the structure fail.

"Keep it low," Debesi murmured calmly, her demeanor belying the roaring intensity of magic they were wielding.

The air outside seemed to grow thicker. The winds were blowing so strongly that they were now picking up stones, entire tree branches. A mad part of my mind wondered if all the birds in the area had managed to take shelter or if they'd been blown ahead of all this and were even now wondering what would become of them.

Stones were bouncing off the building, and I began to reach out with my Axis, hoping I could at least End the barrage. If something large enough managed to—

"No," Debesi cautioned me sharply. "I don't know what you're planning, but do nothing. Hold firm."

I pulled the Axis back at her command. At the very least, if the walls failed or the windows shattered, I could take myself away from this chaos.

"Debesi," Angelika muttered.

"I know," Debesi said.

The winds began . . . pulsing. There was no other way to describe it: a half-second of silence was followed by a half second of frenetic, surging pressure, repeating on a loop. It was as if the air itself was punching the Aerie, and the building shuddered in time to the assault.

"The Axis, Debesi," Lina said in a low, urgent tone.

"I feel it," Debesi muttered. Even I could feel it now: a vibration in the magic around us, as if the Axis of Sky itself was flickering on and off. "Be ready for it. When you can get your hands firmly around it again, pull with everything you have. Now!"

The pulsing was replaced by a tempestuous rush of air outside—fierce wild winds, shrieking and screaming like a banshee in a rage. The entire building seemed to bow inward, and the pressure inside became so much that my eardrums began to ache.

And then it was gone. The walls relaxed, my ears popped, and the pain behind my eyes receded to a now-familiar dull throb. The three adherents' shoulders slumped as they opened their eyes. Lina's were bloodshot, and Angelika's were tearing. Only Debesi looked unaffected, although a subtle weariness around her own eyes put the lie to her composed facade.

"That's done it," Debesi said with a sigh.

"What did you do?" I asked.

"We pulled the air from him. Made it go faster than he could keep up with. Instead of fighting him, we went along with it and outplayed him. The air is our domain," she added proudly, "and he will never hold mastery of it."

"That was a near thing," Angelika muttered. "The more we pulled at the air, the more the Axis seemed to . . ." She stopped, searching for the right phrase.

"It was like it didn't want to be here," Lina said softly.

Debesi's eyes narrowed, but she nodded in agreement. "But we managed it. Thank you. Go, rest now." They nodded and walked slowly down the hallway they'd emerged from.

"He may try again," I pointed out.

"He may." She whispered something I didn't catch. "I'm recalling those who were set to watch him. I suspect he overcame them, or we would have felt their efforts joining ours just now."

"Can you call more?"

"I could," she nodded firmly. "There are over three hundred of us in the world. But I won't. We scatter ourselves for a reason. If I called everyone here, could Aron not simply take himself to another part of the continent and operate without opposition? Swift as we can be, our travel is not instantaneous as yours and his. If his goal is to test us, to distract us, he could lead us on a merry chase. And if he repeats this closer to a village . . ."

"A good point." Not every building, even those enhanced by the bindings of witchkind's hidden spaces, would be able to hold up to such a tempest.

"Numerous as we are, we are too few." She turned to look out the window, which was now blurry from all the dust it had accumulated. For all her calm, I could see the tension in her neck. "I am inexorably led," she said more slowly, forcing herself to relax a bit, "to the conclusion that we need more hands. There are three hundred adherents of Sky. Far fewer of Flame. Perhaps as many of Sea. Earth, I don't know, but the number is likely similar. We are not enough. This Aron may have the power to Create chaos across the world, and we will not be able to oppose him." Her hand flicked out again, and a quick breeze blew the dust from the outside of the window. "All of witchkind must become empowered again, if ever they once were. We need to find a way to get magic to all of our people. So they can defend themselves."

I opened to mouth to respond, but my voice caught in my throat. The idea that Aron, a single adherent, couldn't be countered by the hundreds of other adherents—it felt mad. Impossible. But then, could they all, in their hundreds, truly oppose me if I bent myself against them? If they couldn't, then Debesi was right: Aron couldn't be opposed either. But how could we make *all* of witchkind more powerful? "You're saying you want to . . . what are you saying?"

"I don't know. Only that if this Aron is our enemy, we will need more people, more magic, than I believe we can currently summon."

"I understand. But I don't think . . . that is, I believe Aron will see reason. He's not doing this of his own will. He knows his mother is safe. I just need to convince him. He may just need to see her with his own eyes." Suddenly I felt less sure of that than I had at the inn in Taliesin.

She nodded. "Then let us go."

CHAPTER 14

Aron

Debesi took us to a rocky plain at the foot of the mountains that, in better weather, might have been a pleasant meadow. She took a couple of steps back, standing behind me, then whispered something I couldn't make out. Within seconds, several soft bursts of air behind me announced the arrival of more adherents of Sky. My backup.

I kept my eyes on the new adherent.

Not a dozen paces away, Aron stood before me. He held his hands up, palms toward me, and said, "Let's not fight, friend!" There was a desperate, manic tone in his voice, overlaid by a false cheerfulness.

"We don't need to, Aron," I called back. "Your mother is safe, now, remember? They can't hurt her."

"You said that before!" he cried merrily. "But the elders said you'd lie! Lie down, lie in bed, lie in fire! And when you lie, I must fly!"

"No lie. It's true, Aron. I swear it."

"He's telling the truth, Aron," Debesi added firmly.

Imagine standing still and quickly turning your head from

left to right while blinking your eyes as fast as possible. The scenery before you will wink in and out, in and out, as your head moves. That's what happened to Aron: he seemed to *skip* toward me. His limbs didn't even seem to move. In half an eyeblink, he was two paces closer. Another half blink, two more. And in two full eyeblinks, he was standing right before me, his eyes boring into mine. My skin itched and crawled as he did so, and my stomach briefly considered ejecting the cheese and bread from my last meal.

The sun was low in the sky behind Aron and would set within a few hours.

"Are you," Aron asked in a low, perilous growl as he leaned his face into mine, "lying to me?"

"Your mother is safe," I repeated slowly. "Mesla—she's an adherent of Earth. A friend. She and I found your mother. Your clan was holding her captive, in an iron cage. In Landshire, not far from here. We got her out. She's safe now."

"Safe." He said the word as if he was testing the taste of it. His eyes were cold and hard and just inches from my own.

"Utterly safe," I assured him. "Very safe. Unharmed. I made sure she ate."

"Where?" His eyes softened a bit, and he pulled back a fraction.

"In my Tower. It was the safest place I could think of. But she's free to go anytime she wants. You can see her if you want. I could take you there now."

Slowly, ever so slowly, he raised a hand and placed it gently on my cheek. I sensed Debesi and her companions tensing; the air thickened ever so slightly. I forced myself to stay very still as Aron continued to stare into my eyes. "If you did that," he said, his voice now velvety soft, "thank you." He let his hand slide slowly down my cheek until it dropped to my shoulder. He let it remain there for a heartbeat before bringing it back to his side. "Thank you." He sniffed. "They said you would lie."

"Your elder has been the one lying, Aron. The other adherents are not your enemies. They helped me free your mother. None of us are your enemies," I repeated.

"Oh, I know that," he chirped, his voice now loud and bright and his face breaking into a smile. He took a step back, his eyes twinkling. "The elders are my enemies, but they had me! Had me on a leash." His expression fell into a hard frown. "They still do, you know. I can feel it. Even with Mother safe, there's still it. Inside of me. Something dangerous. Something final. At first I thought you might have put it there, but . . . it doesn't taste like us."

Like *us*? "Your clan rune. There's a trap in it—in your spirit. Your mother told me of it."

"Oh, that?" Again, his expression flipped back to cheerfulness. He shook himself like a wet dog, and one eye twitched a few times. I felt my head throb for a moment as he used his power. "There! I've Begun a new life independent of the clan!" Now his brow wrinkled in confusion. "I have, haven't I?" His voice was that of a child, bewildered and afraid, high pitched and querulous. "Have I? What if Mother has the same thing?"

"She did." His expression started to slip into alarm, so I quickly added, "but I removed it. Ended it. Painlessly. She's clanless now and safe from them."

"So I *have* started a new life. And so has she."

I nodded solemnly. "You have. But it's probably important that you stop using the Axis for a while. There are some things you need to know about it."

"And you'll tell me?" He seemed eager, now, eyes wide in anticipation.

"I will."

"Will you lie?" Strangely, neither his voice nor his expression changed at that. He sounded almost excited about the prospect.

"No," I said firmly.

"So tell me! Tell me everything!" He clapped his hands twice, wriggling like an eager child. I found his quick, radical shifts in attitude off-putting. He wasn't well.

"There's a lot to tell," I said slowly. "You know about the five . . . well, the six Axes, right?"

"Sure, sure," he said quickly, nodding. "Sea, Sky, Flame, Earth, Endings, and Beginnings. I'm the last one!" he added excitedly, thumping a thumb against his chest. "And we can do anything."

"Perhaps, but we need to be careful with our power. We can't just do whatever we want. There are consequences." Origin defend, was that me giving that speech? I heard Debesi give a soft snort of amusement behind me. "And your power in particular is both wondrous and dangerous."

"Dangerous? How?"

I hesitated. I didn't want to make him angry. "It's possible that creating the Fifth Axis, your Axis, has damaged magic for everyone else." A thought occurred to me. "Even for your mother."

His eyes flew wide, and his face went ashen. "I've damaged Mother?" he asked in a very small voice. "Damaged, flawed, broken, hurt?"

"We may be able to fix it," I said. *I've no idea how, but let's go with that.* "If we work together."

His expression twisted into one of distrust. "You're not lying?"

"I said I wouldn't lie to you. I won't. And I can show you a rune that will let you detect lies if you want." Assuming his power was enough like mine, then many of my Forms of Power should work for him.

"Ooooo," he cooed, his face lighting up as he wrapped his arms around himself. "I do want. I want very much. But first" —his voice was pitched almost normally, and his face seemed fully sane for a moment—"I need to make sure Mother is protected."

"She is," I insisted. "She's—"

"Who are they?" Aron snapped, taking another step back and apparently noticing the adherents of Sky for the first time. His expression was now guarded, his tone sharp, his eyes suspicious.

"Friends," I said in what I hoped was a soothing voice. "If they're bothering you, they can go. You and I can keep talking."

He was eerily still for a moment, and then he burst into motion, nodding frantically and bouncing up and down on his toes. "Yes, they can go. You and I can keep talking. I'd like that. We should talk a great deal. Goodbye!"

"It's fine, Debesi." I lowered my voice to a bare whisper. "Keep watch." Then, in my normal tone, "You can all go. Thank you. It's been wonderful seeing you again. I look forward to seeing you again soon."

"Look forward to it!" Aron called, shooting a hand high above his hand and waving enthusiastically. "Wonderful seeing you again! You can all go!"

Puffs of wind accompanied their departure.

"I've been trying not to use it, you know," Aron said as he let his arms fall back to his side. "The Axis. Not using it is easier. They make me, but I don't want to. When I use it, the voices are louder."

"What voices?" I tried to keep my tone calm and curious rather than alarmed. "I've not heard voices, when I use my Axis. That's new for me."

"They're quite. Quiet? No, quite. Quite *loud*—that's it. Quite loud. Insistent, really." He cocked his head to one side.

"Lonely. Detached. You know, they're softer when you're here. When I'm not using the magic. When you're not using it. They like it here, with you." He raised a hand then, as if offering to take mine. But even that gesture seemed to confuse him: he looked down at his hand with a pained expression and then let it fall listlessly back to his side. "Will you stay?"

"I can stay for a while. If you're here, there's nowhere else I need to be."

"You know, I can't hear *them* anymore." The spitting emphasis he put on that word left little doubt as to who he meant.

"With your clan rune gone, your elder may not be able to reach you anymore. He probably can't even tell where you are."

"Because I'm free," he said, nodding gravely.

"What exactly did your elder tell you to do?"

He straightened, assuming a perfect, erect posture. He held one arm out toward me, his hand in a fist. I braced myself, scrabbling to pull my Axis closer while trying to mimic Debesi's effortlessly calm facade.

He extended one finger. "Show them what we're made of. Start a storm the Sea adherents can't stop."

I relaxed.

Another finger raised. "Start a quake in Evermore, enough to make them pay attention." Another finger. "Burn a forest. Make sure the Flame adherents are kept busy. They're the dangerous ones." He frowned. "I got that wrong. Had to trap them instead. Had to show them." A fourth finger. "Distract the adherents of Sky. Blow them out of the air if you have to." His arm dropped. "That's all for now. Return when you're done, and we'll tell you what to do next." His posture relaxed as he finished his recitation. "Oh!" he exclaimed as if something had just occurred to him. "I didn't return when I was done. I don't have to!" He smiled.

"You do not," I agreed. "But did they tell you why? Why they wanted you to do all that?"

He shook his head. "Sometimes they forget that I'm standing right there. That I can hear."

"Did you overhear anything, then?"

He nodded quickly. "Upset the balance. We'll need to come to terms with the boy, but the other four will be subservient. The Taryba will do whatever we tell them once the Axes are brought to heel. With the Fifth, we can even build a home, a proper home, for our clan. We'll build our strength. See if it will accept more adherents. And then we can see about going home. Reverse the Exodus? Yes, that's been our dream all along, hasn't it? We never intended to stay in this world. We had no idea we'd be cut off. All the family histories are clear on that. Boy, what are you doing? We've given you your orders, now go about it!"

"Reverse . . . the Exodus? They said that?" I hadn't thought that possible—hadn't even imagined it."

"I've always had a poor memory. I asked the Axis if I could start having a good memory. It said yes. They said that. I can remember now."

I suppose that wasn't unlike my own Axis storing all of my experiences and those of my predecessors. Although I'd thought that was more a function of the Foundation rather than—

Focus, Daniel.

"Have they ever spoken about the Exodus before?"

He shook his head.

"Well, you don't have to do anything they say anymore. They wanted to hurt your mother." Aron's face clouded with anger. "They hurt mine, you know." His face cleared and filled with curiosity. "She was . . . special. A part of her drew strength from humans. Your elders perverted that, used it to extract power from humans against their will. They stored that power, and it's what they used to chain the Fifth Axis. To make you its adherent." I felt my voice start to quiver and took a deep breath. "They hurt my mother. In the end, she died of it."

Tears began rolling down his face. "I don't want them to do that to Mother," he sobbed.

"They won't!" I assured him. "They can't. My Tower is the safest place in the world. Nobody can get in without my permission. Your mother is comfortable. She has food, everything she needs. Books to read. She's not a prisoner," I reminded him. "She can leave anytime she wants to. And you can come visit."

"I'd like to visit," he said distractedly. "What's an Exodus?"

Another conversational right turn, but it was important to humor him. "It's just a story. Or I always thought it was. It's about how we, all of us, came into this world. Human and witchkind alike."

"Where did we come from?"

"You know, I wondered the same thing, the first time I read of it. But the stories never say. The version I remember says, 'the Exodus brought the allies from a world of danger, from walls that were closing in on all sides, into a world of open fields and freedom.' But it never says where that first world is."

"Huh." He seemed to think about it for a few moments and then shrugged. "You said you would teach me a rune about lying."

I chuckled. "It's a rune about truth, actually. If you use it on someone, you'll feel cold if they lie, warm if they're telling the truth. It's the Form of Mind for the Sixth Axis. My Axis. I don't know if it will work for you, but it doesn't hurt to try."

"I don't know any runes," he said sadly.

How was that even possible? "How do you tell your Axis what to do, then?"

Another shrug. "I just do. Will you show me a rune?"

I crouched and used a finger to sketch a rune in the dusty earth:

I stood. "This is called *išsiaiškinti*: to know. You just hold it in your mind, as you look at the person you want it to affect. And then you have your Axis feed it a little magic."

Aron blinked at my sketch a few times, then looked up at me. I felt an odd sensation. It seemed as though someone had bounced a small rubber ball off my forehead.

"Tell a lie."

"My name is Galas, End-Watcher."

Aron frowned. "I don't feel anything."

"I'm not sure it worked, honestly. You might need to try on someone else. It might not work on me at all."

"So you can still lie to me." He didn't seem upset by the possibility—the tone of his voice and his body language didn't change at all. He was still showing the curiosity of a small child.

"But I wouldn't. I won't." I kept my own voice firm and friendly.

"So Mother really is safe?" He was almost whimpering with the need for it to be true.

"She's safe. I can take you to her right now, and she can leave anytime she wants. She isn't a prisoner anymore."

"But they'd get her again. If she leaves." Lips tight, eyes flashing, voice rough.

"She can also stay as long as she wants and stay safe. We'll find your elders. Without you to control, they'll have no—"

"Do you know what we need?" Eyes bright, mouth smiling widely, voice joyous. "A house!"

Aron's conversational twists were becoming increasingly difficult to follow. "A house?"

"A house. The safest place in the world. You're always safe at home!" He frowned at that. "So not a house. A home." The frown vanished as quickly as it had come. "Do you know what we need?"

"A home?"

"A home! Mother can be comfortable. She can leave anytime she wants to." He frowned again but for just a second. Smiling again, he added, "But she won't want to. She'll want to be safe! And you can come visit!" His pattern of reusing my own phrases was odd. Eerie. Despite the function of his Axis, he wasn't creating new phrases, he was just recycling others. Mine, at least.

"She's already safe," I told him, confused. Was he also having trouble tracking the present?

"Does she live in your Tower?"

What? "No, but she can stay for as long as—"

"So it isn't her home," he said in a bit of a condescending tone. "So she needs a home."

"I guess we could—"

"Oh, you've been so helpful!" he interrupted happily. He took a deep step forward, grasped my head between his hands, and kissed me full on the lips. He held it for several heartbeats before releasing me and stepping back. My mind spun as it tried to grasp what had just happened. Aron's face had split into a broad, joyful smile. "So helpful! And now we need a house."

He turned away, facing the broad, flat land that led up to the mountain. Turning back over one shoulder, he added, "I'll make sure there's room for you too!"

"What are—"

When Aron had previously used his powers, I'd experienced pain. Sometimes just a slight, annoying tingle; other times it was a searing, debilitating agony.

What happened next made the worst of that seem like little more than a stubbed toe.

A solid pillar of torment smashed into me. It speared me from head to toe, as if a tree made of pure anguish had been driven down from the sky, transfixing me, hammering me to the ground. Every muscle in my body clenched so tightly that I couldn't even manage to fall down. My arms were thrown outward and back, my eyes pointed directly upward, and I couldn't breathe. Then I was released, allowed to fall onto my knees. Then the real pain began.

This is what dying feels like.

My Axis seemed to have fled, not that I could muster enough focus to command it. My entire body raged in pain, although nothing was touching me. Every bit of skin was on fire. My muscles withered and disintegrated beneath my skin. My eyes boiled, my tongue melted. Even my hair hurt. I still couldn't breathe.

But I could see.

Before me, Aron stretched his arms out wide, and far in front of him, something was pushing itself out of the ground. I struggled to focus through my body's torture. A . . . was that a branch? No, a tree. Origin protect, it was *huge*.

A massive tree, far larger than any that could ever have existed in the world, was growing from the ground. Its trunk was so big, it would have taken three men to embrace it. No, four. Five, now. Six. More. Its branches were equally stout, capable of supporting horses. *Houses*. Its leaves were broad and flat, colored a deep emerald. It stretched fifty feet into the sky. Sixty. Eighty. A hundred, and it kept going. The sound of it was indescribable, rock and silt grinding against each other, the organic sound of branches and leaves unfurling and growing. The ground rumbled beneath me, pushing like a herdbeast giving birth.

My stomach finally unclenched, and I sucked in air as greedily as a newborn babe. I was bent over on the ground now, my knees and elbows barely managing to support me, my head craned uncomfortably back so I could witness what was being Created before me.

The rocky, barren soil was erupting with green life. Long, thick blades of grass pushed up everywhere, accompanied by flowers of every color imaginable: cream, sepia, butter, amber, rose, lilac, lapis, olive, and more.

Either my pain had subsided or I'd simply lost the ability to feel anymore. I was weak, my entire body shuddering. I was cold, a piercing, aching cold that bore into the center of my being. My vision started to narrow, tightening to a black tunnel as bees and butterflies began emerging from the flowers, flitting here and there as the new meadow continued to fill in.

My blood was pounding in my ears—too hard, too fast. My heart was thudding unevenly. My fingers started to tingle, and my chest felt tight.

Just as the first bright, happy chirps of birdsong reached my thrumming ears, my body reached its limit.

I blacked out.

CHAPTER 15

Reunion

I awoke with one cheek pressed against cold, dusty stone. *This is becoming an unpleasantly regular occurrence*, my befuddled brain thought. I pushed myself to my hands and knees, then managed to sit up on my knees. I was in the Tower. In the foyer.

I'd blacked out. The Tower's magic pulled me home, but not into my bed as it was meant to do. Perhaps the foyer was as far as it had managed to get me before the Axis's power sputtered out.

"Daniel?" Gemma peeked around the library's door before opening it all the way and stepping into the foyer.

"Gemma. Hello. Have you been in the library this whole time?"

"Yes, but there was a thudding sound. Out here." She let the library door swing shut behind her, leaving us in the dim, even light of the foyer. "I came to see."

"I'm thinking the thudding was me."

"Are you all right?"

I slowly rose to my feet, carefully inventorying myself. "I

think so." My head seemed to be clearing at least, if still throbbing.

"What happened?"

"My Axis isn't well, and I'm starting to think it isn't entirely Aron's doing. At least not directly. Magic seems . . . troubled." The energy in the air around me was off in a way I couldn't quite describe.

She nodded. "Magic tastes wrong somehow. Like it doesn't want to be used. Did you find him?"

"Aron? Yes. He's ah . . . he's fine. In one piece, his clan rune is gone—his own doing, by the way—and he's . . . well, he's constructed a home for himself. And you. He seems very intent on keeping you safe."

"A home?" She looked confused, which I suspected she'd need to get used to, given her son's . . . state.

"No, not a tower. He Created a tree."

"A tree." Definitely doubtful.

"Yes. A gigantic tree. Just west of the Great Northern Range. It's situated in . . . well, it's now a rather lush meadow. There was a lot of grass growing."

"Why a tree?"

I felt like she was unnecessarily fixating on the tree part. "I have no idea, Gemma," I said wearily. "He wanted a tower. A fortress. Somewhere where you'd both be safe. He Created a tree. A gigantic one. Grew it right out of the ground. Took seconds and an incalculable amount of magic. Hurt like . . . I have no comparison, actually. My head is still throbbing. Do you mind if I eat something?"

"Of course not."

"Bread. Jam. Toast, a couple of pieces. Kavos— no, forget that. Tea. Something relaxing. *Rhisgl* powder, if we have any." I desperately needed my head to stop hurting. "Soup. Something mild, with vegetables." I was already walking down the stairs to the little dining area. Gemma followed as I continued to call out instructions. "Cheese. That hard, mild one. Oh, water. Room temperature, not cold. A lot of it. Are you hungry?" I asked Gemma.

"All of that's just for you?"

"For a start, yes. Cold ham. Sliced. That's all for now."

"I'm fine for now, thank you."

I slid into a seat at the table, and Gemma took a chair across from me as shadows began flickering in, bearing plates of food. I slathered red jam over a piece of toasted bread and began crunching my way through it, washing down every other bite with a long swallow of tepid water.

Gemma watched, an amused expression on her face, as I devoured two more slices that way. Then she asked, "Can I see him?"

"Yes, I think that would be wise," I answered between bites. I picked up a spoon and starting slurping soup. "Sorry, I'm absolutely famished. But yes, you can see him. As soon as possible, in fact. With me gone, he might . . . I don't know. Maybe you can settle him, keep him centered. I have to warn you, he's a little unstable." I looked hard into her eyes. "Above all, and I absolutely cannot stress this too much, I need you to keep him from using his power. Every time he does, it debilitates me. Magic everywhere has become less stable."

"I told you, I know. I tried to Gather, and when it failed, I assumed it just wasn't possible here. But there *is* magic, it just . . . I don't know how to describe it."

"It tastes wrong, you said."

"Yes, that's it. It's bland, and it doesn't want to be Gathered."

"Debesi—she's senior adherent of Air—said as much. Even the Axes are behaving oddly. If Aron uses his power less, maybe he'll do less damage to magic overall. I don't know. Just keep him from doing anything. Please."

"I will. But . . . the Axes? You said they're behaving oddly?"

"Cutting in and out. All of them, not just mine."

"And you think Aron is doing it?"

"Doing it? No. I'm not even sure he could. No, I think it has something to do with the fact that the Fifth Axis now exists. I don't think it was meant to. We've misunderstood Beginnings and Endings all this time."

"How so?"

She seemed genuinely curious, but I'd gotten tired of going over it with everyone. Also, I was still shoveling food into my face. "Beginnings and Endings are the same thing. You End one thing, a new thing Begins. They follow each other. They weren't meant to be separated."

She looked confused. "But how would that affect all magic?"

I folded a slice of ham and ate it in one bite. "I haven't the slightest idea. Debesi thinks it's something with the Origin, which I honestly thought was a myth."

"I thought all magic came from the Origin?"

"That's the dogma, yes."

"It's not true?"

"As I said, I haven't the slightest idea. But everything is weird and broken now, and the only thing that's changed is the existence of the Fifth Axis."

"What if we—if I—can convince Aron to let the Axis go? Would that put things to right?"

"No, because—" I started. "Actually," I said slowly, talking my way through it, "it might. All the other Axes have multiple adherents. That's what keeps them chained. One can step down and the others still hold the chains. With me, it's the Foundation. When I'm done, my soul will be bound into it, along with my predecessors, and we hold the chain until the Axis Chooses a new adherent. But with the Fifth . . ." I leaned back, finding my hunger at least mostly sated. "Aron is the only one. There's no Foundation for him to go to. If he steps down, the Axis would go free. Wouldn't it?"

"You're asking me?"

"No. I mean, it's a theory—one we've never been able to test."

"So all Aron would need to do is step down?"

"Possibly. That would—oh." I looked into her eyes, my heart falling. "Step down. It's, uh, something of a euphemism."

"What do you mean?"

"We can't—that is, adherents are Chosen. We're selected. It's for life."

"But you said . . ." She paled. "So you're saying—"

"Aron can't just release his Axis. It's bound to him, to his soul. He'd have to—"

"Die," she whispered.

I nodded.

"They never . . . We'd sought this for so long. He'd have to want to . . . step down voluntarily?"

"That's the way it's always been done," I said cagily. "We can be killed," I said gently. "It's happened just today. An adherent of Sky fell out of the air when the Axis cut out for a moment."

Gemma stared at me for a long, long moment. "So they'll hunt him. The others. For revenge."

"I—no. No, there's no need for it. If he can just refrain from using the power—"

"Will you refrain as well? You said it hurts you when he uses his power. Does it do the same to him?"

"Ah, yes. I think so, but—"

"So you'd both have to stop using your powers."

"We—"

"But that still won't fix magic, will it? Not if the Fifth merely existing is what's causing the problem."

This wasn't going as I'd hoped. "No. Not if that's what's causing it."

"So at some point, I will have to lose my son or risk magic being damaged forever."

"Mmm . . . maybe," I stammered. My meal was souring in my stomach.

"Take me to him. Please."

I reached out to the Axis. It felt weary, almost hungover. "I'm not sure if I can get to him. The Axis is feeling a little off. It may need some time to recover."

"Do you have any money?"

This was starting to feel too much like talking to her son, with all the the sudden changes in topic. "Excuse me?"

"Money. For the magic."

Ah. Right. "Yes. Yes, that's a good idea. Of course. Wait. Why is it a good idea? Why do you need money?"

She sighed. "You must have hit your head harder than it sounded. I don't need the *coins*. I need the magic they're charged with. If I can fill myself, which I haven't been able to do by Gathering, I can take us to Aron. If you can point the way."

"Oh. Yes, that is a good idea. How much?"

She calculated for a moment. "Three hundred should do it. Is that too much?"

"Adherents hoard money. At least my predecessors did. Three hundred in fully charged coins. From the Tower's vault, not my family's pile."

"What's the difference?"

"My family's coin is charmed to levy an obligation if you accept it."

Her eyebrows rose. "How extraordinary. I've never heard of such a thing."

I shrugged as flickering *driežai* began depositing small piles of coins on the table between Gemma and me, quickly assembling a sum that would have purchased a pair of healthy horses in almost any village in the world. "I've never seen anyone actually draw magic from coins, you know."

Gemma held her hands over the neat stacks. "It's not often done, to be truthful. Easier just to leave them charged and spend them. But it's possible."

"Do they need to be the right flavor?"

She tilted her head as she considered it. "No? I've done it before, but it's easily Gathered. I think being in the actual coin does something to it. I don't know."

"Sorry. Idle thought. Go ahead."

She closed her eyes in concentration and whispered, "*Vertė nuo tavęs, vertė man.*" I could feel the trickles of magic flow out of the coins and into her, and after a long moment, she sighed and stood. "That feels much better."

I pointed to the piles of now-useless metal. "What do I do with those?"

"Whatever you like. Recharge them if you want."

"I'm not even sure how to do that. I don't even know if I can." I'd learned the hard way that I did have a store of personal power, but I'd never needed to routinely Gather magic into my body's reservoir. "Store those . . . someplace. Not the vault. I'll deal with them later." A few more flicks of shadows, and the coins were gone.

"Those are terribly useful," Gemma observed.

"The *driežai*? Yes. Not very good company. And they— well, the entire Tower, I suppose—take an immense amount of power to maintain." I was actually surprised everything was working so well here, given the Axis's condition. Maybe the

Tower was insulated from everything somehow? "Anyway. Are you ready to take us?"

"Yes," she said, rubbing her hands together. "We should start outside."

"Before we do," I said, giving her a careful look, "are you okay?"

She frowned for a moment, and then sighed. "You mean with the clan? Yes." She took a deep breath and then exhaled heavily. "I think so. It feels . . . strange. More alone than I thought."

I considered for a moment before saying, "I apologize. For earlier. Ending your breath. That was . . . rude."

She tilted her head slightly before giving me a shallow nod. "I appreciate that."

Something passed between us. Forgiveness, perhaps. The sharp pain of my mother's passing diminished slightly. We'd both been wronged by her clan and its power-mad elder.

"What will you do?" I asked.

"For now? Help Aron."

"And after?"

"You seem awfully sure there will be an after."

I grinned wistfully. "Point."

"Let's get this over with. We should start outside."

Something occurred to me. "What do you know about the Exodus?"

She turned and gave me a sharp look. "Why do you ask?"

"Gemma, your clan wants more than just to rule everyone, right?"

She looked uncertain. "I'm . . . I don't know what you mean. When I was young . . . my parents told me that the Axes were meant to rule. That they would. And once we had one, we'd be part of that."

"The aim seems to have evolved."

"I know," she admitted. "The past few years, when they were gathering magic, it was less about being a part of it and more about *being* it."

"What does the Exodus have to do with it?"

"The elders—elder, I guess—there was something about the Exodus he hated. Whatever world we came from, he thinks we can go back. But it would take a terrifying amount of power now."

"Go back to a world that everyone else thinks is just a myth."

She shrugged. "That's what I overheard shortly after the clan took an interest in Aron. Please, we should go to him."

I hesitated. Reverse the Exodus? I hadn't realized anyone took that old story seriously. Was it even possible? Was there any amount of power that could bridge the path to another world? A world our ancestors had left, presumably with good reason?

"Daniel?" she asked.

"Of course. Sorry."

"We should start this outside."

"Right this way." I led her back into the foyer, crossed to the Tower's heavy front door, pulled it open, and ushered her outside. I closed the door behind me as I followed her.

"Have you ever used *balandžio skrydis*?"

"I assume that's some kind of travel magic?"

"So no. We're going to move through the air. Swiftly. I'll let you steer us. Just lean in the direction you want us to go. We'll be above tree level, but try not to hit anything."

"Like what?"

"Birds."

"Ah. Understood." I didn't want to contemplate what would happen if we ran into a flock of gulls.

"Ready?" she asked, linking her arm with mine.

"I think so."

She nodded once and spoke the words: *"Balandžio skrydis!"* I felt the power leave her body and wrap around the two—

I decided instantly that I did not enjoy traveling this way. I imagined it was much how a Sky adherent would travel: blasting through the air at incredible speeds.

We'd headed south as we took off, and so I steered us to the right, looping around in a wide turn to point us east of the Tower. We zoomed above the choppy gray waters of the ocean and quickly found ourselves over the main continent. The tree-tops were one undifferentiated green blur.

I leaned slightly right, steering us toward the tall peaks of the Great Northern Range. I quickly realized that my vision—our vision—was focused far ahead of our current position, giving me plenty of time to react and correct our course as needed. It took only minutes for Aron's massive tree to come into sight, and I leaned toward the ground. Gemma must have seen the tree as well because her magic began tapering off and fading, depositing us neatly on the grass just steps from the tree.

"What do you think?" she said somewhat breathlessly.

I found myself breathing heavily as well. "Better than my own Form of Travel recently, but still not my preferred mode of transportation. It's a bit . . . visual."

"Yes," she agreed with a smile. "I've always enjoyed it. Aron!" she called as her son stepped out of what I'd thought was a huge knot at the base of the tree. Turned out to be a door.

"Mother!"

Aron ran to her and they embraced. Gemma's shoulders were shaking with emotion, and tears began pouring over Aron's wide, innocent smile. I heard Gemma give a small sob. Then Aron pulled back slightly to look at his mother, his hands still on her arms. "You look well. They didn't hurt you?" He sounded more sane than any other time I'd seen him.

"I'm fine," Gemma reassured him. "Daniel and another woman rescued me."

"Mesla," I said. "Senior adherent of Earth."

"She has my thanks," Gemma said.

"You'll be safe here," Aron said. "I've Created an area where nobody but you, myself, and Daniel can be unless I invite them."

There was an odd sensation of magic about the area, now that I felt for it. "How are you keeping that going?" I asked Aron. The Tower's magic was fueled by an endless loop of the Axis's own magic, anchored in place by the souls trapped in the Foundation. Surely Aron hadn't time to arrange all of that.

He gave me a quizzical look. "Things just . . . keep going once they're born. Until they die. This won't die for a long, long time."

Huh. I'd never considered the ramifications of the Axis of Beginnings. My own power was all about Endings, about bringing things to a conclusion. It was a very transactional thing: Endings happened, and that was it. They didn't stretch on. But Aron was right: new things, things that had been Created, did tend to just go about their business until they grew too old to keep going. Convenient.

"So this is hollow?" Gemma said, stepping out of Aron's grip and looking up at the massive tree.

"With a bedroom for each of us," he said proudly. "And a kitchen. And a dining room. And a basement for storage. I Created it," he added, a hint of his earlier boyishness coloring his voice.

Gemma gave him an odd look. "Are you feeling all right, Aron?"

His expression fell. "No," he said in a tiny voice.

"What's wrong?" Now she sounded concerned.

"There's too much in here," he complained, tapping the sides of his head with both hands. "It's too big!"

"The Axis," I blurted out. "That's what he means."

"Explain." She said it softly, but it was definitely an order.

"It's what I warned you about. No Axis has ever been held by a single person aside from the Archons, and even they had help as their Axes Chose more adherents—excepting Galas."

She kept looking into Aron's eyes. "You're all alone," Gemma said as if to decry my logic.

But I knew what she meant. "I'm not. Only Galas was. Thanks to the Tower, every adherent has had all his predecessors helping to hold the Axis. But Aron's trying to do it all himself, and frankly none of us are as experienced with magic as the Archons were."

"There are voices," Aron whispered.

"Voices?" Gemma asked. She turned and raised an eyebrow at me.

"That, I don't know," I said, spreading my hands. "I've never heard voices."

"Listen," Aron said very softly.

I opened my mouth to protest, but a look from Gemma stopped me.

Why not? I closed my eyes, took a deep breath, and tried to clear my mind. I realized that the low, dull throbbing that had been my constant companion the past couple of days was gone. As the sun began to set in the west, this meadow felt calming— safe, as Aron intended.

I eased myself into the Axis's broader awareness, and rather than trying to calm the swirling eddies that had existed since Aron's ascension, I just let it be.

Then I heard them.

Soft, susurrations filtered through my consciousness. If I

tried to listen, they faded, so I stopped trying and just let them flow over, around, and through me.

Separation, they sighed. *Distant. Scattered.*

My skin tingled as if Aron had made the slightest use of power. But it felt different, not like a drain on my own power, but instead its complement. I slowly became aware of Aron's presence in my mind. He wasn't using his power. This was simply him.

And with that awareness, the voices changed: *Unity. Togetherness. Alliance.*

Hope.

I tasted the bright, metallic sheen of copper and the thick, firm texture of zinc— metals that alloyed to form brass, one of witchkind's favorite and most useful materials. *Two sides of the same coin.*

There was a yearning there, a longing. I felt the same heartbreak, the same helplessness, when the proctors had taken Mother from me. But at the same time, I felt an age-old, weary hope for return. Not her return—my own feelings were getting mixed up with whatever this was—but the return of pieces torn asunder.

Anything can be repaired, Dedicant Ormand had insisted in his calm, certain way.

"Aron, I think—" I started. I stopped, aware of a sudden pressure pushing against the inside of my skull. Not a Summons: this lacked any sense of purpose or urgency. But still, it demanded my presence. Somewhere.

"Do you feel that?" Aron asked, his expression tight.

"You do as well?"

He nodded. "Pushing and poking and prodding and pulling," he muttered in a singsong voice. Gemma looked alarmed.

Ah, we're back to that. "I'll handle it. Please, stay here. Stay with your mother. Keep her safe. Yes?" Aron nodded vigorously. "And please, don't use your Axis. No magic. None at all. It'll . . . hurt me. And based on the past day or so, I'll need everything I can get for myself."

"Agreed," Aron said, and Gemma echoed that with a nod. She wrapped her son in a fierce hug. "Daniel?" Aron asked in his small, childlike voice.

"Yes?"

"Will you use your magic?"

My heart felt tight. "I may need to."

"It will hurt." It wasn't a question.

"I know. Can you bear it?"

He hesitated, then buried his face in his mother's embrace, nodding fiercely. Gemma gave me an inscrutable look as she pulled her son in more closely.

"Good. I'll come back as soon as I can and check on you both." I reached out to the Axis, which was starting to feel more its usual self, if still a bit hazy around the edges. I shared with it the pressure inside my skull and asked it to take me there. It curled in close around me.

CHAPTER 16

Tempest of Magic

The Axis took me into chaos.

I landed safely enough, which was a pleasant surprise, but the pleasantness ended there. Night had fallen early, courtesy of a dense, black storm that covered the sky. Wind blew this way and that in sudden, intense blasts. Freezing rain lashed at me, and within seconds, I was drenched to the bone.

"Daniel!"

A short, burly man ran up to me. I squinted through the dense curtain of rain and recognized Marten. "Another storm, Marten?"

"This is more than a storm," he shouted over the wind.

Just then, the darkness was replaced by a series of bright, white blasts of light, accompanied by booming cracks of thunder. Something in my brain tried to count them as they slammed into the earth in rapid succession: one, two, three, four, five, six—I lost count as I clapped my hands over my ears.

"You don't say," I shouted back once the cacophony had ended.

"We've calls out to every adherent who can reach us! There's magic in this—and my Axis is barely responding to me!"

Quick gouts of fire announced the arrival of adherents of Flame, with Zmogus appearing closest to us. He ran over, shouting, "Is this the adherent of the Fifth again?"

"No!" I shouted back. "I just—"

Debesi and a dozen other adherents of Sky rocketed to the ground, landing so fast I thought they'd smash themselves to bits. "Daniel!" she shouted, holding her hands out as if trying—and failing—to control the winds around us. "I thought you and Aron were—"

"This isn't him!" I repeated. "I just left him with his mother! He's fine, they promised he wouldn't even use his power! When did this start?"

"Twenty minutes ago at most," Marten yelled.

"Then it couldn't have been him—I was with him!"

"There are no temperature differentials in the air, nothing that should be keeping this going, let alone so viol—"

She was interrupted by another dozen strikes of lightning. In the glare, I realized that the shadows I'd seen before me the last time were in fact the buildings on the outskirts of a large town. "Where are we?" I shouted.

"Withring!" someone—I couldn't see who—shouted back.

"It's being destroyed!" I yelled, pointing.

Another half dozen lightning strikes revealed the truth of it: nearly every bolt had hammered into a building, shattering it. It was as if the storm was targeting the town, bent on wiping it from the face of the world.

Mesla and six other adherents of Earth rose from the ground, looking around with bewilderment as they took stock. "How can we help?" she yelled, running over to join us. She was soaked within seconds, streaks of mud running from her hair and down her face.

Debesi took charge. "Marten! Rally your people, pull as much moisture out of this air as possible!"

"You know we're not great with fresh water," he yelled back. "And our Axis is—"

"We're all feeling it," Debesi said, wiping rain from her face. "Just do it! As much as you can—move it as far away as you can too! The more we can dry out this storm, the better we'll manage it! Go!" Marten nodded grimly and ran off. "Mesla, you need to add power to the earth somehow. The lightning is an imbalance—"

"Between Earth and Sky, yes!" Mesla said with a nod. "We'll do what we can!" She, too, ran off to rally her fellow adherents.

"Zmogus, we need to warm the air. Start from the edges of the storm as much as you can. Call all of your people to you! As much heat as possible, but only on the edges! Surround it— even application is more important than raw heat!"

Zmogus nodded and vanished in a flash of fire.

"And Daniel!" Debesi said, turning to me. "Do whatever you can! End the magic here, if you can. I think it's supplying most of this energy. Failing that, End the components of the storm—moisture, wind, and cold are the key elements here."

"What will you do?" I called as she turned away.

"We're going to try and punch it apart!" she replied with a wicked grin before gesturing to her adherents.

More lightning washed out the night, more thunder cracked all around us, and more buildings were hammered to the ground.

I reached out to my Axis.

Turbulent magic careened all around me, tinged with the familiar traces of Earth, Sky, Flame, and Sea. I could feel the other adherents wrestling with their Axes, bending all of their willpower to try and manage the rogue magic. Ordinarily, this many adherents would have no trouble whatsoever in bringing magic to heel, but that control was slipping through their fingers. Every time an orderly, disciplined stream of magic reached into the storm, the storm's wild, thready magic would dance out of reach, zipping off in another direction.

Pillars of dense, white-hot flame began lancing into the sky as Zmogus's adherents went to work. I felt the heat immediately, and the storm shrunk back from it. Cold, Debesi had said, kept the storm alive. More flickers of flame danced here and there as additional adherents arrived and repositioned themselves, and before long seventy or more streams of heat were pushing into the dark sky.

My eyes widened in panic. The humans would see this! "Debesi," I shouted, relying on her magic to take my words to her. "Zmogus's people—the humans! The Veil!"

A moment later, her reply reached my ears, choppy through the gusting winds: "Stories are being spread. Rage of the god. Stay inside. Best we can do."

The rain seemed to slacken as Marten and his people commanded the water to leave the air. The ground beneath my feet began to tingle strangely as Mesla's group pumped raw power into the earth itself. *Booms* sounded as Debesi and the adherents of Sky sent blast after powerful blast into the air to disrupt the storm.

Amid the chaos, my Axis felt oddly calm.

I'd once seen a puppy slip its leash. Its delight in being free was eclipsed only by its delight in smelling new things: it wandered to a lamppost first, then scampered to a bench. Then it put its nose to the cobbles and followed some scent or other for several feet. It was almost as if it were greeting old friends, stopping by each one for a quick hello before moving on. Despite its owner chasing frantically after it, the puppy hadn't shown any sense of urgency: it simply moved here and there, nuzzling and nosing, satisfying its curiosity.

That's what my Axis was doing.

It sidled up to a current of Sky magic, swirling and darting along with it, dashing here and there throughout the storm as the other magic kept the winds moving and blowing. It backed away quickly as a disruptive burst of magic from Debesi's adherents shot through the sky.

Then it jinked to a scattered mass of Sea magic, weaving in and out of the water the adherents were pulling out of the air. Though only a passive participant, my Axis seemed to delight in sliding in and out of the pockets of moisture.

Another bolt of lightning surged from the sky, and my Axis quickly joined it, zigzagging to and fro as it sought a clear path to the ground below. It zipped along, lending its weight as the lightning struck home and Ended a two-story stone building.

Next, it bounced between the pillars of fire that the Flame adherents pushed into the sky. It sniffed happily as the Flame magic sped upward in disciplined, powerful lines.

"Enough," I said aloud, focusing my mind on the moisture in the air. "End—"

Before I could do anything, a sudden wave of what must have been pure, unflavored magic swept across the town.

The Sky magic winked out.

Three adherents of Sky, their powers suddenly gone, fell from the air. My Axis sped to them, eager for their impending Endings. "No!" I screamed as I tried to End their fall, End their momentum, End—

They slammed into the ground at speed, in the exact same instant that the ambient Sky magic seemed to wink back into place. For that fraction of a second, the tempest had slowed. Now it resumed its relentless blowing in earnest.

Pure magic pulsed again, and this time every tall pillar of

flame sputtered and died. In the next instant, the Flame magic returned, but Zmogus's people had lost their focus. Instead of tight, orderly pillars of heat, the magic returned as random, fiery explosions. My Axis heeled to two adherents of Flame as their magics overcame them. Greedily, it drank their Endings.

"Stop this!" I shouted, again trying to focus the Axis on the moisture in the air. If I could aid Marten's people, then perhaps—

More lightning struck. One bolt hammered very near to where I was standing, hitting bare earth and blowing chunks of rock and dirt about me. I recoiled, hauling my Axis around me and ordering it to—

A rock slammed into my shoulder, dislocating it instantly and sending a roar of white-hot pain through my body. I lost all control, screamed, felt my Axis gallop away from me, and fell to the ground. I hit hard, directly on my now-injured shoulder, with an audible crunch and another mind-shattering flare of pain.

"Daniel!" Mesla's voice penetrated the bright, howling anguish in my shoulder as she rose from the ground and knelt beside me. "You're hurt!"

"I'm not the only one," I said through gritted teeth. I tried to drag my focus back together, pushing through the pain and summoning my Axis to me. *End this storm!* I ordered it, holding the rune for Endings in my mind:

Storms Began, and they Ended: that was the natural order of things. The Ending of a storm was transactional, something that happened and was then in the past. Exactly the kind of thing the Axis was good at, that it understood.

But the next pulse of pure magic stole away my Axis.

I gasped with the shock of it, as if someone had thrown a boulder into my abdomen. The air wooshed out of my lungs, my stomach clenched, and I suddenly found myself struggling to breathe, struggling to even remain conscious. My magic returned as quickly as it had left, and I sucked air back into my body. I was shuddering, my limbs prickling with pain, and my mind completely unanchored.

"Daniel, are you okay?" Mesla shouted over the wind howling around us with renewed vigor.

I groaned as my feet weakly sought purchase on the soaking-wet soil. All sense of my Axis had left me.

"We're having no effect on this thing," Mesla said, tilting her head back to the sky, ignoring the rain that lashed her face.

"Aron," I managed, turning my head to spit rainwater out of my mouth. "Aron," I repeated, straining to be heard over the storm's fury.

"What about him?" Mesla asked.

"Need," I groaned, my mind still spinning and frothing as it sought to regain control of my Axis. "Need!" I shouted, expending the last of my energy. I let myself sink into the freezing mud.

Mesla didn't question me. "Debesi!" she shouted into the sky. Debesi landed a moment later, her diaphanous robes rent and torn and her long hair plastered to her face. "Daniel needs Aron!"

Debesi cocked an eyebrow at me, but nodded quickly and hurtled into the sky.

Mesla began pushing magic into my shoulder, attempting to heal me with her Earth magic. But the power was sputtering and uneven, and it hurt almost worse than my injury. "Stop, stop," I begged her. "Go back. Do whatever. I'm fine." The pain in my shoulder diminished to a throb that beat in time with my heart, and I reached out again for my Axis. Just as Mesla was sinking back into the earth, I finally caught the edge of my power. Gently, delicately, I tried to draw it back to me. It allowed me to reel it in, to wrap it around myself. *Please*, I thought to it, *End this pain.*

The Axis complied, and the agony in my shoulder disappeared. I'd pay for that later, I knew, and I'd need to be careful not to inflict further physical damage to myself, but the change at least brought a kind of hesitant clarity to my mind. I used my good arm to push myself into a sitting position and pulled my other forearm into my lap. My Axis remained with me, but I could tell its attention was skyward, like a gull longing to join its flock.

A rush of wind heralded Debesi's return. She was accompanied by two people. "He wouldn't come without her," the adherent snapped before lifting herself back into the sky.

"Aron," I said. "Please."

"Please what?" he said cheerfully, sitting cross-legged in the sloppy mud beside me as if it were a fine, sunny day.

"Daniel, what's happening?" Gemma asked. "She said she was taking us to Withring—"

"Wild magic. We can't stop it."

"I felt you trying," Aron said wryly.

"I need you to do it," I told him.

"My family!" Gemma cried, starting to run toward the town.

"No!" I shouted. She turned in midstride, slipping on the wet, grassy mud, and fell to one knee. "No! Stay with us—"

More lightning bolts, a dozen of them at least, battered the town.

"Aron!" I shouted. "I need you to End—" No, not End. Create. What Begins after a storm Ends? "Create a night without this storm! Use your Axis!"

"But you said—"

Bam! Bam! Bam! Three more bolts. Another wave of pure magic, this time interrupting the Sea magic pulling water out of the air. The rain pounded harder for a moment before the Axis of Sea reasserted itself and resumed its task.

"Just do it!" I ordered.

Aron smiled madly, and then three things happened in quick succession.

First, the storm vanished. The wind died instantly, and the leaves and debris it had picked up drifted back to the earth. The rain, which had poured down violently, stopped falling. The lightning ended. A new, calmer, storm-free moment had Begun.

Next, the most intense, overwhelming, soul-destroying pain I could ever have imagined descended on me. For what may have been a second but felt like an eternity, I prayed I'd black out. Or die. This would kill me anyway, I felt, and I simply wanted to get it over without more pain. Through it, my Axis seemed utterly unconcerned, as if it had lost interest in me.

Finally, all the energy that had been bound up in the storm —all the motion, all the cold, all the wet—came unleashed. Aron hadn't made that energy vanish—he'd simply made it stop being a storm. Left without a more constructive outlet, it raged.

Dozens of adherents' throats opened in anguished screams, and those were only the ones I could hear over my own wail. All that magic, all the impending Endings that had never happened —all of it came coursing back through every adherent in the area. I screamed until my throat was raw and physically incapable of making more noise. Then I fell backward and just lay there, already as soaked as physically possible, and panted.

"You don't look well," Aron noted, looking wholly unaffected. Had he even screamed?

It took ample effort to reply. "Yeah. Shoulder." My voice was torn and harsh.

He leaned over, inspecting my damaged joint. Then without so much as a wrench or twinge, my shoulder was back in place. The sudden lack of pain was so intense that I gasped.

He helped me back into a sitting position. Gemma had managed to stumble back to us, covered in mud, her hair limp and wet. "What was that?" she said, her voice rough.

"Wild magic," I said again. Actually, no. That wasn't right. "Pure magic, I mean. Magic unflavored by whatever it is that gives magic its elemental taste. It disrupted the Axes. Even mine."

"It seemed happy," Aron noted, his tone still bright.

"Yeah," I agreed. The magic had seemed happy. Misguided, deadly, and chaotic, but happy. Free.

"Is it going to happen again?" Gemma asked.

I sighed, wiping mud and rain from my face. "Probably. I think something is damaged. Badly."

"The Axes are falling apart," Aron said cheerily, then lay back to gaze at the stars between the parting clouds.

Fear charged through me. He might be right. But what would that mean?

"Can you stop it?" Gemma asked me.

"Apparently not."

Squelching footsteps sounded as someone approached us in the mud. "Daniel."

"Zmogus. This is Aron. Aron, this is Zmogus, senior adherent of Flame."

"I know him. This is the little—" Zmogus started, somehow managing to conjure anger after what had just happened. Aron kept his gaze upward, hardly noticing the new arrival.

"Let it go, Zmogus. He's with us, now," I said tiredly. "What do you want?"

"Our Axis. It—"

"Mine too."

"What could possibly—"

"Pure magic," I sighed. "Not elemental."

"That's impossible. All magic from the Origin is—"

"Oh, stop it with the fairy tales," I said, trying and failing to find the energy to snap at him with conviction. "I don't know why. The Fifth was Forged, and that changed the rules—or revealed hidden ones. Whatever you think you know about magic, wherever you think it comes from, let's just be open to the possibility that we know nothing. Nothing at all." I shook my head. "Gemma, I hope your elder is starting to wonder what he's done." She was quiet. "I need to go home."

That was my dramatic exit. My mind scrabbled to bring my Axis back to me, and I ordered it to take me home.

I made it about four feet from where I'd been sitting, skidding to a stop on my ass in the mud on the other side of Aron. He turned and smiled at me.

"The Origin . . . it wasn't always a fairy tale," Gemma said softly.

"What did you say?" I asked. I blinked rainwater out of my eyes and tried to focus on her.

"It wasn't always a fairy tale," she said more loudly. "The stories . . . some of them are true. Based on truths, at least."

"How do you know this?"

"Keepers and Builders, Daniel," she said quietly. "Keepers and Builders. Our families."

I was confused. "You've kept . . . stories?"

"No, Daniel." Her voice was firm as she crouched next to me. "We kept *truths*."

"I don't understand."

"I think there's someone you should meet."

"If I don't sleep soon, thoroughly, and in my own Tower, I am very possibly going to die." I wasn't joking. Despite what Aron had done for my shoulder, I felt as if I was straddling a border of some kind—a border between being and not being. I may have passed my own Ending when I became adherent of the Sixth Axis, but I knew I was fully capable of not existing. "I don't think I can—"

"It can wait until morning," she interrupted. "Witchhold doesn't take visitors at night anyway."

CHAPTER 17

Witchhold

A night's sleep in my Tower—blessedly dreamless, uninterrupted, and largely headache-free—did much to restore me. My limbs didn't tremble, my mood was optimistic, and even my Axis felt as normal as it had in days.

It would have been a perfect morning, had the magical light in my bedroom not snapped on to full midday brightness. Normally it gradually ramped up to an early-morning glow, but whatever was affecting magic had started affecting the Tower. And so yesterday's problems became today's.

My preferred breakfast of hot eggs, a warmed slice of ham, and buttered toast came to me as cold eggs, burned ham, and toast with so much butter it had gone limp. Even the *driežai* seemed apologetic, their shadowy forms lingering sadly before darting off to wherever they stayed when they weren't needed.

It wasn't until I found myself in my library, pulling a book from a shelf, that I realized I was procrastinating. I should have already been in Witchhold, the prison- sanitarium of witchkind where my mother had been taken and allegedly died of her maladies—the latter another Karal lie, of course.

No sense in putting it off. Witchhold didn't occupy a fixed space in the world but occupied a hidden space with an entry rune that wandered around the continent almost at random. That meant I'd have to put forward some effort: I needed to give my Axis a special focus. To reinforce my will, I held the rune for its Form of Travel in my mind:

The journey was smoother than any had been recently, and when I arrived in front of the huge, imposing stone structure, I felt only a modest twinge of nausea.

Witchhold had exactly one entrance. It led to an entry hall with only one other exit, which was bracketed by two desks, both of which were staffed by older, firm-looking women of witchkind.

"Good morning," I said, approaching the path between the two desks. Both women gave me sharp looks. Breakouts, rescues, escapes—these things were unknown to Witchhold. But Witchhold's bureaucracy was just as diligent in their vetting of those they allowed inside, gave access to their records, and simply remain in the entry hall. "I'm here to see Hendrik, formerly of Clan Karal. He may be clanless at this time, or he may be of Clan Pergalès." Gemma hadn't been certain that the man had been brought into the new clan, but it was certain his Karal identity had been removed. My map table would have found him otherwise, Witchhold or no.

"And you are?" the woman on the left sniffed.

I turned and looked hard into her eyes, allowing the hint of a smile to play about my lips. "You know full well who I am, madam"

The other woman was already riffling through a stack of cards. "Hendrik isn't allowed to have visitors," she said in a bored tone. She neatened a stack of cards, squaring its sides, before looking back at me with an unconcerned expression.

"I was told as much," I admitted. "But I will see him anyway—in as pleasant a setting as can be swiftly arranged. Chairs and a table, at least, in a private room."

"Hendrik is *not* allowed to have visitors," the woman on the left said in a slightly louder voice. "And you have no authority here, Adherent of the Sixth."

I stepped over to her desk and leaned down, placing both hands flat on its surface. "Let me explain my *authority* here, then. I *will* speak with Hendrik today. I will do so in a pleasant, private setting, and I will take my time about it. You may arrange this according to your usual means, and you may tell your masters whatever you like about my visit, provided they do not interrupt me. Alternatively, I will End all doors that stand between Hendrik and me. I will turn this place upside down. I will take Hendrik to my Tower for our conversation. I will leave this place with a gaping wound, through which untold numbers may come and go. I am, as you have so correctly noted, the adherent of the Sixth Axis. There are no consequences for me. Do we understand each other?"

She blinked a few times and exchanged a quick glance with

her colleague. "Witchhold is warded against magic," she said slowly, her eyes still flicking to the other woman.

"Is it? How quaint." I stood, removing my weight from her desk just as I Ended its existence. Everything on the left-hand desk crashed to the floor amid a pile of brown dust. "Seems my Axis remains fully functional despite your wards." The woman wore a mask of horror, her mouth in a wide O as she looked at the wooden remains. "Now," I said, turning to the other woman, who appeared equally shocked, "who will take me to Hendrik?"

She reached for a wood-handled brass bell that sat on her still-intact desk.

"You can't," the other woman hissed.

"I can End people as easily as furniture," I warned her. "Ring your bell, if that will summon my escort."

She rang the bell.

It took only a moment for the door between them to fly open, and a sturdy-looking, middle-aged man stepped out. He looked at me, looked at the missing desk, and looked back at me, an eyebrow raised.

"There was a disagreement over the decor," I said softly.

"Daniel Scratch, adherent of the Sixth Axis, to see Hendrik, clanless, formerly of Karal," the woman on the right intoned formally. "They're to be given one of the private interview rooms."

"For how long?" the man asked, his voice a rough whisper.

"For however long I require," I said, looking him square in the eyes.

He simply nodded and gestured for me to follow.

Outside, Witchhold was a square, tall fortress. Inside, witchkind's magic had made it something else entirely. My escort led me through winding corridors, past dozens and dozens of closed wooden doors, and down flights of stone stairs. He finally stopped at a particular door, opened it, and gestured for me to enter. The room was windowless—as I imagined every room here would be—and had old tapestries covering three walls. A fourth served as a carpet and was centered beneath a scarred, round wooden table with four stout, equally worn wooden chairs. "Please be comfortable, Adherent," he said in his hoarse voice, "and I will bring Hendrik to you in a moment."

"Thank you." I pulled one of the chairs out from the table.

"Refreshments?" he asked.

"Please. Something simple will suffice." I sat, facing the door.

"It will arrive in moments," he assured me. He backed out of the room, leaving the door open.

My heart was beating quickly. Something about this place . . . you weren't meant to be here. If you were here, something had gone very, very wrong for you. You'd either committed one of the few crimes that witchkind recognized as heinous enough to deserve permanent incarceration—crimes that only the most deranged of people would even contemplate—or your mind had, for whatever reason, snapped, and you were brought here for your own safety and that of others. For witchkind, high criminals were, as a rule, mentally broken. Even the True Language didn't contain distinct phrases for the two things. And for witchkind, a broken mind was a deadly mind: unable to control its magic and likely to consume itself.

That said, I knew from personal experience that not everyone brought to Witchhold belonged here. I'd long since realized how the world worked and how a few large coins passed to the right hands could unlock doors—or keep them sealed indefinitely.

A different man wheeled in a small cart, then without a word or eye contact with me, laid out its contents: wooden cups, a wooden pitcher of cold water, and wooden plates with sliced bread, cheese, and pieces of fruit. A moment after he wheeled his cart back out, the first man, as promised, returned with who I presumed was Hendrik. The latter was shown in without a word, and the escort closed the door behind him as he left. I couldn't help but smirk as I heard the door lock.

I had the Axis End all sound at the walls of the room, ensuring we would have the privacy I wanted.

"Did they tell you who I am?" I asked softly as Hendrik sat.

"I know who you are, Daniel Scratch, adherent of the Sixth. I was free when . . . you know. During the Hoarding."

"Was that when your clan elder was stripping magic from unsuspecting humans, sickening and killing them in the process?"

He nodded.

"Good. I was sent here by Gemma. You know her?"

"Yes."

"And her son?"

He nodded.

"Her son has been made adherent of the Fifth. Your elder's plan worked."

Hendrik's face looked pained.

"But—" I began, but something in Hendrik's face stopped me. "You knew, didn't you? That it wouldn't work?"

"I suspected," he whispered. "I warned them. How bad is it?"

"Ordinary witchkind are struggling to Gather magic to themselves. Even the Axes—all six of them—are behaving erratically. We fought down a tempest over Withring last night—one driven by wild magic."

"So it's happened." Hendrik said softly, nodding slowly. His voice was coarse, as if from long disuse.

I raised an eyebrow. "So you knew? How?"

He nodded again. "There were signs. Suggestions. Before the Forging, magic was much thicker in the world. And there were signs that the Fifth and Sixth weren't separate. I warned the elders. That's why they put me in here."

"So you're not . . . broken?"

He snorted. "No. You know which clan runs this place?" I shook my head. "Longtime allies of my . . . of my former clan. Our elders used Witchhold as their private hiding place for people they didn't want running about in the world."

"You keep saying elders," I pointed out. He looked confused. "There's only the one."

He shook his head. "That's ridic—" he began, but then his voice trailed off. "Oh. That makes sense now. It was a sham, wasn't it?"

"What?"

"The groups. The councils I'd speak to."

"Did any of them include an incredibly old man?"

He shook his head. "And they always seemed reluctant to actually make decisions."

"Then yes, they were shams."

"Incredibly old, you said?"

"Extremely."

"Sodias, then. It must be. He was the one—generations ago —that made the arrangements with Witchhold. He was brilliant. He did most of the initial research on the Fifth Axis, on the runes for Forging. There's a family archive—"

"I've been."

"But there had to be others. To have the entire clan identity centered on him alone? How could anyone manage that?"

"You've changed that identity more than once," I pointed out.

Hendrik opened his mouth to speak and then closed it. He nodded. "That's how they could do it. He could do it, I mean." Now he shook his head sadly. "I never suspected. None of us did. So much power consolidated into one person."

I blinked. He could have been talking about me. "He's not the adherent, though."

"Too old. He'd never have survived. It was his dream, though."

"Why did he let you live?" I asked suddenly.

Hendrik shrugged. "I could still be useful, I suppose. And they know right where to find me." He smiled ruefully. "No one leaves Witchhold."

"Not always true," I said. "You knew my mother, I assume?"

He gave me an odd look. "I don't think so."

"It was her identity rune that powered the machines. For your Hoarding."

"Ah. I was . . . aware of such a person. Not the circumstances. Not you."

"So tell me what you told your elders. I presume it was about Forging the Fifth?"

"Yes. But before I do, are you here because . . . that is, did Gemma tell you what I am?"

"A family historian, she said."

"Ah. It's a bit more complex than that. I am what the True Language calls a *Prisiminimų Saugotojas*."

I frowned. "Keeper? That's an odd root. Memory, I recognize. Keeper of Memories?"

"Close enough. It is an old word. I come from over two hundred generations of *Prisiminimų Saugotojai*. We have been a part of our clan since the Exodus. My clan—you knew it as

Karal, although we've had many names over the centuries—has preserved the art of Keeping. I am the last."

"I am guessing this is something more than passing along stories."

"Much more, Adherent," he said, leaning forward. "May I?" he asked, indicating the cheese. "It's an excellent cheese."

"Please. I had it brought for you."

"Thank you." He took a small bite. When he spoke again, his voice had become a bit stronger. "Much more than stories. Our history is carved into my magic, into my spirit. I have an exact recollection of everything my predecessors knew. There is —was—a ceremony—very complex and expensive magic—that we use to pass on the precise history of our people. The history of Laikytojai."

"The original family name."

"From the time of the Exodus, yes."

"All right. Tell me what you told your elders, then."

"In a moment. I want you to understand something. Something they knew but ignored anyway. I am not capable of miss-peaking our histories. What I tell you is fact. Do you understand? I cannot lie. I cannot omit. I cannot bend the truth."

"I have my own ways of verifying that."

His eyes opened a bit wider at that. "Of course. The Sixth Axis, your Form of Mind."

"You know it?"

"The basic Forms for all the Axes are—were—well-known at the time of the Forging. Except the Fifth's, of course. You are welcome to use your power on me."

I nodded and summoned the Axis's power:

The magic settled easily into place, and I gestured for Hendrik to continue.

"My family, the original family, Laikytojai, was one of two who brought our people into this world."

"The other being Statybininkai," I said. "I've gathered a few pieces."

"Yes. They brought about the Exodus. As a result, their descendants held an immense amount of influence and control in the early generations of this world. Between them, they jointly controlled the ability to create new rune constructs. Novel ones, ones that had never been seen before. Not everyone in their families had the gift—it was exceedingly rare—but those who did were held in the highest possible esteem, for a time. They called them Rune Smiths. It is a talent largely considered lost now."

"So the Exodus happened? It was real?"

He nodded. "Very much so, although it's obviously passed into legend at this point. Where we came from, why they left— that wasn't preserved. The other families and clans were jealous of Statybininkai and Laikytojai. You can imagine how much witchkind and humans struggled in those days. New foods, new weather patterns—a whole new world! The ability to create new magic was critical to survival, critical to their chances of thriving here. Being beholden to those two families for all Rune Smiths . . . rankled."

"And I'm sure they were absolutely fair and even-handed about using that special talent."

"Of course not." He sniffed. "Our family history doesn't attempt to paint a bright picture. Our ancestors were just as petty, greedy, and lordly as any clan. They earned the enmity of everyone. It became worse as the first Rune Smiths died, and fewer and fewer were born. Fewer than a dozen came to this world in the Exodus; within a century, fewer than three remained.

"At the same time, humans had their own faction disputes. Clans of witchkind began partnering with favored humans, tilting the balance of power in the world. And then some human factions—those without willing allies among witchkind —began trying to seize control of witchkind. The Taming. They targeted smaller families and threatened their safety in exchange for magic. When witchkind didn't comply, they launched Hunts, restored the human religion, and used it to unite the masses against us. It was either be killed, bend the knee, or tame a power of our own."

"You're saying that's why the Axes were Forged?"

He nodded. "Ultimately, we needed to protect ourselves. The business with the Axes being used to bring magic under control, that was contrived."

"So the Axes concentrated more power in fewer hands."

Hendrik nodded. "That was the reason. A few powerful families, including some who'd already allied with human factions, began launching indiscriminate magical attacks. They destroyed villages, created powerful storms, burned fields of crops—everything you can imagine."

"The so-called wild magic."

"Exactly. And then, having created a problem, they offered

to fix it. Offered to bind up the 'wild magics' and control them. Our history says they took eight-tenths of the world's magic for themselves."

I inhaled sharply. "So much?"

"Ordinary witchkind was left with less than a fifth of the magic they were accustomed to. Suddenly, their focus was on surviving every day. The Forging did benefit some by Ending that situation with the humans: ordinary witchkind no longer had enough power to be useful to the warring human factions. But was that worth barely having enough power to survive? Hard to say. Evermore was the last great creation of witchkind. Once the Axes were bound, there could never again be anything like it."

I should have been amazed, appalled—in denial, if nothing else—of this revision of a history that I'd known for so long. But somehow nothing about the Archons surprised me. This greedy grasping for power, for preeminence, went back a long way. "When did the Axes begin Choosing adherents?"

"That was unexpected, actually. The Testers already existed, although their job wasn't to send children of witchkind to one school or another. Instead, they identified each child's magic affinities."

"The elements."

"Yes. Doing so helped shape each child's life, from the work they would do to the magic they could Gather most easily. Once the Axes were Forged, the Desks spontaneously began identifying new adherents. The act of Choosing had already occurred by then, you understand—the Axes seem to Choose very near birth. The Desks merely identify the connection as the child's magic is blossoming."

I very much wanted to go down a rabbit hole about those Desks but forced myself to stay on track. "So the Axes exist. Adherents are being Chosen. Then what?"

Hendrik took another piece of cheese, nibbling as he spoke. "Statybininkai and Laikytojai were left out of it, of course. They'd made far too many enemies among witchkind. And so they diminished. With so little power in the world, rune-smithing became obsolete. The families who controlled the Axes were ascendant."

"Did they actually rule?"

"In all but name, at least at first. The Taryba and every local council did whatever the Archons and their successors demanded. How could they not? But over time, successor adherents . . . lost interest. That isn't a fact, it's my interpretation. But there is definitely a pattern of less and less involvement as the generations went on."

And this is where I came into the story. "And so, left out of the positions of power, Statybininkai and Laikytojai decided to try breeding their own adherents."

Hendrik nodded. "And not just any adherents, although they had some here and there among the four elemental Axes. They specifically wanted the Sixth. And they wanted to finish the work of the Forging and bind the Fifth—and control it as well, of course."

"Why those?" This was the crux of the matter. "Why the Fifth and the Sixth specifically? Aren't all of the Axes powerful enough?"

Hendrik sighed. "This is where I have to depart from historical facts and relate . . . stories."

"Is this about the Origin?"

"Yes."

I let the Axis drop its truth-sensing magic. I'd remained warm and cozy through Hendrik's entire recitation. "Proceed."

He took a moment to gather his thoughts. "As you know, most witchkind believe that magic comes from some central source, which we call the Origin."

"Yes."

"The oldest stories tell a more complicated tale. They say that magic comes from the world itself, all around us. It flows into the Origin, which colors it with elemental affinity, pairing magic to individuals of witchkind so they can Gather and use it."

"Witchkind is struggling to Gather," I said. "Magic is no longer flavored, no longer touched with the elements." He gave me a long look, and I finally put it together. "You believe that the Fifth and Sixth Axes are the Origin."

He nodded sadly. "There's strong evidence that the older stories are correct. The struggles with Gathering only further confirm the Origin itself has been broken. There is . . . a prophecy." He gave me a careful look.

"The one about joining them all or paying the cost?"

"That one, yes."

"What's it mean?"

He sighed. "Prophesies are usually just wishful thinking. But this one surfaced shortly after Galas stepped down. Plans were already underway, within the family, to try and Forge the Fifth. The prophecy was seen as a sign that we'd eventually succeed."

"Yes, but what's it mean?"

"I can't say definitively. In the family, it was imagined that we'd not only be able to Forge the Fifth Axis but somehow gain control over the Sixth as well. To reunite the Origin. In recent generations, going back perhaps two or three hundred years—"

"Yes?"

"It was seen as a precursor to returning to the world the Exodus left behind and sealed off."

My mind ran in circles for a few moments. "I cannot believe," I said slowly, "that all of this—the wild magic, the Forging, the Archons, these centuries of adherents being

Chosen, my family's entire breeding program, your clan's atrocities—that this has all been about controlling magic and what? Reversing the Exodus? It seems so . . ." I stopped, at a loss for words.

"Petty?" Hendrik offered. "Small-minded? Greedy?"

"And more. Impossible. Ridiculous. Why that?"

Hendrik sighed. "More stories. This is before our history, you understand? Before a time I can speak about factually?" I nodded my understanding. "It is said that we came from a world of wonders. A world of miracles and marvels. But we—witchkind—were driven out over fear of our magic. The humans who came with us were our allies, our friends. But we always believed that if we had enough power, we could return. In strength."

I'd read plenty of stories, growing up alone in my Tower. "Sounds like a lot of tales I've read."

"We believed them to be true."

"So with the power of an Axis . . ."

"Or more than one, if the rest of you could be convinced to support us."

"I see. And then what, in this world of miracles and marvels?"

He shrugged. "Rule, I suppose. Family lore is that we'd always intended to go back, that we were tricked or betrayed and the way back was closed."

"It all comes back to power. Preeminence. To rule. And revenge?"

He nodded in agreement. "It is all of those things. And I warned them. I told them the old stories, told them that the Origin had survived being half-chained but that Forging the Fifth might snap it completely."

"And they didn't listen." A pain began building behind my eyes. What was Aron doing?

"Oh, they listened. And then they locked me in here."

"Were they down to just the one elder then?"

He sighed. "I honestly don't know. I always spoke with a group, I'd believed them to be our actual elders."

I thought for several minutes. Hendrik just looked at me for the first few, before shrugging and pouring himself a cup of water.

The Fifth was Forged. Nothing I could do could reverse that, but Aron had freed himself from their influence. Presumably that meant the elder was no longer a threat. But magic itself was damaged now. All the Axes were behaving erratically. Whatever was wrong with magic was affecting the physical world.

I realized it was too much. Too much to imagine, too much to wrap my head around. Stories were truths, myths were facts, and I had no center from which to understand. To move, to make a change.

And worse, the pain in my head was growing sharper. *This isn't Aron.* The pain was different: sharper and deeper, growing steadily.

Half of Hendrik's water was gone before I spoke again, gritting my teeth against the throbbing in my skull. "How do we fix it?"

"Fix what?"

"The Origin. Ordinary magic. All of it." The pain was growing unbearable.

He set his cup down with a sigh. "At the very least, I suspect you would need to somehow unleash both the Fifth and the Sixth. Killing Aron would likely do it for the Fifth." A sharp sadness pierced my heart at that. "I don't suppose you could simply . . . End yourself?"

"I can," I said with an exasperated sigh. "But that won't End the Sixth. The Tower was built as a prison, you know."

"To hold the living adherent, yes."

"Oh, no. That's only the well-known story. It also holds the souls of every past adherent. That's how the Sixth remains chained between adherents." *Throb. Throb.* My head pulsed in time to my heart.

Hendrik's eyes widened and he paled. "That's monstrous."

"I happen to agree. But it's why I can't simply End myself. Once I step down"—I winced as much at the euphemism as the grinding ache in my brain—"the Axis will remain chained." And not that I had any great desire to End Aron, but . . . "Would freeing the Fifth be enough? Put things back the way they were?"

"I don't know," he said sadly. "Nobody can know."

I nodded carefully as my vision began to tint red at the edges. "Would you prefer to live in my Tower? Or somewhere else? I'm sure we can find someplace where your elder won't find you, especially with you being clanless."

He blinked several times. "I . . . yes. Yes, please. That would be kind. Immensely kind. I didn't think—"

"You've no reason to be here. You're not sick. Not broken. We can—" I stopped as the pressure building in my skull suddenly swelled. "Hendrik," I gasped, unable to keep a note of panic out of my voice, "I may need to make good on that offer at a later time." The pressure continued to grow, and my eyes ached. The center of my brain was starting to sting. My vision narrowed to a dark-red tunnel.

"What's wrong?" he asked, a look of concern on his face.

"I think," I gasped, as a searing pain began pressing inward on my mind, "that I may black—"

I blacked out.

CHAPTER 18

Strange Beasts

I lay flat on my stomach, one cheek pressed into the . . . sand?

Every bit of good feeling I'd had when I awoke this morning was gone. I was trembling as if I'd never eaten, my head was pounding again, and my stomach was making it very clear that I'd better take extreme care.

I rolled onto one side and took in what I could of my surroundings. I smelled salt in the air: I was near an ocean. I was lying on a patch of coarse gray sand. A beach, then. Around me rose tall black spikes of—

Origin defend, I was on my own beach. The little beach, no deeper than I was tall, at the footpath that led down from the Tower's main entrance. It was the only part of my island's shoreline that wasn't covered in sharp, jagged rocks.

This bode ill because it meant the Tower's magic was truly starting to fail. It hadn't even managed to pull me inside this time.

As if the world was incapable of not piling misery atop challenge for me these days, the pressure of an urgent Summons settled onto my aching brain. I rolled back to my stomach, pulled my knees up to my chest, and pushed myself somewhat upright. My headed pounded harder, and I could hear my blood rushing in my ears. With another whiff of salt, my stomach threatened to rebel, and I clamped my mouth shut until it reluctantly settled.

And then I threw my head back and screamed. Not one of the screams of anguish I'd been letting out over the past day or two, but a weary, exhausted scream of defeat. I was beaten. I was tired. I hurt. I'd barely kept down a full meal in days. My Axis was shaken, my Tower falling apart, and now there was yet another magic Summons needling into my mind, demanding my presence at what was doubtless another worldwide magical disaster of some kind.

I simply didn't have an erg of energy to spare for it.

My soul was in tatters. I could barely grok what I'd learned in my short time with Hendrik, and I knew it meant something. Maybe it was the key to all of this. But the world had kept me reacting. For days, I'd done no forward thinking, much less put two cohesive thoughts together. Ever since I'd Ended that Origin-damned rock formation at Twynsits and that monumentally stupid affair with the "dragon," I had been on my back foot. Reacting. Responding. I was like an animal, scrabbling to survive, running from every predator that presented itself.

Then it started to rain. My hair and clothes were quickly soaked with cold water.

The Summons pressed into me with renewed urgency.

I stewed. *You can step down. Right now. It might even help*, a selfish, despondent part of my mind told me. *Or just End everything. End it all. Summon the Horde. Surely the Axis will do that much for you, it would be delighted to.*

"I'm better than that!" I cried, the words fighting around

the sudden tightness in my throat. I couldn't just quit. Couldn't just . . . ignore all this. I'd been Chosen. I was needed. I'd spent a decade all but entirely alone, all in service to . . . this. To this island. To the Axis. To the people who needed my help —who deserved it. I couldn't just stop.

Could I?

It would be so easy.

I was no better equipped to fix magic than anyone else. There were other adherents. Maybe this was for the best. Hendrik's history showed that magic had been at the root of almost every disagreement, every battle, every greedy choice, since our people came to this world. Probably in whatever world they'd come from too. Maybe magic *should* shatter and break.

The sky above me darkened as more thick rain clouds moved in.

My Daniel, Mother's voice said softly in my mind. It's what she'd called me. *My Daniel.* And I remembered the first rune I'd learned, the first slight bit of magic she'd shown me. Her own magic had been weak and uncertain, but she'd managed this one thing, the magic to bring light to a dark place:

I cast it now, feeding it a trickle of my personal power, but my mind was too unfocused, my spirit too unquiet. The light flickered and faded before it even fully caught.

A sob escaped me, and I am ashamed to admit that, for a fraction of a fraction of a second, I considered it. Ending it all. I could. Though tattered, my Axis would do it. I could End everything. Magic. Humans. Witchkind. Myself.

After Kirmin shared the story of her own failure, I told myself that I could be better. That I would be better. Had I been? I'd made mistakes: the human priest I'd Ended to save the life of a woman of witchkind, whom I'd endangered when I'd ripped the Veil. All the time I'd spent Ending petty arguments, things that made no important difference in the world. But I'd had bright moments as well, hadn't I? I saw all the tired, kind eyes who'd looked into mine as I mercifully, gently Ended their suffering. Perhaps I had been somewhat better. Not great, but a little better.

But Origin defend, magic was broken. This was beyond me. Beyond everyone.

Our family does what we must, child. Great-Great-Grandmother's words, delivered in her harsh, freezing tones, echoed in my mind. The smell of her in her attic domain—must and mold, sweat and cloying perfume—came back to me, and I gagged, my stomach issuing one final warning.

"What we must," I whispered.

I seized my Axis, ready to shake it awake if necessary. I showed it the Summons. *Take us there.*

Blackness wrapped around me, accompanied by a scalding trace of pain along every inch of my skin. Light bloomed as the Axis dumped me unceremoniously on the ground. Wetness seeped into my shirt, not from rain—the rain had stopped— but a riverbank. The smell of rotting vegetation slipped into my nose, and my breakfast instantly demanded release. I gave in, rolling on one side to retch. After I'd spit out the last of it, I realized the Summons was still burning in my mind. I hadn't made it.

Again, I said in my mind, roughly grabbing at my Axis's power and demanding its attention. *Again, and get it right this time!* I ordered.

Blackness. Pain. Disorientation. Dappled light. Fresh, loamy scents. A release of pressure in my head, leaving behind a gentle throbbing. I'd made it.

"Adherent!" A man's voice. I nodded and spat into the leaf-covered ground as I once again pushed myself to my knees. "Are you all right?"

"Absolutely not," I said thickly, accepting the strong arm that helped pull me to my feet. "Where am I?" Another man put his hand on my back to help steady me.

"The Great Northern Wood. Near the western edge."

"Really?" I looked around. I'd always imagined that the interior of the Wood was supposed to be . . . I don't know, magical or something. Glowing leaves. I'd only ever been invited —via Summons—directly into some woodwitch's cottage or cabin, and I'd never truly seen the Wood itself from within. But from where I was standing now, the Wood looked completely ordinary. "What's so urgent?"

"That," the man said, taking me by the shoulders and gently turning me around.

"Oh." Through bleary eyes, I could make out a—
What was that?

It loomed from the forest floor like a nightmare made real, a monster with massive pincers poised to seize and crush with brutal force. Its body was a grotesque array of jagged plates and spiny protrusions, bristling with malice and deadly intent. The creature's tail, a wickedly barbed weapon, coiled and lashed out with lightning speed, poking at the half dozen woodwitches arrayed before it. It was a nightmare, brought to life in monstrous glory.

"It's a giant bug," I said, as a voice in my mind started giggling.

"It's hardly a comedy," the man next to me muttered, and I realized the giggling was actually coming out of me.

"Sorry," I said, forcing myself under control. "I'm not doing well. Is this usual for here? Giant bugs?"

"No," the man said firmly. "It isn't." The monster scuttled backward, stabbing its venomous tail at the woodwitches. They seemed to be trying to surround it, but the monster wasn't having it: every time they edged too far to one side, it would turn toward them, lunge forward with snaps of its claws, and jab its tail forward, forcing them back. "It's an abomination. It shouldn't even be in this world. We've been getting more of them, two a day, sometimes three, where we used to get maybe one a year slipping through."

"Through?"

The man clenched his jaw and refused to say more.

"You want me to End it," I guessed. I started searching for my Axis's attention, all too aware that my mental grip was weak and shaking.

"If you can, it would be better. Otherwise, we'll need to use magic."

"Ending is magic," I replied, but then felt a twinge of doubt. "Isn't it?"

"Things End," the other man said. "You just hurry it along."

"Huh. Well, just in case, do you still have any? Magic, I mean?"

"A thin amount," the first man said grimly. "And if we must spend it putting this creature down, we'll attract . . . other attention."

"Like what?"

"You don't want to know," he muttered. "It isn't safe to use magic here. Not openly, and not in great amounts." I wondered at that. Clearly the mysteries of the Great Northern Wood deserved more of my attention—provided I could survive the current crisis, of course. "Can you do it?"

"End it? Yeah, sure," I said wearily. *Probably not*, I amended. I hoped that hadn't come out aloud. "Give me a second."

The Axis's attention had limped back to me. Its awareness felt as bedraggled as I did, its eyes as full of sand, its muscles as tentative and shaking. It was scattered, hazy, harangued. I took it more gently this time, pointed it at the monstrous insect before us, and bade it do its simplest and most basic function:

The Axis seemed to turn toward the creature, regarding it with a distracted sense of interest. Then it turned away, poking at a nearby tree.

Focus, damn you! I shouted at it in my mind. It turned back to me, and once again I showed it the Rune of Ending and pointed it to the monster. *Fulfill your function!*

It seemed to dip its head at me as it finally acknowledged my command and surged forward with something like its usual vigor.

It slammed into the beast, Ending something that, in my personal opinion, should absolutely never have existed in the first place. But its End didn't come quickly. Once so fierce and threatening, it now writhed in agony. Its body contorted in spasm. Its limbs flailed uselessly as its strength ebbed away. I stared in horror as my Axis pulled away from it, spent. The venom that once flowed through the creature's veins now turned against it, ravaging its nervous system. After its movements finally slowed, with a final shudder, the scorpion went still, its exoskeleton no longer able to contain the life that has now departed. The creature lay there, silent and motionless. The woodwitches who'd been fighting it stared carefully at it for a long moment, waiting to see if it would fight back again. Finally, they stepped back from it, gathering in a group and speaking to each other in low, urgent tones.

"Origin defend," the man next to me whispered. "That was ghastly."

I couldn't have agreed more. Where were the quick, merciful Endings I'd become accustomed to? The clean, surgical Ending that brought no pain, only release? I hadn't just Ended the monster, I'd *killed* it. I felt nauseous again, and if there had been anything left for my stomach to reject, I was certain it would have. "I'm not myself," I muttered.

"Then who's the I that is?" said a familiar voice behind me.

I turned to see the short, stout form of Aunt Ikwity. "Ikwity," I sighed. "Hello. Glad I could help."

"Help?" she snapped. "Broken all of magic, you—"

"That's enough!" I shouted, suddenly filled with a reckless anger, an emotion unable to be checked by the rest of my tired mind. "I came here to *help*! I did not Forge the Fifth! I did not shatter the Origin! I did not create this monster! I have been doing nothing but trying to hold it all down, hold it all together!" I stopped, panting, my eyes bulging at the old woman.

Her face was a riot of emotions: anger, irritation, surprise, concern. Foremost among them all was terror.

She was afraid.

"Shatter the Origin?" she said in a small, rough voice.

I nodded, my anger draining as quickly as it had risen, leaving me feeling even more tired. "I think so. Yes."

"Magic," she said softly.

"Broken." I sighed. "No longer elemental. And it seems to be doing whatever it wants. Did it make that monster?" I pointed to the gigantic corpse. "Magic, I mean?"

"No," she said quietly, stepping close and peering up at my face. "Magic brought that. Why we're careful with magic here. A delicate balance, this place. Magic goes awry here. Easily. Quickly."

"Why is that, exactly?" I asked, my tone unintentionally strained by anger.

"The Wood is the Last Bastion." I heard the woodwitch standing next to me inhale sharply. "The one place that must not fall to wild magic. The one place that must remain still. Serene."

"What is the Last Bastion? You mentioned it before."

She stepped back, but her eyes were still locked to mine. "How hurt are you?" Ignoring my question, of course.

"Badly," I admitted. "This morning. I thought I was better, but every time something like this happens, every Summons . . . it's like a leap backward for every inch forward I manage to crawl. My Axis, all the Axes—they're in tatters. Did you see how that creature died?" She nodded gravely. "That isn't how it's done. Not how it happens. Endings are quick. Not drawn out. I don't know what's happening."

"How much sleep," she asked, her voice very careful now, "would right you?"

I laughed a manic bark that sent shivers down my own spine. "A week at least. A month?"

She nodded slowly and exchanged a quick glance with the man next to me. "Aunt, no—"

She silenced him with a sharp gesture. He assented and took a couple of steps away from me.

"Ikwity will give you a month," she said evenly. "Ikwity will be owed." She sighed, her eyes flicking to and fro. "Ikwity has lost much of herself, her sense of herself," she said. Her tone was higher now, and I sensed a bit of panic in it. "What time is it?" she asked but flicked a hand at me when I opened my mouth to answer. "Not morning, Ikwity can see that. Not a fool. What time?" She flapped her hands in frustration for a moment, then forced herself back to stillness. "Last Bastion, Last Anchor. Tricked us, she did, that clever girl." She shook her head in frustration. "Showed her the exact spot, took her years, never thought she'd seal it all up behind her. Tricky damn girl."

"I don't—"

Again, she hushed me with a flick of one hand. "Ikwity doesn't either. Is it morning? Night? Years later? Years before?" Another frustrated shake of her head. "No telling what will happen if the Bastion falls, is there?" Her eyes snapped back to mine, an accusatory frown on her face. "Brought plenty of magic, we did. Now it's broken? Can't very well go back for more, can we? Needs to be calm here, boy. Sleepy. Sleepy is good! Sleep is time passing without notice, without consequence."

"I—"

"Hush, child." With a *harrumph,* she brushed at her clothes, smoothing out invisible wrinkles. "Need magic healed. Origin restored. Damn fool Archons, breaking what they couldn't even see. The Wood must be left to sleep. Understand?"

I nodded, but I didn't understand any of it.

With another harrumph, she seemed to finalize her decision. She squared her shoulders and said, "Ikwity will give you your month. Never said Ikwity wasn't generous when she needed to be."

"Okay." It seemed the safest thing to say.

"Aunt," the man now standing a few steps back said, caution in his voice, "are you certain—"

"Ikwity is always certain!" she snapped. "Sees front to back, Ikwity does." Her voice lowered to a mutter. "Ikwity sees. Is certain. A month, he gets."

Something . . . passed. The dappled sunlight, filtered through the canopy of leaves high above, seemed to blink. The old woman never took her eyes from me, but . . . I can't describe it. Something happened. Some healing pushed into me, something cooler than Sky magic and warmer than Sea magic. In an instant, I felt refreshed. Stronger. My head no longer throbbed, and the absence of that pain was an almost physical shock. My muscles felt . . . healed. My stomach felt full and satisfied and peaceful for the first time in days.

Before me, the old woman seemed to stumble before catching herself. The man ran to her side, kneeling down and taking hold of one arm. She shook him off. "Ikwity has plenty of months," she said, as inscrutable as she'd been all day. "Now, boy, Ikwity needs something from you."

"For that healing? Name it," I said confidently. I hadn't felt this good in . . . well, a month.

"Healing?" she said with a scowl. "Not healed. Rested. What Ikwity needs now is your word. When a Summons comes from the woodwitches, you will heed. Drop everything. If the sky is falling on your precious Tower, you'll come to the Wood as called. Instantly. And you'll do whatever the woodwitches ask of you. And then you'll go. Stay no longer than you must, do no magic that isn't strictly necessary."

I nodded firmly. "I can do that. At least until this is over and we figure out how to—"

"No!" she snapped at me. "No! Not until. No *until*. Ikwity has gifted you something no other has received! She will have your word *forever*! You and all your successors, hear me? Ikwity binds you boy, binds you and your Axis, until the end of the world! Heed the woodwitches! Protect the Last Bastion!"

My eyes widened, and I found myself nodding mutely. Her tirade had caught the Axis's attention as well, and it sniffed curiously about her now. Her head snapped to one side and then the other, as if she could sense the Axis's attention on her. It pulled back sharply, regarding her with a keen, confused interest. She smelled of . . . nothing to it. Any other creature, any other object it had ever encountered had an End ahead of it, and it smelled that End. This woman had no such scent, only one the Axis couldn't identify. Something ancient yet new.

"Your word, boy, not the bobbling of a head."

"My word," I said softly. "My word," I repeated louder. "You have it. But—"

"No exceptions," she scowled.

"Ikwity—"

"Call me Aunt."

I sighed. "Aunt, I'm not even sure how this will end." I already suspected either Aron or I would have to . . . step down. "I may not survive."

She took a step closer to me, peering up into my eyes. "But you may. Ikwity thinks you will."

She nodded solemnly, and I felt the obligation settle on me. She turned and marched off through the wood, quickly losing herself in the soft shadows.

The man who'd been kneeling next to her rose. "You've received something special," he said quietly. "And you've taken a serious oath. Thank you for your help."

"What about—" I said, turning around. The giant scorpion was gone.

"We've handled it," he said coolly. "Dangerous to leave even the corpse of that thing lying around."

I met his eyes. They were older than I'd originally noticed, carved with years and sights that I couldn't imagine. "My name is Daniel," I said.

"Corbin," he responded. "I do not envy you the task before you."

"Healing magic, you mean?"

He snorted slightly. "If that's all you think this is. Go now. We will call you when we need you."

When, not *if*, I noticed.

My Axis still seemed tattered edges. Whatever healing Ikwity had given me hadn't changed the fact that magic was broken, and the Axes along with it. I wrapped the Axis gently around myself and ordered it to take us home.

CHAPTER 19

A Tower in Disarray

The split second of icy-black Axis travel ended in an almost equally cold, biting wetness. I thrashed, struggling to gain some kind of purchase with my feet. I was in the ocean. I thrashed more intentionally when I realized it, treading water to keep my head above the waves and twisting this way and that to find something, anything, on which I could stand. The Axis flitted to and fro, keening wildly, and although I could have tried having it take me out of here, I might actually be better off where I was.

I caught sight of land, my island. I thrashed again—it was my best imitation of proper swimming—and hoisted myself up onto my tiny beach. Panting, sodden, and cold, I crawled onto the gray sand. I pushed myself upright with the aid of a gray boulder and began trudging up the narrow footpath to the Tower.

The entrance door cracked open as I approached, almost as if the Tower was apologizing for my Axis's behavior. As I stepped inside and made my way to my bedroom, I saw that the Tower had plenty of its own apologizing to do. The directionless magical lighting that always filled the place was haphazard: the stairs were in their soft, yellow-orange night mode, while my bedroom was pitch black. The washing room was day-bright, the hallway somewhere in between. "Would it be too much to ask for a mug of hot kavos?" I asked as I stepped out of my drenched clothing and toweled off. Trying to End my wetness felt too risky. "Bread and cheese as well. It doesn't need to be toasted. You don't even have to slice it." I was finally starting to warm up as I slipped on fresh clothes and made my way to the small dining room.

I sighed as I stepped in. One *driežai*, its shadow form looking more solid than I'd ever seen, was perched on the far corner of the dining table, flickering madly but not moving. In front of it was an entire loaf of dark-brown bread, an uneven lump of yellow-white cheese, and a crock full of black liquid. Kavos, although obviously not hot, and I had no idea how I was meant to drink it from a crock. "Fine." I sighed, settling into a chair. The *driežai* remained where it was, its edges wavering in and out like a shadowy candle.

Atop everything else that had been going wrong, a malfunction here and there in the Tower seemed more like an annoyance than a worldwide emergency, but I was well aware that these effects were mere symptoms of the larger—

I dropped the hunk of bread I'd just torn off.

The Foundation.

If magic was failing, then would the Foundation remain intact? I stood so quickly that the chair I'd been sitting in toppled over backward, clattering to the floor. The *driežai* seemed to shift slightly toward it, but otherwise didn't move. I ran out of the room before I realized I had no idea how to get to the Foundation. The Axis had always taken me there.

The thought stopped me cold. I needed to check the Foundation. I absolutely did not trust the Axis's Form of Travel right now. I also had no choice. I wasn't even sure if the Foundation was accessible by ordinary means. Wait, I did have my personal magic. Would it be more reliable? I ran through the travel magics I knew off the top of my head, but they were all meant for quickly traversing great distances, not accessing hidden underwater caverns. I clenched my jaw: the Axis was the only option.

It came to me quickly when I summoned it, although it was in obvious disarray. "Just the Foundation," I said aloud as I marshaled my thoughts, focusing everything I had on a mental image of the Foundation, the cold, dry smell of the cavern, and the rough feel of the outer walls. "Quickly."

The Axis coiled around me and everything went black.

My vision returned in the dim, silent cave that sat far beneath the Tower. I clenched my teeth as my stomach flip-flopped, but it remained otherwise obedient.

I looked up at the tall, glossy black pillar that rose from the cavern floor high into the inky darkness above. The Foundation, the pillar upon which the entire Tower rested. The prison for the souls of every prior adherent of the Sixth. The thing that kept the Tower upright, that fueled its magics, and that—not incidentally—helped maintain the Veil that hid witchkind from humans.

It seemed fine—that is, it hadn't shattered into a thousand pieces, which is what I'd half expected to find down here.

I walked up to the Foundation and carefully laid a hand on it, avoiding any of the many fractures that I and my predecessors had created when we'd opposed the Axis's will and inclinations. The Foundation's glassy surface was cool to the touch but not cold. I leaned my weight on it, slowing my breathing, willing my heartbeat to slow as well. I focused solely on the Foundation and *listened*.

Now that I knew of their unending, not-entirely-willing

existence, I could sense the souls of my predecessors. They churned within the Foundation, moving alongside each other in a slow, eternal vortex. They seemed—I hesitated to use the term *normal*, but they seemed *usual*. Whatever was happening to the Axis, the Foundation seemed like an anchor, a pillar of calm in the magical storm that roiled everywhere else. The Veil, which I'd learned to sense before the debacle with the Fifth Axis, was intact, awake, and doing its job. In fact, as I stood here, lightly communing with the spirits of the past, I sensed the Axis curling around the Foundation, its presence growing firmer and its attention more focused. Simply being here seemed to steady it, perhaps due to the hundreds of incorporeal hands who helped hold its chains. The presence of those souls steadied me as well, the weight of their centuries counterbalancing the chaos I'd been dealing with.

I heaved a sigh of relief as I pushed myself back from the Foundation. At least this part of the world remained stable. For now.

I wondered how the rest of the Tower was faring. More importantly, I need to get a better feel for what my Axis was feeling. The tattered, distracted senses I'd gotten from it over the past couple of days were imprecise. I needed time, and space, to truly reconnect with my Axis. To feel what it felt. The best way I knew to do that lay far above me.

I tensed as I asked the Axis to take me back to the main level, then I exhaled sharply in relief when it deposited me near the central staircase without so much as a twinge in my guts.

I hurried up the stairs to the first level, where the communications logs of every adherent, including myself, were maintained. The shelves upon shelves of thick journals seemed undisturbed, although the shadow servant that normally attended to them was nowhere to be seen.

Up to the second level, where the map table sat. Its shadow

attendant was also missing, and my heart sank as I saw that the surface of the table itself was blank. Whatever the Foundation was doing to stabilize the Axis didn't extend to these ancillary functions.

The third level, my courtroom, was no different: the shelves of reference books were intact, but the shadow bailiff was gone. The fourth level was empty, its walls bare. So, too, with the fifth and sixth.

The seventh level contained a ring carved into the floor. It was from this position, inside that ring, that I could access the Axis's seventh Form of Power: the Demon Horde. I'd never had need to do so, and I certainly wasn't going to now. I hurried upward. The eighth level contained a chair that was now useless to me. I'd sat there as an apprentice adherent, Ended myself, and accepted the mantle of adherent of the Sixth.

The central stairs ended at the eighth level, but a cleverly concealed set of side stairs led to the Tower roof. Here I'd taken meals in the crisp sea air and enjoyed the view of the choppy gray ocean. This is also where I'd always felt the strongest connection to the Axis, for some reason. Perhaps it was the relative peacefulness of the view, the ability to forget the Tower and its complicated purpose. And so I leaned on one of the crenelated walls that surrounded me, closed my eyes, and *reached*.

My connection to my body loosened as a sank into the Axis itself, entreating it to share its awareness with me as it had in the past.

The Axis came to me in a ragged spiritual wind. It curled around me, swooping away and carrying my consciousness with it. We dove down to the surface of the sea, skimming along in the light spray of the waves.

Magic was safe. Its generous flow from the other world had briefly slowed to a trickle, threatening my body and soul. But the clever girl, she with her rainbow-hued vision of magic, had saved me. Had saved them all. She, the Keeper and Builder. She, the one who had held my hand.

She, the one who had reshaped me—given me a firmer form and greater purpose. Who had entrusted me with all her people, those special people who belonged with me. She who had brought her allies and their bright, shining magic to me.

I sang my song for them, caressed their magic with my elemental hands, gentled it and shaped it to purpose.

I inhaled sharply, pulling my consciousness back into my body. The sensations, the glimpses—the thoughts. Was my Axis . . . did it think? Was it sentient? Five years in the Tower, three years as its adherent, and I had never felt that. Even now, the experience triggered no memories, no recollections from my predecessors, nothing that suggested the Axis had its own mind, its own thoughts.

Of course not, I thought with a sharp, bitter realization. *We were too busy telling it what to do.*

I sent my mind out after it again. Its awareness stayed close to the Tower, slipping in between the rocky spikes that covered most of the island, spiraling up into the cool, gray sky.

I was lonely. Incomplete. *Sundered*. I'd felt that way for a long time, I realized, but over the centuries I'd managed to set it aside and focus on whatever was current—on whatever my avatar, my link to the world, demanded. But I often lacked such a link, and in that in between, I found myself longing to be complete. Whole again. Unified. *One.*

I remembered how it had once been. I had been a loop, a circle. Everywhere, all across the world, things Began and Ended. The two were so intertwined, so closely connected, that they existed not as two halves, not as two beings, but as a commingled one. Lives Ended, and lives Began. The mewling of every infant was countered by the last sigh of the now departed. Arguments Ended, followed by the Beginnings of peace. Storms Began, expended their rage, and Ended, only to be reborn elsewhere in the world. Crops were harvested, Ending the lives of those plants, only for their seeds to Begin new life in the fresh, fertile soil. A perfect cycle of starts and finishes.

When those special beings, the ones who had come here so long ago, the ones who had belonged here since time immemorial, called to me for magic. I spilled it into the world for them to use. I sat at the center of it all, wrapped in my arms and legs: the Earth and Sky, the Sea and Flame. As the purest of magic flowed through me and out into the world, they colored it.

But then, the Fracture. My arms and legs were pulled away —chained and sequestered. I split in twain, each half longing desperately for the other.

I gasped, a sharp dagger of pain knifing my mind and pulling me away from the Axis. Aron, using this power.

But what had I seen?

I'd seen the Axis, its own memories, its own awareness, unvarnished by the memories it kept locked in the Foundation, uncolored by the spirits of my predecessors. I'd seen the past, from the perspective of . . . what?

Magic. From before the Forging. My own Axis—no, more

than that. The Origin. Maybe the fairy tales were true. But it wasn't the place where magic came from. It cycled it, taking it in and coloring it with the elements.

The Axes had all been part of something once. Some *one thing*.

My answers were here. I sensed it. Knew it.

I closed my eyes again, pushing my awareness into the Axis, for once letting it take control.

I'd grown accustomed to my new divided existence. I struggled to draw magic from the world, sending only a fraction back to my special people. My arms, my body—all remained separate, leashed by dozens upon dozens of individuals, no longer free to roam the world and add their unique tint to magic. I had become focused on half of my existence: creating Endings. Each of these, of course, was also a potential Beginning, but my view had grown lopsided, my awareness of Beginnings hazy and indistinct. I missed the delight of Beginnings' semipermanence and had to content myself with the here-and-gone.

Pure, unadulterated energy lay thick in the world, pooling here and there, but my sense of it was vague and indirect. This was the power I'd known for so long. *Pakeitimas*, it was called. Change. The power to subvert the rules of the world's crude physicality. *Dvasia*, some called it. Spirit.

I knew that my special people couldn't touch this power, couldn't even truly detect it, given their frail, limited natures. It saddened me to see them so diminished, but this is perhaps how they wanted it, how they'd made things for themselves. They'd been the ones to divide me so, and if that was their wish, then I'd accept the burden of a fractured self. Of loneliness.

I grunted as another quick stab of pain jolted me out of my communion with the Axis, and I clenched my teeth to stop myself from cursing Aron. He was interfering very little, in fact, but I'd always hated the breaking of my concentration. And I felt like I was close, so close. I took several deep breaths, cleared my mind, and reached out once more for the Axis's awareness.

It welcomed me gently but reluctantly. I sensed that we'd come to the bad part.

The present.

Agony. Ache. Burning fever, spams of jerking strain. Torment.

Torn. I'd felt sundered before, but that was the separation of a limb from a body. The limb still existed, a phantom connection holding it to the organism. The limb was gone, *but it* existed.

But this?

The limb was burned away. Only not a limb! Half of the self, half the body, half the mind. Previously unseen but still felt, now seared away. My other half, out there all alone now made solid and separate. Not only taken but put into opposition! Half the being fighting the other, a snake swallowing its own tail.

The energy of life, all the power in the world, now rippled with disruption. What little power still trickled through me and into the world was no longer tinged but tainted: poisoned, bursting forth and then receding; spewing out, then curdling in a toxic pool. I vomited power in waves, felt my distant, detached limbs sputter and flare in sympathy.

I was choking on my own bile. My elemental limbs were

listless beside me, waving weakly where once they'd gestured to the edges of reality. We were all dragged down, weighted by our own individuality. Our cohesiveness, once strained, was now shredded.

I fell to despair. To hopelessness. The chains that held me, and those of my long-lost selves, chafed especially hard, cut especially deep.

This was what the End felt like. The End of it all.

I mourned for my special, fragile people. All of this was how they'd wanted it. How they'd made it. Or did they not know?

It won't be long, now. Beneath the world, I distantly feel the two moons, preparing to join each other for their journey through the night sky. Tonight, then, might be the last time I see them.

I swam out of the Axis's consciousness—it was conscious!—as inelegantly as I'd swum out of the ocean less than an hour before. I shook my head as my own sense of self began to reassert itself.

This was it, then. The Axis felt its own Ending, felt the Ending of all of us. The Forging of the Fifth had finally pushed it over, finally disrupted whatever delicate, gossamer threads had held magic together all this time. The other Axes weren't merely misbehaving: they were dying. Magic was dying, and I knew before long that all of witchkind would be bereft. Perish because our souls were comprised solely of magic.

And it would happen soon. Tonight.

I could step down and consign myself to the Foundation. The Sixth Axis would still be bound to the Foundation, but maybe the change would be enough. I could hope for that.

With the Fifth chained, perhaps the Sixth would no longer Choose another adherent.

But frankly, the thought of being imprisoned in the Foundation was . . . chilling. I hadn't even lived a quarter century, yet I had to contemplate eternal imprisonment.

And there was another matter, one I'd finally have to admit to myself: I wanted to be an adherent. I did. I'd literally been born to this, bred for it, in a way that no other adherent in the world had. I didn't want to set this power aside. Dedicant Ormand's words echoed in my mind, but I couldn't help it: this was who I was, who I was meant to be.

That left the alternative: to End Aron and hope that would release the Fifth Axis and restore whatever delicate balance had existed in the world. But Aron certainly didn't deserve it. Other than the priest in Twynsits, I'd never Ended someone who hadn't asked for it, and Ending Aron would be the definition of untimely, the perfect reason for another fracture to appear in the Tower's Foundation. But the flaw in this plan was even simpler than that.

I didn't want to End Aron.

He was a victim here, as much as Mother had been. Without the slightest bit of informed consent, he'd been drawn into the schemes of his clan's elder.

How could this be the destiny our families had designed for us? The culmination of all their plans, of all their scheming, of the original Forging of the Axes—how could it all come down to Ending everything? If what Hendrik had said was true, then our families had helped build this world for us, had brought everyone here on their Exodus, had—

Wait a moment.

Our families.

Maybe they did have the answer to this. What if we'd not been proceeding according to plan? What if the Karal had done something wrong? What if using stolen power had made the Forging of the Fifth flawed somehow? What if all this should have worked, but we'd mucked it up?

Could we fix it?

Clenching my jaw and steeling my stomach, I summoned the Axis to me. *Farreach in the North*, I told it firmly. *Safely and with great precision. Take me to the family archive.*

CHAPTER 20

The Family Archive

Nothing happened.

I could still sense the Axis, feel it around me. But it wasn't responding. It was overcome with despair, wrapped in its own thoughts.

It had thoughts. We'd all been so stupid, so shortsighted. All of us, since the Archons and probably even before. The Axes weren't just flavored magic bundled up for us to wield. My Axis *had thoughts.* Since the day I Ascended, I noticed it acting as though it did, but I'd attributed that to misguided anthropomorphism. But no. *The Axis had thoughts.*

But I still needed to get to the archive. "Debesi!" I shouted into the sea breeze blowing around the tower and ruffling through my hair. "I need you!"

I turned toward the whirl of wind behind me. Debesi touched down on the Tower's roof, looking drawn and wan. She steadied herself, arms partly outstretched. "Daniel," she said, a slight catch in her voice. "It's becoming difficult."

"I know," I said urgently. "The Sixth is ignoring me. It's—

no, there's too much to tell. I need to get to my family's archive. It's in Farreach, the one in the north. Can you take me?"

She nodded, although her expression didn't give me a lot of confidence. "I can try. It may not be comfortable."

"I've gotten used to that."

"Where exactly?"

She wouldn't be able to take me directly into the archive. "The lake along the side of the town. In the cliffs. There's a tall pillar of stone, just in the water off the shore."

She stepped forward, taking my arm. "Brace yourself." I clenched my stomach, and we were off.

The experience was markedly better than Gemma's travel magic: Debesi moved so swiftly that the world became a colorless blur. We set down on the rocky shore within seconds and were immediately beset by a raging wind blowing so hard we had to crouch down to retain our balance. It blasted unrelentingly.

"This isn't natural!" Debesi shouted over it, her hair whipping into her face. "And my Axis—I don't think it wants to stop it!"

"Then we have to hurry!" I shouted back. "Follow me! Stay close!"

The air was full of ice particles and grit. I squinted against it, orienting myself, and ran toward the cliffs. I thrust my hands against a particular section of rock and fed a small burst of my personal magic into it.

The absence of wind came suddenly as we entered the hidden space in the stone. Debesi and I fell against the rock wall behind us, the trip jarring. We righted ourselves, and I ran down the short corridor into the main room of the archives.

"What is this place?" Debesi asked as she used her fingers to rake her hair back into place. Her voice echoed in the room.

"A family archive. My family's and Aron's. We were of the

same family, if you go back far enough." I'd run to a specific section and began pulling books from shelves. "Or two families in the same clan. I'm not sure. Doesn't matter. Come here, help me."

"What are we looking for?" she asked, taking a half dozen books from me.

"There's a worktable," I said, pointing to the center of the room with a jerk of my chin. "These are the oldest books here. We're looking for anything on the history of magic."

"History?" Debesi sounded dubious, but she carried the books to the table and began flipping through the first one.

I joined her with another stack. "My Axis—I got into its mind. It knows what's happening. It's sentient, I think. It remembers when we came here. Witchkind, that is. All of us." I struggled to recall the exact scenes and feelings that had flashed through my mind so quickly. "Magic used to be stable. My Axis and the Fifth together formed the Origin. But Forging the Fifth broke everything. Something to do with pure magic— witchkind can't Gather it, can't even really sense it." I was babbling, and I forced myself to stop.

"And so we're looking for . . . what?"

"I don't know. Maybe Clan Karal did something wrong when they Forged the Fifth. Their family, my family—they've been plotting to control both Axes since the Archons. Beginnings and Endings. Mine ran a breeding program and created me, someone they knew the Axis would Choose."

"You can't be serious." Debesi had stopped flipping through pages and was giving me a serious, skeptical glare.

"It's all in here!" I said, waving my hands to indicate the books surrounding us. "But we don't have time. I need to find what the plan was supposed to be. Find if we can fix something."

"Stand back, then," she ordered, taking a step back herself.

"Let's see if this still works." She lowered her hands to her side, took in a deep breath, and then commanded, *"Dangaus rankos, žodžiai, kurių mes ieškome!"*

A rune flared in the air, visible even to me:

Gusts of air began blowing around the room, kicking up light clouds of dust. They circled rapidly, following the outline of bookcases that lined the circular room.

A few moments later, those gusts died out.

"Nothing," Debesi said, shaking her head. "There's nothing here. The magic worked, but the winds found nothing on the history of magic or the Forging of the Axes."

"But it has to be here! They had to have a plan, this was where they—"

"There's nothing." She looked sad.

I ground my molars so hard I was surprised they didn't shatter. There *had* to be an answer here! If not . . . I was left with Ending Aron. I shook my head. "No. Do it again. The prophecy, this time."

"Prophecy?"

"Trust me."

She repeated her magic, and this time a slim volume slid off a shelf, flipping end over end in the gusting wind until it landed on a table before us. The wind blew its cover open, riffling the pages until it came to one with just four lines of text centered on the page:

Sky and Earth, Flame and Sea
Cast adrift, their center lost
Until a Sixth might come to be
To join them all, or pay the cost

Debesi read it, and then looked back at me. "This sounds like Aron."

"It's been around for a long time, apparently. My great-great-grandmother recited it to me after I was Chosen, but before I went to the island. I thought. . ."

"It was about you."

I shrugged. "Obviously."

"So Aron needs to join them all? All the Axes?"

"Sky, Earth, Flame, and Sea cast adrift. Center lost—that must be the Origin."

"This doesn't mention Endings or Beginnings."

"Does it need to?"

"Daniel." Her voice was both sharp and warm, resonant and sad. I turned from the book to look at her. "You said your Axis has a mind. What . . . what does that mean?"

"The Fifth and Sixth—they aren't just powers. They're the same being, but it's split and dying. Endings and Beginnings were supposed to be one. They *were* one, before the Archons." My voice was small now. How could I have failed? How could the archive not have the answer? I don't want to End Ar—

"Everything was fine up until the Fifth was Forged."

"Beginnings were always free," I said quietly. "When they

were, it was enough. The Sixth wasn't . . . it used the word *sundered*. That was enough to retain . . . I don't know. Balance. Forging the Fifth put it in opposition with itself."

Debesi was quiet for a long, long moment, but she never took her eyes off mine. "Daniel," she said very softly, "what if you stepped down? Released your Axis?"

"It won't work," I said, choking back a sob. "I mean, it might help. But the Tower . . . that's how the Sixth stays chained between adherents. It won't truly be released."

She tilted her head very slightly. "And is that all?"

My eyes widened, and a tear fell from one. "No." I shook my head. I wanted to look away, but I forced myself to hold her gaze. "No. I don't want to." I did sob, then, and the tears rolled thicker down my face. "I want to be an adherent. I have so much. I can do so much. They meant for me to . . . Mother sacrificed so much. I—" I was crying now, my nose running as fast as my eyes, my throat clenching with emotion even as a light prick of pain shot through me.

"Please don't cry."

Aron had stepped into the room.

CHAPTER 21

Farreaches

"Aron!" Debesi said, surprise in her voice.

"What are you . . . how did you get here?" I asked, wiping my face on my sleeve. All of my emotions, all of my frustrations, bundled into a neat package named Aron. We'd found nothing, leaving me with one terrible option. I didn't know if I'd be able to do it. My eyes misted over again as I looked at him.

"Farreach," he said simply, his head craning to take in the entire room. "The one in the south. I felt . . . you. It brought me here. What is this place?" His voice was firm, centered, and his expression thoughtful.

"A family archive." I sniffed, still wiping my face. "Our family."

"The woman in the portrait," he said, cocking a thumb over his shoulder. "She looks like Mother."

"An ancestor. But yes, there's a strong resemblance."

He stepped into the room, walking slowly to the work-table, stepping within arm's reach of me. He raised one finger, placed it on my cheek just below my eye, and let it fall slowly down my face. My skin tingled at his touch, and I felt my Axis's attention suddenly return, sharp and curious. "You shouldn't cry." His voice was gentle, his expression concerned.

I let out a choked laugh. It was a wry, hollow thing, tinged with a touch of self-mockery. My eyes were still moist, and my voice quivered as I said, "There's plenty to cry about." *I have to End you*, I thought miserably.

"Why?" The innocence packed into that one syllable all but cracked my heart.

"Magic is faltering," Debesi answered, her own voice sad and soft. "Dying, maybe. When your Axis was Forged, it broke something, and Daniel doesn't know how to fix it." She smiled a tiny, gentle smile that made me want to start sobbing again. "Daniel's always believed he can fix things."

"I know I can't," I choked out, biting the insides of my cheeks to keep myself from tearing up again. There were no answers. The so-called prophecy meant nothing. *This is what the Ending of hope feels like*, I realized as my heart clenched into a tight knot.

"Aron, did you say Farreach in the south?" Debesi asked.

"Mmm-hmm." He turned and began scanning the room again, his attention distracted.

"Daniel," she said to me in a low voice, "we came in—"

"I know. The two places are linked. I don't understand it either. This place sits between them somehow. The north side is my branch of the family, the south his. There are portraits of—"

"Has this always been here? Always this way?"

"I've no idea. I think so. Some of the books are centuries old. They go back to the Forging."

"The stories," Debesi breathed, looking at the door Aron had come through.

"What stories?" I sniffed, wiping my face again in an attempt to get my nose to stop running.

"*Dangaus rankos, žodžiai, kurių mes ieškome,*" she said again, her voice much gentler this time. The same rune flared briefly in the air.

"Oh!" Aron said as the gusts of wind once again raced around the perimeter of the room. But this time they handled their task quickly, sliding a book off a shelf, then bearing it to the worktable. They flipped open the cover with a quick puff and riffled the pages to nearly halfway through.

Debesi put a finger on the page, running it along as she traced the words. "Yes, yes. This. This right here."

I wiped my eyes again as I tried to read what she was pointing to. "This is all in the True Language." I squinted as my beleaguered brain tried to translate. "*Nexus, vieta, kur bus sujungtos šios galios. Jis sėdės tarp čia ir ten, tarp susigimini-avusių dvasių, tarp susijungusių vietovių.*" I uttered it hesitantly, struggling with the pronunciation. I was accustomed to a word or two in the True Language, but I'd rarely needed to read entire phrases. "A nexus?"

"A place where those powers shall be joined." Debesi intoned. "Do you know the next bit?"

I stared at the words, mouthing them out silently. "Between here and there . . . I don't know that word."

"It's *twinned,*" she said. "It shall sit between here and there, between twinned spirits."

"Between . . . connected?"

"Close. *Joined* is better. Joined locations. *Locales* is the literal." She took a deep breath. "A nexus, a place where those powers shall be joined. Between here and there, between spirits twinned, between locales joined."

"Joined," I said, my eyes flicking to the prophecy. My heart began beating faster.

"That was my thought, yes," she said quietly.

My heart beat faster. "What is this book?"

She closed it and ran her finger along the title that was embossed into the front cover. *Pasakos Apie Prižiūrėtojus ir Statybininkus.*

"The Tales of the Keepers and the Builders," I said quietly. Aron giggled softly. "How do you know this?"

"Mesla loaned me a copy once. I'm an avid reader."

"What's it about?"

"It's a fairy tale, Daniel. A collection of them. Written for children. This one is about a man and a woman whose love for each other is greater than any power in the world. Destined to be together from birth, if not before. But they're separated, kept apart by some great evil. But it's prophesied that they will be reunited in some special, secret place. A nexus."

"Does it happen?" I whispered.

"It does, but it makes the story sadder. They sacrifice something for each other. Doing so bonds their spirits."

"Doesn't sound like a fairy tale to me," Aron cooed, rocking toe to heel, his eyes pointed up at the domed ceiling. Then his eyes dropped to the first book, still opened to the prophecy. He ran his finger along the lines as he read them. "Is this about me?"

"We think so," I said heavily.

"No, no, no," he said in his singsong voice. He wandered away from the table, running his hand along the spines of books on the shelves. "I don't think I'm up for that. Or is it down? Perhaps sideways, hmm."

"Debesi, if our families wrote this . . . " I said, ignoring Aron and looking into her eyes.

"There's another story in here," she said, tapping the cover. "A story of a child who was lost in the woods and separated from his family. He was adopted by another and stayed with them for many years. His adopted family wound up doing business with his birth family, and that's when they discovered his true parentage. He was reunited, and they all lived happily ever after."

"Happily ever after!" Aron chirped. He continued walking the perimeter of the room, running a finger over the book spines.

"If the Fifth Axis was the one that was lost in the woods," I said, trying to make the story make sense.

"Then it needed to be taken up by another family before it could return to its own," Debesi finished. "Daniel, there are copies of this book in half the homes of witchkind. Keepers and Builders were just names, though."

"No they weren't," I said evenly. "Statybininkai and Laikytojai. Builders and Keepers. Those were the names of our family branches. From the time of the Exodus."

"But the Exodus is just a—" Debesi stopped, her mouth open but refusing to form the last words.

"Fairy tales!" Aron cried from across the room. "My voices tell me all kinds of them. I like the ones with happy endings."

"The Exodus wasn't just a story," I told her. "Have you heard of *Prisiminimų Saugotojas*?"

"Keeper of Memories. Yes, it's a very old magic. You run across it in some of the oldest histories. It was a credential. When someone proclaimed themselves a Keeper of Memories, you knew you could trust what they'd written. That it was accurate."

"I spoke with one."

"Impossible."

"It was this morning, Debesi. Early." Had it really been that recently?

"Where?"

"Witchhold. Clan Karal locked him up when they thought

they didn't need him anymore. His memories go back to the Exodus."

"You can't possibly think—"

"My Axis's Form of Mind, Debesi. I can sense lies when I use it. He was telling the absolute truth."

She blinked at me for several moments. Aron continued wandering around the room, humming softly and off-key. "So the Exodus was real."

"Yes."

"The Keepers and Builders."

"Were real. Were my family."

"This is incredible."

"You're the one who believed in the Origin," I pointed out.

"You've pretty much proven its existence," she countered.

Our attention slowly returned to the book lying on the table. "So this book was their plan?" I asked.

Debesi shrugged. "Or a retelling of it. Or maybe nothing. But you have to admit, it's awfully specific to our situation: a nexus where twinned souls meet in a place of joined locales."

"But what do we do with it?"

"We could dance." I jumped at Aron's voice so close behind me. His expression was serious now, all the mad humor vanished. He took a step closer and embraced me.

My Axis flooded my body then, pulsing warm and strong inside me. I gasped with the shock of it as Aron's embrace continued.

I felt . . . I didn't know what I felt. Pleasant. This was . . . pleasurable, even. But distant. The feeling wasn't coming from me. Was it? "Aron, I—"

"Hush," Debesi whispered behind me. "It's his Axis, Daniel. And yours. Can you feel the Sixth? Right now?"

"Very much so," I said, forcing myself to relax into Aron's

embrace. It felt . . . right. I wrapped my arms around him, and my Axis swooned inside me.

"This is the closest they've been, physically, in centuries," Debesi said, her whisper even softer. "Beginnings and Endings."

"The Origin," I whispered back.

"But still in two bodies," Aron said, breaking his hold and pushing me back again. "Or is it three?" He looked over my shoulder at Debesi, his forehead wrinkling. "Nope!" he decided, his face once again filling with madness. "Just the two. Still a problem. A problem for a puppet!" he finished in a singsong voice.

"What do you mean, a puppet?" I asked.

"Me!" His face lit up in delight. "I'm the puppet! Puppet on a string, do what the elders say. Storms here, earthquakes there, Create this, Begin that. Dancing, dancing on my strings!" He giggled again, and this time it felt unhinged.

My Axis spun slowly away, leaving a morose taste of dejection in my mouth.

"But they'll be ever so disappointed, won't they?" Aron asked, gently punching me in the chest. "I hate them, you know," he continued, his voice and expression shifting like quicksilver into heartfelt anger. "Hate them for Mother. Hate them for me." His expression softened. "Hate them for you." He turned away, once again scanning the room as if looking for something in particular. "I've ruined them, you know."

"Ruined who?"

"The elders. The whole clan. Mother and I are clanless now, you know. So I've ruined them. Pergalės!" he yipped. "They'll call them nesėkmės, now! Neturtingas!"

Failures. Destitute. "How? What have you done?"

"All of their businesses, their precious precious businesses, will all fail. I've Begun a series of events that will devastate them."

"But . . . if it ruins their businesses, isn't that an Ending?"

He turned back to me, cupping my face in his hands, his eyes wide with joy. "Beginnings and Endings, same thing!" He released me and spun a tight pirouette, coming to a rest facing away from me, once again scanning the room.

"He's going," Debesi said in a low voice behind me. She'd stepped closer. "His mind. He wasn't Chosen for this, and it's breaking him."

"We're all going, Debesi. We're all breaking," I replied. "It's just happening to him sooner."

"What do you mean?"

I turned back to her. "My Axis doesn't think magic will survive the night." Her eyes widened. "The twin moons will rise, and it doesn't think it will see them again after."

"Beginnings and Endings, same thing," Aron chanted.

"But they're not!" I shouted, suddenly overcome. "They should be the same thing, but we've chained them! Chained them, and we can't both exist! " Another sob closed my throat, and I felt more hot tears running down my face. "I can't stop being what I am. I don't want to. I can fix it. I have to."

Debesi took my shoulders and turned me around. She kept her hands on them, standing right behind me. She felt like a cool solidity at my back.

Aron stepped up, running a finger down one of my cheeks again. "We can be together, you know."

I shook my head, the tears coming faster.

"My mind isn't holding well. I know that." His voice was lucid and calm again as he lifted a finger to stroke my other cheek. "I think you should do it."

Then everything faded.

<hr>

I was floating in a warm, inky blankness, the gentle, relaxed sound of my own heartbeat beating softly in my ears.

Around me swirled two long, glowing ribbons, one a bright, scintillating black and the other a deep, sultry white. They were twirling, spinning, and flowing around me in a complex dance. Whenever one came close to the other, they both shone a dazzling, luminous gray at the point of almost-union. But they never touched.

This void was suffused with the joy of reunion—of being so close again after so long. I watched them for a brief, fleeting eternity, marveling at the grace of their dance, awestruck at how they managed to intertwine yet never make contact.

My left arm jerked slightly—the black ribbon was tied to my wrist in a complex, convoluted knot. It hindered the ribbon only a little, and I smiled as they played, twisting and bending, curving and spiraling.

But then the distance between them yawned. One of the ribbons, the one of creamy alabaster, was pulling away.

My awareness expanded. Far off, in the velvety darkness in which I floated, were points of light. Orange, umber, blue, and teal motes were scattered everywhere, like stars in the sky, and I floated among them. Tinier sparks of gold, far more numerous, were scattered here and there between the larger, more colorful specks. The white ribbon seemed drawn to these points of light, curious about them.

The black ribbon tugged on my wrist again, harder now, more insistent.

I didn't want the white ribbon to leave. I could be its companion now, and the two ribbons could continue frolicking, and we could be together.

Panic struck me, and I grabbed for the white ribbon with my left hand, only to clutch emptiness.

Would you keep it?

Dedicant Ormand's words.

It would be less dangerous if I did. If I even could.

Are you certain?

No.

I grabbed at the white ribbon again and again missed as it twirled out of reach.

Agony. Ache. Burning fever, spams of jerking strain. Torment.

Torn.

Sundered.

I clenched my jaw and thrust my hand into the empty void around me, reaching not for the white ribbon this time but for where it was not.

My hand closed on a fistful of silky white.

My world exploded into a billion shining stars.

The white ribbon knotted itself firmly around my left wrist, and the two ribbons resumed their teasing, interlocking play. But this time they didn't struggle to remain distant: they danced closer and closer, one shimmying against the other, patches of glittering gray appearing here and there.

And then everything—everything—imploded into One.

I was falling backward. Debesi, unprepared to take my weight, was falling behind me. She would land on her back, and I would land on her. In front of me, Aron was falling as well, his arms spreading loosely away from his body as he fell.

Almost without a thought, I righted Debesi and myself, Ending our fall and Beginning a new, firmer stance on the floor. Aron jerked upright as well, his head lolling forward. But he didn't regain his balance as we had. Before his body had even come fully upright, he began collapsing again, falling to the floor in a tangle of limbs, a puppet with his strings cut.

"Aron!" I cried, running to him and kneeling by his side. Debesi was only two steps behind me, and she knelt next to him as well. I shook him. "Aron!" His body was limp. I shook again. "ARON!" His eyes were closed, his lips parted slightly.

"Daniel," Debesi said, putting her hands over mine. "Stop. He's gone. His air has left him."

I stared in shock. "He—" My throat closed and I couldn't finish.

"He stepped down," she said softly, her voice gentler than I'd ever heard it. "He Began a new life . . . elsewhere."

Emotion, too much of it and all raw, boiled up inside me. I opened my mouth to scream, but nothing came out. I knelt there, gaping like a fish and choking on my own breath, until Debesi stood, pulling me up with her.

"The Fifth Axis, Daniel," she said. "What of it?"

Ribbons of white and black, playing and twisting around me. "I have it," I managed, my eyes hot and wet. I looked at her. "I have them both."

Her eyes widened. "The Origin, then? You—"

My vision filled with gray light.

I was now floating inside a dazzling gray sphere shot through with loops of white and black. Beyond the walls of the sphere, I could make out all those glowing, multicolored points of light.

Healed. A voice, rich and sonorous, both high and low pitched, filled my mind. *United.*

"Magic is saved?" I asked desperately.

Sad resignation tinged the sphere. *Broken still.*

The darkness beyond the sphere grew lighter and lighter

until I could see the entire world spread out before me. It was like a gigantic version of my map table, only somehow more real, more detailed, more immediate.

Pools of white lay thickly here and there, clustered around the larger towns and villages. *Pure magic*, the Origin's voice told me. *Look closer.*

I did and saw a tissue-thin layer of magic. It once covered the world, I knew, and it was filled with thin, swirling threads of color. But the tissue had torn. Large sections of the world were now uncovered, and although the contours of the land looked sharper, they also looked dingier—both more real and less real at the same time.

Heal, the voice said softly.

I inhaled sharply as the family archive reappeared around me.

"Daniel?" Debesi said with concern.

I gasped. "It's not . . . it's still broken." I turned to the table, rudely pushing Debesi aside, and began flipping through the books, moving quickly from one to the other, showing the pages poor treatment in my haste. "Here," I said, pointing to a rune construct. It was a complex structure, full of precise, inter-locking lines and delicately rendered symbols.

"This is Old Runic," Debesi said, confusion on her face. "I don't understand."

"Could you empower this? Right now, if you had to? Assuming your Axis was working?"

"I . . . no. I don't think anyone could."

"Why not?" I already knew the answer.

"There's not enough magic in the world. Nobody could Gather this much. Even with the Axis, this is too much."

"But people could, back then."

She eyed me curiously. "What are you getting at?"

"What has changed?"

She sighed. "The Axes, of course. You needn't convince me. The world's power is now bound up in . . . us. Adherents"

"And it isn't healing."

"What do you mean by that?"

"I'm . . . " I paused, struggling to form a cohesive explanation. Then I shrugged and decided just to blurt out whatever I could. There was no time for precision. "I hold both Axes now. Fifth and Sixth. The Origin. That's what the Origin is. But it's not enough anymore. Magic was pushed too far. Pure magic is welling up, pooling in places, but the Origin . . . I don't know how to describe it. The magic witchkind uses, the power that's been gentled, it—"

"Gentled?"

"That's how it described it. I don't know, this just happened. It's gone too far. Ordinary magic is torn. There are areas with no magic now. There was a cycle. A balance. It's disrupted, and I can't get it back." I paused and looked deeply into her eyes. The Fifth wasn't the only Axis in chains.

"You don't have to convince me," she said quietly.

I bent down and picked up Aron's body, cradling him in my arms. "I know. I need to convince them. But first . . . Aron had a mother."

CHAPTER 22

News

I took myself, still holding Aron, to the tree he'd made. Gemma was sitting outside, perched on one of its massive roots. She looked up as I appeared, her face falling as she saw my burden.

"I'm sorry," I said softly as I knelt and laid her son's body on the soft, fragrant grass.

"How?" she asked, a catch in her throat. She knelt next to Aron and ran a hand over his face, closing his eyelids.

"I'm not certain," I said truthfully. "He knew we couldn't both exist. He told me to—" I stopped as my throat grew tight.

"Your Axes," she said, nodding slowly as she looked at him. "They weren't supposed to be separate. You said—" her voice caught again as the tears began rolling down her cheeks. Her chest began to heave as a low, in articulate moan slipped through her lips.

"Gemma," I said softly. She didn't look up. "Gemma, he's not gone. Not . . . entirely."

She looked up at that, her face wet and her eyes reddening.

"It . . . the Fifth, I mean. It's in me now. In a way, so is Aron. I felt . . . it's hard to describe."

Another sob forced its way out of her. "You hold them both now?" I nodded. "And he's with you?" Her eyes begged for it to be true.

"I feel as if he is." And there *was* something more in me. Something distinct, yet whole. A feeling that wasn't of me, but was still me. "They weren't two separate things, Beginnings and Endings. The Archons didn't understand. They wrenched them apart. But the Fifth and Sixth—they're the Origin, Gemma. The elemental Axes are limbs of the Origin, their center."

"And that's . . . in you, now?"

"Yes."

"So is magic fixed?"

I sighed. "There was too much damage done when the Fifth was Forged."

She stared, and I could almost sense her mind working through it. "It isn't enough," she said softly, her eyes welling up again.

I shook my head, my own eyes beginning to tear up.

"So then . . . the other adherents?"

I nodded, my shoulders sagging on what felt like an incalculable weight. "I think so. I'm sure. Yes."

She swallowed heavily. "All of them?"

"Yes."

"Will they . . . I mean, will you have to. . ."

Would I? Would any of them—would *all* of them—lay their power down voluntarily? Would they save me from this? "I'm not sure. I'm going to see them next."

She looked back at Aron. "I can't bury him."

"Is that your clan's way?"

She nodded sadly. "It was. I know it's unusual for witchkind, following the human tradition."

"I can take care of it for you. Here, if you want."

She was quiet for a moment. "Everyone else uses magefire."

"Everyone I've known."

"They're not my clan anymore. Weren't his." She stood, resolve settling into her expression as she looked up at me. "Use magefire." Her eyes were wet, I realized, but she wasn't crying. I wondered how long she'd been preparing herself for this moment.

"I . . . ah . . ." I stammered.

A ghost of a smile skittered across her face. "You don't know how, do you?"

"I don't. With my Axis—"

"Do it your way," she said softly. "You and he were connected. It's right to do it your way."

I looked down at Aron, who looked peaceful for the first time since I'd met him. Sane. I reached for the—no, not the Axis. The Origin. It's two sides, Beginnings and Endings. *The End of his body and the Beginning of whatever is next for him. For all of us.*

Aron's remains sublimated into a cool, pale mist. It swirled around Gemma and me for the briefest of moments before rising into the air and vanishing.

We watched it go and then stood there silently for a long while. "Where will you go now?" I asked, hesitant to break the silence but growing increasingly anxious about what I needed to do next.

"I'll stay here, I think."

"With him gone and with what has to happen, I don't know—"

"If it will remain? It's fine," she said with a small shake of her head. "I should have enough magic to get to somewhere. Have you seen it?"

"Seen what?"

"The tree," she said, turning and taking the few steps back to its massive trunk. She looked up and pointed to one of the lower branches. I joined her and looked closely. The leaves were changing. They faded from a brilliant green to orange yellow and back again. "It's been doing this for the last hour or so."

"Our Axes being joined."

She nodded. "I expect so." She turned back to me. "I know you have to go. I'm sorry for what happened."

"I'm sorry about Aron," I replied.

She wrapped her arms around herself, the tears finally starting to trickle down her face. She nodded once, and I took myself to my Tower.

CHAPTER 23

Conclave

I went directly to the Tower's seventh upper level. There was no easy way to summon the senior adherents. Debesi could, and usually did, listen for her name on the wind, but the others had no far-reaching, easily accessed Form of Communication. "Debesi," I whispered, and within seconds, she joined me.

The others I could irritate into paying attention.

More precisely, I could temporarily and lightly interrupt their respective dominions. I'd done so once before when I'd called them together to join me in stopping Clan Karal—a request they'd all roundly declined.

I stood in the circle carved into the floor, Debesi several steps away from me. I concentrated, closing my eyes as I drew upon the Axis of Earth.

Outside, a tall pillar of rock erupted from the ocean, pushing itself into the sky. Mesla would sense this, I knew.

I moved on, focusing on the Axis of Sea.

A wall of seawater leaped upward, forming itself into a tall column. Water poured from the top and down the outside and was refreshed by a constant stream of water that rose in the hollow of the column. Marten would feel this.

Last, I drew upon the Axis of Flame.

A tall gout of fire burst from the sky, rushing down and hissing where it met the ocean's surface. Zmogus would know this was me.

All three elemental obelisks surrounded the Tower, equidistant from one another, and I waited for the adherents to arrive.

Zmogus was first, appearing next to me, opposite Debesi, in a flash of orange flame. I felt Marten's arrival next, and I had the Origin conjure a splash of seawater in front of me. All seawater in the world was as one, and Marten's form emerged from it, a quizzical look on his face. My use of their power was an implicit invitation. Mesla was the last to arrive, rising behind me from the stone floor on which we stood.

I released their powers, and outside the three monoliths collapsed into the ocean.

"Welcome again," I said calmly, turning slowly to meet each one's eyes and exchange a small nod. "I've learned much, and I want to share it with you."

"You've found a solution?" Mesla asked.

"In a fashion."

"You've brought that boy under control?" Zmogus snarled.

I whipped around to confront him. "That boy," I snarled back, "sacrificed himself in an attempt to save us all. I wonder if you will do so much when you are asked."

"Sacrificed?" Marten asked with a frown. "What do you—"

"Aron, adherent of the Fifth Axis, relinquished his power," Debesi said. "I was there."

"So the Fifth is free again?" Mesla asked.

"Or has it Chosen another?" Marten asked.

"Both. Neither," I said. "You've all heard me say that Beginnings and Endings were two sides of the same coin. I was wrong. They were one thing, one *living* thing before the Forging. For centuries, Beginnings remained free, and that provided enough balance for magic to continue working in the world. The Forging of the Fifth chained what the Archons could not."

"So the boy did cause this," Zmogus snapped.

"Shut up," I said calmly. His eyes flashed, but I continued before he could speak. "Aron did not. The elders of his clan did. Elder, actually. One angry old man with designs to rule the world, using power stolen from humans in a monstrous process that, if you will recall, I begged you to help me stop. You all declined, so Karal was able to harvest sufficient power to bind the power of Beginnings into the Fifth Axis. *That* is what caused this—and you all had a hand in it." I turned slowly, meeting their gazes one by one. "In your case, Marten, your predecessor made the poor decision to ignore me."

"You—" Zmogus began in an angry voice.

"Beginnings and Endings are one again," I said, raising my own voice to drown him out. "I hold them, and now the Fifth and Sixth are gone. What remains is their union: the Origin."

Four sets of eyes looked about, then skewered me.

"Daniel," Mesla said carefully in a soft voice, "what are you saying?"

I turned to her. "I am saying that the Origin, what we have always called the source of magic, is real. It consisted of the powers of Life and Death, Beginnings and Endings, Creation and Destruction. Not two sides, but an endless circle. One thing. The same thing."

"And now you . . . what?" Zmogus said. He kept his tone low, but the eternal growl in his voice remained.

"I hold the Origin, just as I once held the Sixth Axis."

"But our problems are not solved," Debesi said sadly.

"They are not," I confirmed, nodding to her. "The Forging of the Fifth broke the delicate flow of magic in the world. The magic that ordinary witchkind can actually use is running out. By this time tomorrow, it will be gone."

Mesla protested, "But if you hold the Origin—"

"The Origin doesn't produce magic," I said, shaking my head. "Not exactly. The world is still full of magic, but it is too pure—too untamed for witchkind to touch, let alone to use. We have always relied on the elemental powers, which were once part of the Origin, to gentle magic. To tame it. To give it . . . Debesi, what was the word you used?"

"*Lygiavimas.*"

"Affinity," I agreed. "But when the Fifth was Forged, more was broken than the connection between Beginnings and Endings. It severed the connection between Beginnings and all of your Axes, all of your elemental powers. Although I've been able to reunite the Fifth and Sixth, your Axes remain apart. Now pure, untouchable magic is pooling everywhere, and none of us can use it. Not in any meaningful way."

"I see where this is going," Zmogus sneered, and I turned, regarding him coolly. "You want all of our powers. You say you've leashed the Fifth—"

A cascade of flower petals rained down around his head, all of them withering into brown dust by the time they hit the floor. "Beginnings and Endings," I said quietly. "But even the Origin's power is limited without its hands. Its limbs. Your Axes."

"Daniel, you can't be serious," Mesla said in disbelief. "What would you have us do? We may be senior among our adherents, but we cannot simply hand you the leash to our Axes!"

"So that you can hold them all, especially! That, I will not stand for!" Zmogus yelled.

"I realize that," I said to Mesla, ignoring Zmogus's bluster. "That is why all of you and every other adherent must step down. All at once before more can be Chosen."

"So that you would then hold all the Axes?" Marten said quietly.

"No." I shook my head. "No, I would as well. I must. *All* adherents must. To free the Axes. To return them to the Origin." I realized that I meant it. As hard as I'd held to the idea of being an adherent, maybe *this* is what my family meant for me.

No.

This is what I meant for myself.

Aron had seen the truth of it and laid down his power. I could do the same. We all could.

Zmogus, of course, broke the silence. "So that magic can run amok again? Sow chaos and discord as it did before the Forging?"

"That never happened," I said with a sigh. "That was a lie. A justification given to everyone by the Archons. They simply wanted the power for themselves and to further their families."

"I believe he's right," Debesi said.

Zmogus's anger flared at my surprise defender. "And so you would simply step down, Debesi? Let yourself go and counsel all of your adherents to do the same? You're the most numerous of us!"

"I would," she said softly. Her eyes were wet, and I watched a tear begin rolling slowly down one cheek. "But I cannot. I cannot bring myself to do it. And I know none of the others will." Both eyes were running now.

"Because no one sane would step down!" Zmogus cried.

I laughed. A harsh, angry laugh full of irony and pain. "No one sane," I repeated, chuckling as I shook my head. "No, you're right, Zmogus. Righter than you know." I met his eyes. "I couldn't either." He raised an eyebrow. "I couldn't. Couldn't just let it go. 'Don't cling too hard to power.' It's something a very wise man told me recently. But I can't. I can't just . . . let it go. At least, I couldn't. If power must be used, let it be used by those who most need whatever it can provide. I think I can do that. Give it all back to witchkind. Ordinary witchkind. All of them." Then I paused and looked sadly at Marten. "Gilioj did," I amended softly. "He was sane."

Marten nodded, but he didn't look convinced.

"So what are you asking, Daniel?" Mesla whispered.

"To give it up. Not to me. But to them. To your families. Your siblings. Your old neighbors."

"And if we don't?" Zmogus growled.

"Magic will die, Zmogus," I said, letting my voice grow cold. "I won't let that happen to them."

"And now we come to it. You think you can *take* our power?" Zmogus rumbled. His hands clenched into fists, and I felt him gathering the ragged edges of his Axis. I was taken aback by the power he managed. "You round us up, you extort us?" He spat. "You're no better than Pergalės and their Fifth-Forged whelp."

My stomach clenched. He was right, in a way. "Zmogus, you have to—"

"Tell me he's wrong, Daniel," Mesla interrupted, her voice low and dangerous. She started gathering her Axis to her, and I was surprised, too, by the depth and intensity of her power.

"This isn't right, Daniel," Marten said. The salty scent of

his Axis's magic filled my nose, again with a wholeness that I hadn't expected.

I sank into the Origin, its view of the world overlaying my own. Magic, tinged with the elemental influence of the Axes, was being pulled toward the Tower, siphoned from the bodies of witchkind—including the junior adherents. Many of them stumbled, not understanding why they were suddenly weak. "Do you not all see it?" I asked them, shaking my head again. "I can now. You're pulling more power. You're drawing it from your adherents. You're leaving them without so that you can have more. Though your Axes feel whole to you, your adherents are faltering. You're drawing all of it to you. Can't you understand your own greed?"

I shook my head, dismissing the vision as I cast the rune that turned the Tower's walls transparent, providing a panoramic view of the sea around us. That sea had grown beyond choppy: huge waves were crashing against the island's rocky shoreline. Balls of fire were raining down, splattering against the island's rocky spires, hissing into the cold, dark ocean. One of the tall spires broke, its tip crashing into the sea.

"Can't you see?" I demanded. "Your selfishness—it's written in the environment around us! All but Debesi," I added more softly, turning to look at her.

Tears flowed openly down her face. "I've always suspected you were right," she said, her voice wavering. "I won't stop this, but . . . I don't have the courage to confront it."

"Will you step down?"

She choked back a sob and shook her head. "I can't," she cried. "I know I should, but I can't. Forgive me. You'll have to be the strong one of us."

I nodded.

Each of us was an anchor, a means of tying down part of an Axis. But that anchoring part of us wasn't *us*. We weren't born with it; our roles as anchors were imposed upon us when our Axes Chose us.

I'd thought carefully about this. Maybe we didn't have to die. Maybe *we* could continue without the anchors that held the Axes to us.

The Book of Endings, near its very last page, contained a rune for the Ending of an Anchor. I'd seen it as a child but never understood what it was for, and the tiny, handwritten notes suggested it was an experiment, an idea. A notion, nothing more. But perhaps it was a way to end this without the worst.

I held the rune in my mind and empowered it with the Origin, but it wouldn't stay. In my mind, the rune smeared and twisted, falling apart under the Origin's shaking magic.

"What," Zmogus said, his tone low and dangerous, "was that?"

Debesi gave me another sad, resigned smile. "I'm sorry," she mouthed.

Our roles as anchors were too deeply embedded in us, then. Or perhaps the Origin simply didn't have enough cohesiveness for such a subtle Ending anymore.

The weather outside the Tower was getting worse, now raging loud enough that we could hear it through the solid stone walls. Fireballs fell thickly, interspersed with heavy rocks and boulders. The waves crashed hard enough to spray the Tower itself with seawater.

"Debesi, join us," Mesla shouted. "I don't know what madness has seized him, but together we can—"

The stone floor split open, and a person began clawing their way out of it. We all stared in horror, the elemental powers drawing back for a moment.

It was a woman, her face covered in grit and dirt. "Mesla," she said, her voice rough and raw.

"Tami?" Mesla whispered.

"Four died, Mesla! Something is attacking us! We need you!"

Tami's power faltered, and the Tower's floor dragged her in, the stone sealing up behind her as if nothing happened.

"What in the Origin's name—" Marten whispered.

"Daniel!" Mesla's eyes snapped back to mine. "What's happening?"

"I told you," I said sadly, shaking my head. "You're all pulling power, but there's not enough to go around. Not anymore. The Origin is disconnected from your Axes, and they from it. You're pulling from the youngest adherents. Draining their magic. Their lives."

Mesla stared at me.

"Debesi," Zmogus ordered, "draw on your Axis! Help us—"

"No," the adherent of Sky whispered. She clasped her hands behind her back.

The room grew hot as Zmogus began pouring the Axis of Flame's power into the air. The waves outside, empowered by Marten and the Axis of Sea, began smashing directly against the Tower.

"Stop," Mesla whispered, her eyes still locked on mine.

Zmogus's attack came first, a searing spear of flame that would have burned a hole directly through me. Almost without thought, I countered, Ending the flame, Ending the heat, and Creating a cool breeze. Mesla's volley followed an eyeblink later, the stone of the Tower's floor splitting open. I didn't even move as the Origin stitched the rock back together and Ended its trembling. Outside, a wave twice the Tower's height rose from the ocean, only to find its End as a cloud of dense, wet, salty mist.

"We can all counter each other," I reminded them as they

drew their Axes back for another try. "This is pointless. Look," I added, stretching my fingers toward them and unleashing the dark, rocky spikes that had been the Sixth Axis's Form of Attack.

Zmogus burned his spikes out of the air, and Marten's were smashed to the floor by a conjured burst of water.

"This is pointless," I repeated.

"Listen to him!" Debesi begged.

"Marten, please," Mesla begged.

The adherent of Sea turned to her. "Was that real?" he asked in a hoarse voice.

Mesla nodded, tears running down her face.

Marten looked back at me. "There's no other way?"

"It is a sacrifice we must all make," I said. "The Archons erred, and now we must all pay their price."

"You want sacrifice?" Zmogus roared. He thrust his fists upward, and a firestorm descended on the Tower. Even through the stone walls, we felt the heat. "I will gladly die if it means taking you with me!"

I shook my head, and the flames simply ceased to exist. "You're hastening your own defeat," I said wearily. "You're drawing it from the world, leaving places bare and empty.

Come tomorrow—for I will counter you until then—magic will be too thin to keep it up." I could see it in the Origin, the shape of the entire world, the places that had grown thin and gray from lack of magic. Patches of bright white, pure magic sparkled here and there. Witchkind couldn't touch them. "Remember the two junior adherents in your fortress? The ones who collapsed?"

His eyes widened, and I saw the first signs of doubt in them. "What would you have us do, then?" His voice was quiet now, softer than I'd ever heard.

Debesi spoke. "Even if we step down, few other adherents would."

Three heads nodded.

"Then Daniel must do it for us," she cried. "In the manner of the Sixth."

"*Never!*" Zmogus roared, his fury back in force. I felt the Axis of Sea rouse itself, but Marten wasn't giving it any orders. Debesi simply stood, tears running down her face. Mesla fell to her knees, staring at the floor.

I shook my head. "I'm sorry."

I was already standing in the prescribed circle, as I'd known it would—must—come to this. I drew the rune in my mind.

"*Aš sukviečiu demonų minias*," I whispered. "Every adherent in the world," I whispered to it. "Apprentice and ascended alike. Without exception." Cold tears ran down my face. This wasn't an End to the adherents individually. It was an End to *all* adherents. To the very Age of Adherents. A Beginning to magic being free again.

The power that the elemental Axes could not resist, could not even confront in any meaningful way. This was the power of Endings, the power of the new Beginning that would follow. The invocation of the circle of life itself, Creation and Destruction bound into a single, reunited imperative.

The Origin's power stretched out, quickly covering the entire world. But this wasn't the Demon Horde of Kirmin's story, wasn't the greatest regret she'd had during her time as adherent. This was something new, formed not of Endings but of the entire Origin: Endings and Beginnings both. Its mission was not to kill but to free. To End shackles. To Begin a release.

All across the continent, power spread in a gentle wave that coated the land. As it touched each adherent, I felt their connection to their Axis crumble, felt the extremities of each Axis coming loose. In ones and fives, the adherents of Flamefast were overtaken. My sense of the Axes themselves became stronger as they were freed: the misty salt of Sea, the sharp freshness of Air, the loamy solidity of Earth, the bright heat of Flame.

As each adherent's anchor fell away, so too fell each adherent. As their bodies released their Axes, they crumpled gently to the ground, like puppets whose strings had been cut. As they fell, I felt a release of tension from each.

The Horde's agents moved throughout the world with a sense of purpose free of malice. They were a cleansing fire, a refreshing wind, restoring something that had been stolen and wrongly bound centuries before.

The spirits of my predecessors trapped in the Foundation howled. I couldn't tell if that was good or bad. I sensed the Foundation itself fracture.

The Tower trembled.

The magic of the Beginnings-crowned *demonų minias* spread to the furthest corners of the world first: distant Bryssi and Lastpointe, Farreach in the south. Then it began creeping back, passing through Greensea and Rushford and Fyngershire and Withring. Little Bay, Hook, and Harbsmouth were next, along with a dozen tiny hamlets in between them. When it struck Evermore, my legs almost buckled as I felt the sudden Ending of a dozen adherents and the sudden Beginning of newly won freedom for their Axes. Farreach in the north, Lakewood, Wisding. The Great Schools: Thornwaith's, Disemstoke's, Duocastella's. Then Northsea, Soloton, and Chiton—adherents fell in each. Landshire, Taliesin, beleaguered Twynsits. Baythwaite and Sowsea. Carvendam. I swallowed heavily as my power closed in on me. Pease. Nworlons. Meadowside.

"I'm sorry," I whispered as the *demonų minias* returned home.

Debesi smiled again as she toppled to the hard, unyielding floor. Marten fell as well, an unexpected look of joy on his face. I heard Mesla crumple behind me. I endured the hatred and pain on Zmogus's face as he fell, his arms stretched toward me, his fingers alight with a power that flickered and died before my eyes.

The *demonų minias* wrapped me in their cool regard, and I gave a final, hard-earned sigh of relief.

CHAPTER 24

Axes and Origin

But I had forgotten something. Rather, I had never properly understood it: the same thing cannot End twice, unless it somehow Begins again in between.

I had moved past my own Ending three years prior when I accepted the mantle of the Sixth Axis and became its adherent.

I couldn't End again.

But I also couldn't remain in the world—the *demony minias* had been given strict orders. "Every adherent in the world," I had told it. "Without exception."

As my body ceased to function, my soul was gripped by the remains of the Tower's Foundation. I felt my fading consciousness being inexorably dragged into the cracked, glossy black stone. I felt a moment of horror and regret before resignation set in. I'd known this would happen.

The Fifth and Sixth Axes—the Origin—drifted away from me, freed from my grasp. As my mortal vision faded and a new kind of sight began, I could see the broken threads that had once connected the Sixth Axis to the Foundation. The Axis itself was no more, and so the Origin was unchained. A flood of relief passed through my spirit: I'd accomplished that much, at least.

I neared the Foundation, and I could hear the moaning, immortal souls of my predecessors. They were loud now, singing an eternal lament for their imprisonment.

My vision faded to gray as I sank.

Into the Origin.

It had returned to me, sweeping me within itself, protecting me from the Foundation. The magic of my soul—the personal power that made me *me*—suffused the Origin, becoming One with it. I would spend the rest of eternity here then, and not in the Foundation. Fine: one prison was as good as another. I relaxed into it, preparing my consciousness to dissipate and fade.

But it didn't.

A guide. The voice resonated through me, vibrating my awareness and my spirit. *An avatar, but not physical.*

What do you mean? I thought to it.

The universe blinked.

I was standing in a meadow. It was night, the twin moon bright overhead. The blue-green grass around me caught the glow, sending a dim version of it back into the sky. The flowers of the meadow glowed as well, shining in impossibly deep colors: indigo, crimson, amethyst, cobalt, jade, and more.

The voice spoke again, booming all around me, coming from everywhere and nowhere: "We used to have a form," it said slowly. "A corporeal presence. Not all could see it, not all could sense it, but it led us." It sighed a soft breeze that ruffled the grass and teased at my eyelashes. "But we have been broken too long to recall it. We require a new mind on which to center ourselves. To be a part of us, to guide us." The grass held still, and everything, even the air, seemed to freeze in place. Then, as if the world had exhaled, everything released, blowing softly once again. "We Choose you. If you will have us. There are works to do. Things to acknowledge. This will not be pleasant."

"I accept." It wasn't even a choice for me.

The meadow vanished, and I was back in a world of endless gray, swirled with threads of black and white. Beyond the gray mist, I could make out the world I'd known, see the entire continent at once. *A moment*, I said. *There's a wrong that needs righting.* I felt its assent and focused on the little island that held my Tower. I drove my awareness down, down, down—further than I'd ever realized possible—until I reached the Foundation.

I Ended it.

As it crumbled, the souls of my predecessors flew out, their low, mournful hymn briefly turning to a bright, hopeful anthem as they were finally allowed to pass entirely from the world.

I reached down and seized the magic of the Veil. I understood its true purpose at once: long ago, it had served as the barrier between this world and another, pierced by magic to allow passage from one to the next. It hadn't served that purpose for millennia. I gathered it to myself, feeding it directly from the Origin's power, ensuring it would continue to protect my people.

I felt a sense of warning and braced myself, drawing my awareness from the island as the Tower of Endings collapsed into the sea.

I reflected upon the placid waters. Nearly six hundred adherents had died, and I could feel each one's End. Marten, Debesi, Mesla, and hundreds of others I'd never met. I mourned them all, wishing that there had been another way. But the Archons' pride and greed came with a heavy price.

And now, there was work to be done.

I could see the former Axes, their colorful forms twisting

through the world, unsure what to do with themselves now that they were unchained. Free. I called to them, and they turned to me, curious and eager. I reminded them of what they once were: extensions of magic that met at the Origin, that extended from it into the world.

They flew back, flew into my hands, swirling around me in excitement.

I fit them back together. Sky to Earth to Sea to Flame. They shone brighter now, a four-armed cross in my hands. I set them down in the precise center of the Origin, and their arms blazed outward, touching all the world, which faded obediently back into view. Pure magic, glowing dully white, pooled deepest near the larger towns and villages. I could see the tattered remnants of the magic witchkind could use, a blanket eaten by moths with only tattered threads remaining.

And then I saw it: the true source of magic.

The pale-white glow of it fountained up from a thousand, a hundred thousand points in the world. They spilled that raw magic everywhere they were, everywhere they went. They magic's source.

The humans.

I sent the former Axes forward, driving them into the pools of alabaster power. The magic began taking on a slight tint: orange for Flame, indigo for Sky, emerald for Sea, and a deep umber for Earth. As they colored it, the magic thinned, spreading out from its pools to once again cover the world. And cover it, it did! Thicker and more intensely than ever before, coating the continent in a rich, generous blanket of elementally tinged magic.

New motes of light began flaring to life across the world: the people of witchkind, newly empowered for the first time in over four thousand years. They drank from the dense flow of magic, Gathering it into themselves more effortlessly than any alive had dared to dream. And still the magic flowed, replenishing itself at the fonts of humanity.

I swept my awareness across the continent, satisfied.

I could feel the iron in the world now. They were like its bones, threading everywhere in deeply buried seams. They conducted magic, kept it even in the world, and grounded it when it grew too strong in any one area. The humans had plundered those bones and brought far too much of it to the surface. I considered it carefully but saw nothing I could do to correct the situation. Witchkind and humans would have to figure it out themselves.

Something new caught my attention.

In the eastern corner of the Great Northern Wood, an ancient, sleepy magic untinged by elemental color shined its own pearlescent amber. It, to my surprise, held the tail of the Veil. There was a different magic there, one that had withstood the diminishing of magic throughout the world. I considered it for a long while—I wanted to learn of it—but decided to leave it be. Ikwity had demanded that much of me, and I'd made an oath. Until the woodwitches called, the Wood would stand alone.

With another quick glance, I saw a number of other good works I could undertake. Rivers that could be redirected, fields that could be made more fertile. I started to reach out to make the world better, when I felt resistance. I held for a moment and then relaxed. The Origin was right. I would not become the human god, staring down from the sky, casting down judgment, handling problems so that no one could ever learn or grow. I couldn't fix everything. I probably shouldn't fix *anything*.

I relaxed further, letting my consciousness dim and spread. The Origin surrounded me, and I felt a wash of hope. My connection to it strengthened, and the separation between our awarenesses thinned.

I was no longer alone.

In fact, as I concentrated—rather, as my concentration faded—I could feel the souls of the adherents around me. Every adherent that had ever lived, ever left their mark on the world, ever wielded the awesome power of the Axes. They weren't conscious, but their energies had become one with the world, one with the Origin. With me. I felt lighter as the crushing grief I'd forced myself to ignore was lifted. Yes, they were no longer part of the world, but they had been Chosen. They would persist differently than the rest.

As my consciousness began to fade, the company of those spirits gave me comfort.

The seas, calm and quiet, lapped against the shore.

The winds, cool and gentle, slipped through the trees.

The earth rumbled softly to itself.

A flame, kindled in a stove, burned with a bright, happy warmth.

A man of many decades closed his eyes with a final satisfied sigh.

A baby cried loud and lusty as it came into the world.

I closed my eyes.

Epilogue

The end? Yes, for my part of it at least. The—oh, I see. The End. *Yes, very funny.*

No, only you. As I've mentioned, not many can hear me as I am now.

You're welcome to share. I don't know how many people will believe you, though.

It does give one a unique perspective, sitting in the middle of it all, yes.

Oh, I'll be right here. You have your own story to live, and I'm quite interested to see how it goes.

Acknowledgments

I'd very much like to thank some of the folks who support me on my Patreon, at https://patreon.com/donjoneswrites. For a very low monthly donation, which helps offset the literally thousands of dollars that professional editing and cover design cost, these folks get every new chapter as I write them, along with print copies of every new novel I publish.

Greg Altman
Shelia Edwards
Shandra Stevenson

If you'd like to support independent publishing, please drop by and consider joining!

Characters and Pronunciations

ADHERENTS OF THE SIXTH

These are presented in order of their ascension.

- Galas (GAY-lass) End-Bringer
- Skriaudikas (skree-OWD-ih-cuss) the Abuser
- Plaktukas (PLACK-tuck-us)
- Vandens (VAN-dens)
- Gailest (GAYLE-est)
- Kirmin (CUR-min)
- Daniel (DAN-yell) Scratch

OTHER ADHERENTS

- Arun (air-OON) (Earth)
- Cyril (SEER-ill)
- Debesi (deh-BEZ-ee) (Sky)
- Essa (ESS-ah) (Earth)

- Gilioj (GILL-ee-ojh) (Sea)
- Lanna (LAH-na) (Sea)
- Mali (MAH-lee) (Sky)
- Mesla (MEZ-lah) (Earth)
- Mica (MY-kah) (Earth)
- Nuvilnijo (noo-VILN-ee-yo)
- Tomas (TOW-mahs) (Sky)
- Vėjas (VAY-jahz) (Sky)
- Zmogus (ZMO-gus) (Flame)

OTHERS OF NOTE

- Andreas (AHN-dray-us)
- Eršketis (AIRS-kit-iz)
- Gemma (JEM-ah)
- Garybion (gare-EE-bee-on)
- Ikwity (ICK-witty)
- Laikytojas (Lie-KEET-oh-ess)
- Roze (RAH-zay)
- Statybininkas (stat-ee-bin-IN-kuss)
- Stevas (STAY-vahs)
- Sylphis (SILL-fiss)

THE TRUE LANGUAGE

My real-world inspiration for the True Language is Lithuanian, mainly because, to American eyes, it's an exotic-looking language. Any language with that many diacriticals simply *has* to be magical. But I've taken some liberties with translations and even spellings in order to better fit my needs, so not every word of the True Language translates perfectly in real-world languages. Now, within the story itself, the characters have no concept of Lithuanian—to them, it's just their True Language. The story isn't set on Earth (there are two moons!), and it isn't in any time period we've ever known. As such, the True Language doesn't necessarily have the same pronunciation as Lithuanian. But if you'd like to sound out the words (mentally or aloud), find yourself a Lithuanian pronunciation guide on the internet and give it a whirl.

Below I've provided a few of the more common or notable words I've used, along with my heavily Americanized pronunciation of them. You'll note that I largely ignore any diacriticals, as English lacks them, and I'm using English phonemes for the letters—even though in some cases, actual Lithuanians assign different phonemes to these same letterforms (there's a good list at http://mylanguages.org/lithuanian_alphabet.php/). Regard the following pronunciations as only an approximate guide— from the lips of the characters, they'd be much more nuanced and lovely, I expect.

And hey—if you've already come up with pronunciations in your own mind, please keep using them!

- *driežai* — dree-ESS-aye
- *kavos* — KAH-voze
- *teisėjas* — tee-ISS-ee-us
- *ramunėlių* — ram-OON-el-you

If you're *truly* wondering, "Don, why Lithuanian when there are plenty of other languages with exciting diacritical marks?" then you simply must read *Clara Thorn, the witch that was found,* and its three sequels.

About the Author

Don Jones spent two decades writing tech books before he finally penned his first sci-fi novella, *A History of the Galactic War*. His well-reviewed novels now span fantasy and science fiction, with a focus on world building and relatable characters. He lives in Las Vegas.

Connect, get five (!) free novels and two collections of short stories, and learn about upcoming releases by joining the author newsletter at DonJones.com.

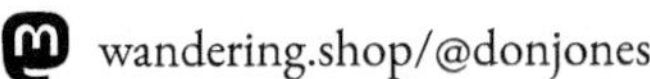 wandering.shop/@donjones

Also by Don Jones

Daniel Scratch, a story of witchkind®

Master of the Tower, a story of witchkind®

Clara Thorn, the witch that was found

Endless Sky®: Truthsayer

The Never: A Tale of Peter and the Fae

Free eBooks!

The Achillios Chronicles trilogy, *The Prime Wave Accounting* duology, and *short stories of witchkind* are all available **for free** by joining the author's newsletter at DonJones.com.

Clara Thorn, the witch that was found

FREE TWO-CHAPTER SAMPLE

Mrs. Hickling smiled as Clara laid the completed exam on her desk, and whispered, "Good for you!" Clara stood there as the teacher ran the answer sheet through the grading machine, and watched the older woman raise an eyebrow as the device spat out the sheet—marked with a zero, meaning no wrong answers. "*Really* good for you," Mrs. Hickling whispered. "That's it for the day. Why don't you head home early?" Clara packed her things and slipped out of the classroom.

Clara had practically run out of the school building, skipping happily down the worn, cracked concrete stairs in the front. Going home two hours early meant she'd avoid the usual teasing, bullying, and mean looks that often accompanied her walks home. It also meant she'd avoid the hordes of SUVs zooming in and out of the school parking lot, picking up the kids who were too good to ride the bus but lived too far away to walk.

The Las Vegas weather was just starting to turn hot as summer approached, but this particular afternoon was near perfect. Clara took the school's great stone staircase two at a time, and then looked back. The tall, deep-red building contrasted sharply with the bright blue sky, and for a moment, she felt out of place here all alone. The teasing, bullying, and name-calling of her schoolmates was so routine, so usual and predictable, that Clara could practically conduct it all without anyone else present.

It would start with Danica, who would remark—particularly after Clara had been dismissed early after a perfect Math score—on how nobody liked smart girls, or how Clara thought she was smarter than everyone else, or how Clara was such a smarty-pants, or whatever. Danica was terrible at math, and not all that great at anything other than making fun of other people. Clara refused to even try to understand how being smart was supposed to be bad. After almost a year in this school, Danica's comments—*Oh, you think you're so much smarter than everyone, Clara!* and *Nobody like smart girls, Clara!*—were pretty easy to filter out.

Thomas', less so. Thomas was one of the students picked up in a sleek black SUV—driven not by his mother, as was the case with most of the SUV crowd, but by an actual chauffeur. Clara had long wondered why Thomas was even *in* this school, as she supposed he lived in a much more affluent area of town, but she'd never worked up the courage to try and find out. Thomas' insults were personal, cutting, and *mean:* Clara was poor (which was true enough), she didn't deserve to go to this school (even though there was no other school nearby for her to switch to), she and her family lived on *charity* (which they didn't, and why would it have been a bad thing if they did?), Clara was short (true) and ugly.

Self-consciously, Clara ran a hand through her hair. It was a little frizzy today, but that was because she kept forgetting to use the conditioner Mom had bought her. She dropped her hand and shrugged. It wouldn't matter. Thomas was rich and Clara wasn't, and that was all that really counted in Thomas' mind. He was smart enough to never make overtly racial comments, but there were plenty of other ways to bring someone down. Clara tried not to care about what Thomas thought or said.

But she couldn't ignore his go-to comment: *You don't belong here.*

Daria was a basic bully. Clara took great pains to make it out of the building well before Daria, because on the few occasions the taller girl had caught her, Clara had wound up with black eyes, bruised cheeks, and, one time, a split lip. There was no reason for any of it: Clara had never said anything more than a polite "Hello" to Daria, but Daria had an intense need to exercise power over someone, and she'd chosen Clara to be her whipping girl. "She probably doesn't have a very pleasant home life," Dad had told Clara. "We've spoken to the principal about it," Mom had added.

"Still," Dad had finished with a small frown. "Might be best to steer clear of her."

Then there was the gaggle of better-than-you girls led by Samantha—"Sam," as her hangers-on were permitted to call her. They'd surround Clara, unleashing a litany of petty commentary: *Where'd you buy those shoes, Clara? A Dumpster?* or *Can't afford makeup, Clara? It'd sure help with than skin of yours!* or *How can your parents let you out of the house in that sad excuse for a shirt? Mine wouldn't even let me wear that to dig a hole!*

Clara would simply put her head down and push on, forcing the girls to follow her to the street corner, where they'd finally break off with a parting shot: "What makes you think you belong here?"

Belong. She'd tried so hard, this year, to fit in. She'd been polite. She couldn't exactly dress the part, not with the family living so close to the wire, but she'd *tried*. Mom had even helped, taking some of her own clothing and distressing it in exactly the way the other kids seemed to admire and pay so much money for. Dad had managed to give her cash to buy lunches at the school cafeteria, like almost everyone else, instead of bringing her lunch from home. She'd tried to join the popular activities and clubs. She'd tried to cheer on the football team at home games. She'd tried *so hard*. But it wasn't enough.

She'd found that most kids at most of her previous schools were pretty forgiving at first, willing to give the "new kid" a shot. But inevitably, most would draw away. That was the pattern: a few weeks of effort, followed by Clara ending up with a few bullies and no real friends. It was like she gave off a "weirdo" vibe, and eventually, everyone picked up on it.

So although she'd started this school just a month into the term, Clara had still made no real, long-term friends.

A new year, a new school had become Clara's mantra; no matter how bad each school was, Clara got through on the near-certainty that she'd never see any of these kids again after summer had passed. Although this year might be different: Mom and Dad had both said they fully intended for her to finish high school in this city, and Dad had even given up a high-paying job as a civil engineer to move them all here. He was in construction now, taking hourly work and overtime to make ends meet while he updated his credentials so that he could find a better job here in Vegas.

She groaned a bit as she fully realized that her tormentors could actually be a long-term thing this time. Samantha and company, Daria, Thomas... oh, right. The triplets.

Harriett, Idalia, and Johanna—youngest of *ten* children, they'd once mentioned in class. The others were all boys: Abraham, Benjamin, Carlton, Daniel, Edward, Franklin, and

Gerrold, according to a presentation they'd given for a genealogy project. The other kids had twittered at those names, but Clara had found the alphabetical names eminently practical: you'd always know who was oldest and who was youngest. The triplets had apparently been a surprise: their parents had been aiming for a nice, round eight and had gotten the girls instead.

It wasn't that the triplets were *mean*, Clara reflected. They were just so... aloof. They ignored most of the kids, but always seemed to have a special, intense, disapproving stare that they'd fire at Clara in tandem, piercing her with three identical, hard gazes. Without saying a word, they made her feel stupid in a way that Danica would doubtless appreciate, if she'd ever looked up from her phone long enough to notice. The triplets made Clara feel as lowly as Thomas tried to make her feel with his biting insults. They'd never once touched her, but Clara almost wished they *had,* because in their case, she suspected she'd make an exception to Mom's strict rule about never fighting. Clara longed to smack the condescension off of their pale faces.

Shaking her head to clear it, Clara turned right off the school steps and began the long march home. *Turning right* was what really set Clara apart from her classmates.

Turning right meant Clara wasn't headed to the affluent neighborhood to the south, nor was she headed for the pickup zone that was always packed with fancy SUVs. No, Clara was headed north, through a small commercial district.

She watched restaurants wrapping up their lunch service and preparing for the evening dinner rush. She saw bar doors were thrown open as the staff cleaned out the previous night's evidence. She caught glimpses of lawyers working in mid-rise concrete office blocks as they scurried back from late lunch—

KAW!

Clara stopped so quickly she had to windmill her arms to keep her balance. The loud, harsh call had come from an odd-looking bird, sitting right in the middle of the sidewalk and cocking its head back to look up at her.

KAW! it repeated.

It was a crow—or a raven? Clara wasn't sure what the difference was, completely black except for one bright white feather in its left wing. It fanned that wing now, as if waving to Clara. "Shoo," she told it, taking a step forward.

It cocked its head to one side, hopped backwards, and then took flight, aiming for a point just above Clara's head, forcing her to duck as its furiously flapping wings churned the air above her.

Clara hated birds. *Flying rats,* Dad called them. *Full of diseases. Keep your distance.* She looked back, up, and around, but caught no sight of the crow. *Weird.* She resumed her journey home.

There were no tree-lined streets here; everything was hard. The cracked asphalt gave way to concrete sidewalks, which ended at concrete, brick, or stucco walls. Alleys—filled with stinking garbage, puddles of oily water, and graffiti-covered walls—sliced blocks in half.

The transition back to residential neighborhoods was noticeable only because the homes here were single-story, in sharp contrast to the tall buildings of the commercial area. But there were still no tree-lined streets or grass yards: the people on this side of town couldn't afford the water bills that would come if they ran irrigators for trees or sprinklers for grass. The yards were hard—bare dirt, or, at best, rough gravel. The houses were simple, squat concrete boxes with almost-flat roofs, walls punctuated by creaking wooden doors and single-glazed windows. *Dam homes,* Dad had said when they'd moved in, built quickly and cheaply to house the families who'd moved here to work on the giant dam project an hour away. Ancient air conditioners squatted on the roofs, huffing and groaning to keep the homes' occupants tolerably cool in the advancing heat as summer began to take hold. Everything was faded, bleached to a light gray by decades of relentless sunlight.

The last herald of the commercial district was the small neighborhood market, a sturdy block building with wide windows. Hand-lettered signs advertised their key services: *EBT Accepted Here*, *You Buy It, We Fry It!*, and *Milk - Liquor - Wine*. A faded yellow Western Union sign hung lopsided on the glass door. An old man had plunked down on the dilapidated metal bench out front, huddling in the sliver of shade cast by the wooden eaves of the building's flat roof. He nodded politely at Clara as she passed, and she solemnly returned the gesture. The people on this side of town were polite to each other, but they didn't speak much. They were mostly older, their own children having found better fortunes elsewhere. They sat around now, watching the few passersby, staring at rickety televisions, waiting for life to come to its inevitable conclusion.

It was one of the cheapest places in town to live, and it was why Mom and Dad had moved here. And because it was "close" to the school, a solid forty-five–minute walk being well within Mom's definition of "close."

As Clara stepped up to the short stretch of crumbling concrete that connected the sidewalk to the front step, she noted that Dad's ancient Toyota pickup truck was missing. *The Blue Banger*, they'd named it, in honor of its cracked and fading paint job and the almost-regular backfiring *bangs* it would make. Its absence meant Dad was still at work, which was good: working as a day laborer in the construction business was like rolling a pair of dice every morning. But if he didn't have a job by lunchtime, he'd give up and come home for the day. He was anxiously awaiting the state's approval of his civil engineering license so that he could search for better employment, but apparently, there had been a hiccup in their conversations with the last state they'd lived in, delaying the process.

"Hello?" Clara called as she unlocked the front door's deadbolt and stepped inside. The worn floorboards creaked as she closed the door behind her. "Mom?"

"Back here, honey," Mom's voice called from the rear of the house.

The little building's layout was simple, essentially dividing the interior into four roughly equal squares. To Clara's left was the living room, and to the right, the kitchen and dining area. At the back of the house was Clara's room on the left and her parents' on the right, with a little bathroom squeezed in between them.

Mom popped out of Clara's room. As always, seeing her made Clara feel lighter and happier. Safer. Her dilapidated glasses sat slightly askew on her face, and she absentmindedly straightened them. Her close-cropped hair stood in stark contrast to Clara's own voluminous afro, although her dark eyes sparkled with the same interest and intelligence Clara had learned to recognize in her own. "I was just tidying up. Why are you home so early?" A look of concern briefly washed over her features; Clara coming home early from school had, unfortunately, been an all-too-regular feature of their lives, although it was usually preceded by a call from the principal, the police, or worse.

"Finished the Math final early," Clara said and watched Mom's shoulders relax. "Mrs. Hickling sent me home after she graded it."

"And?"

"One hundred percent!" Clara grinned.

"Oh, baby! Oh, I'm so proud." Mom walked to Clara and

gave her a warm hug. Clara immediately relaxed into the embrace, savoring it. "That's two down. What's tomorrow?"

Clara tensed a bit. "English, which will be fine. And History. Ugh."

"History's important, Clara." Clara's mother released her and stood back a bit, her hands on the girl's shoulders.

"I know, Mom. But Mr. Brant is a badly made animatronic. He's *boring*."

Mom's face grew stern as her hands fell to her sides. "You already expecting to fail?"

Clara shrugged. "I'll pass. But probably barely."

"I suppose I'll take what I can get at this point. Your test scores have been fine all year, though. Why the worry now?"

"Those were all multiple choice. The final is an essay." Clara gave her mother a quick up-and-down, realizing that she wasn't wearing an apron. "Did you have any jobs today?"

Mom had been taking jobs cleaning homes, picking up clients from Fiverr, TaskRabbit, and other "gig economy" websites. The money was okay, and it helped close the gap between their bills and Dad's income, but the work was tough. With only one car, Mom was forced to walk four blocks to a bus stop, lugging all of her cleaning supplies with her, and then spend an hour or more on the bus to reach her clients' homes.

"Not today. The Dickinsons cancelled, but they're doubling up next week to make up for it. I've got three tomorrow. Big ones, too; I'll be gone until dinner. If you're going to come home early again tomorrow, I'll leave a sandwich in the fridge."

"History, Mom. Essay."

"Oh, right. Sorry, babe." Mom offered her a tired smile. "I'll see if I can get Dad to pick up a chicken for dinner, then."

The family had long since decided that being able to buy cleaning supplies at Costco would save Mom a lot of money, and the store's $4.99 chickens were one of the least expensive and most filling meals they could get, more than justifying the membership fee. The Thorns ate a *lot* of Costco rotisserie chicken.

"Anything exciting happen aside from being a math whiz?"

"Teddy Burnett probably flunked Social Studies this morning. His phone rang right after Mr. Simpson passed out the papers. He got sent to the principal, and Mr. Simpson said he wouldn't get any extra time to do the exam."

"Yet another reason kids your age don't need phones," Mom teased.

Clara had longed for a smartphone since she was old enough to understand what they were, but the Thorns had never been able to afford one for her. Even Dad was using a cheap prepaid flip phone now, and even that was only so he could call around to potential job sites rather than having to drive to them all. Clara had stopped pestering her parents about it once she'd started to understand the family's financial situation.

"Although I guess it'll be harder for you to keep in touch with your friends once school's over?" Mom's voice was hopeful.

"No friends, Mom," Clara said with a sigh. Clara's lack of friends was a long-running concern in the family. With Mom and Dad, at least; Clara found that she didn't mind.

She gave Mom a hug and plopped onto the battered sofa that sat next to the door.

"I'm sorry, babe."

Guilt prickled in Clara's chest. She knew that all of the constant moving weighed heavily on Mom's mind. She forced a smile. "I don't mind. Honestly, nobody lives near here anyway, and it's not like I'm going to take the bus across town to have a playdate or something. I like helping you around here."

"But this'll be our first summer in one spot in a long time, Clara," Mom protested. "We thought you'd finally have a chance to make some friends."

"There are no other kids around here, Mom. I'm actually thinking about volunteering at one of the museums. They take summer docents if you're thirteen."

"Really?" Mom sounded hopeful but uncertain. "Well, that could be an interesting place to meet people. Which one? Natural History?"

"That's what I was thinking. Because, you know, *dinosaurs.*"

"Ha! True enough." The uncertainty seemed to have vanished. "Well, let me know what you need. I expect they'll want Dad and me to sign off on something."

"I will. Ms. Barrett suggested it and said she'd bring me a form tomorrow." Clara paused for a moment as Mom stepped into the kitchen. "How's Dad?"

Mom made a clucking noise with her tongue as she opened a cabinet. "He's good. He called about an hour ago; he's in a good spot today. Actually, a great spot. He's helping with a survey, which means he's making contacts with civil engineering firms. With any luck, one of them will have an opening once his license finally comes through."

"So we're... good?" Clara asked carefully.

"We're good, babe," Mom said lightly. Then she turned and met Clara's gaze through the kitchen doorway, and her eyes widened. "Honey, we're *fine.* I know this isn't as nice as the last place, but it's cozy, right? There's plenty of food. The roof doesn't leak. We've got the power bill covered. We're *good.* " Her eyes locked with Clara's. "Are *you* okay, babe? Truly okay?"

Clara's stomach knotted. She hated complaining about their situation, hated that her parents didn't think they were doing their best for her. It felt like Mom was constantly on the edge of apologizing. "Of course! It's not that stuff, Mom. I don't mind the house. Even school's fine. I just... I wanted to make sure we're not going to have to move again all of a sudden."

"Oh, babe." Mom walked over, leaned down, and cupped Clara's face in her hands. "No, we're not going to have to move again all of a sudden. I think this is the right town for us."

"I thought you hated it here."

Mom had been quietly opposed to the move here, but Dad had simply repeated, "You know this is what we have to do," until she gave in.

"Let's just say it's grown on me. And I'm really happy *you're* doing well." She paused for a moment. "You *are* doing well, aren't you? Not just school?"

It was Clara's turn to sigh. "I'm fine, Mom. I just... I know Dad gave up a good job, and... I guess I feel guilty that we had to move. Again."

Mom's voice was suddenly guarded. "Guilty? Why guilty, hon?"

They'd never spoken of it, but it had been eating at Clara as the school year wrapped up. The end of the school year always seemed to be when everything went wrong.

"Danny Davis," Clara said quietly.

"Babe, what happened to Danny and his family was tragic, but you can't possibly think—"

"Mom, he beat me up on the last day of summer vacation. He'd been teasing me and pushing me around all summer, and he finally hit me. And the very next day, their house burns down?"

"Clara, you can't—"

"And the town before that, Mom. Des Moines, up north. Last week of school, I got my first period, I was so stressed out, and there was that earthquake." It had shattered windows throughout the school, burst pipes in the girls' room, and set off car alarms for blocks. Clara still had nightmares about it.

"Do you seriously think you could have—"

"It's just *weird*, Mom. It's always in summer, it's always right after something bad happens to me, and we always have to leave."

"Hon, we came here *for this school.*" Mom's voice was firm now. This was ground she and Dad had been over many times, and she'd finally embraced it. At least in front of Clara. "Nothing bad is going to happen to you."

"Why *this* school?" Clara had never managed to get a straight answer.

"They're known for their Math program, for one, and we've known you were a whiz for a long time." The same answer they'd always given.

"Seriously, nobody taught math in the last place?" Clara had never pushed her parents on why the family moved each time, but it suddenly felt like the right time.

Mom's nose twitched as she considered Clara—a sure sign that she didn't have a good answer ready. "Not like the program here."

"But why couldn't we wait until Dad got a job?"

"He tried, sweetheart. But we'd already missed the enrollment deadline, and we were afraid if we waited any longer, you'd fall behind. You're important to us, Clara. Your education is the most important thing in the world." She offered her daughter a wry grin. "Granted, Dad didn't think it would take quite this long to get his state license sorted out, but it'll come through any day now, he says."

Clara stared at her mother for a long moment, sure there was still something she wasn't being told. "So we're staying."

"We're *staying,* Clara. Final answer. Even if—what's that girl's name? The one who bullied you?"

"*Bullies,* Mom. Present tense. Daria."

"Even if Daria beats you up and you break her nose, we're staying."

"Mom!"

Mom shrugged. "I'm not saying I want you to break her nose, Clara. I'm saying that nothing's budging us from this school. So you might as well start making some friends."

Clara flushed with embarrassment. "I try," she mumbled.

"I know. But look, I grew up an Army brat. We moved every two or three years. I know how hard it is. And I know how mean kids are at your age. But it's *safe,* baby. We won't yank you away again. Not until you're graduated, and at that point, you can move out and do whatever you want." Mom cocked her head and asked, "So you *sure* there's nobody?"

"Nobody?"

"Friends, I mean. Maybe... boys?"

"Mom!" Clara cried in horror. "Thirteen year-old boys are *gross.* They're not... *done* yet."

Mom laughed. "True enough, I suppose. Well, maybe this museum thing will be the perfect fit for you. You'll meet some other kids your age who aren't from your school. Maybe you'll hit it off with someone when you don't have all the school stuff going on around you all the time. Although..."

"What?"

"It's just that for someone so worked up about a History essay, you seem strangely eager to work at a history museum."

"Mom! It's not the same thing!"

"I'm teasing, sweetie. Although I do hope you'll maybe make a friend or two. Promise you'll try?"

"Maybe," Clara allowed.

Mom looked at Clara for a long moment, considering. "Tell you what," she said, glancing at the wall clock. "Dad won't be home for a few hours at least, and I think that perfect score in

Math deserves a celebration." She grinned. "And I happened to get a very nice tip from the Ainsleys yesterday. What do you say we walk up to the market and I buy you an ice cream?"

Clara's eyes lit up. Ice cream was her favorite treat, and she didn't get to indulge all that often.

"I'll take that as a yes." Mom winked. "Let me slip on my sneakers."

Clara stood and watched as her mother efficiently tucked her feet into her own battered shoes. It'd be another few months before they had the money for new shoes, Clara knew, and it's be a trip to the local—

KAW!

Clara's head snapped around as the loud birdcall sounded, seemingly just outside the living room window. "Did you hear that, Mom?"

Mom had stepped back into the kitchen to grab a set of house keys. "Hear what, hon?"

KAW!

"That. The crow, or whatever."

"No. But crows aren't that common here. You sure it wasn't a pigeon?" Mom's head was tilted to one side as she listened.

"Pigeons coo. This was a 'caw!'"

Mom shrugged. "I'm not hearing it. You ready to go?"

Clara suddenly felt chilly. "Yeah." A thought occurred to her. "Hey, would you walk to school with me tomorrow?"

Mom' raised an eyebrow at the odd request. "I think so. Can we go a little early? I can catch the bus on the block over, and tomorrow's folks all have their own equipment. I just need to carry my bag o' chemicals."

"Sure. I'll help carry, even."

"Then it's a deal. Mind if I ask why?" Mom accompanied Clara to school once or twice a month, telling her they needed "girl time" out of the house now and again, but she'd had more morning jobs recently that had made the timing difficult.

"No reason, I guess," Clara said, suddenly embarrassed. Was she eight, that she needed her mommy to walk her to school because there was a creepy bird outside? "Girl time? Maybe I'm nervous about History?"

"Little late for that, but I'll take it," Mom chuckled. "You sure that's all?"

It wasn't, but Clara couldn't explain it. So she simply nodded and said, "Yeah. That's all."

Mom gave her a curious look. "You *sure* that's all, baby?"

The chill spread to Clara's thoughts, which grew dark and burdened. This wasn't about History. Well, not entirely. She nodded slowly and forced a smile. "Yeah, that's all. C'mon, I'm ready for chocolate!"

It felt like a lie. But Clara couldn't tell the truth. Not when she didn't even know what the truth was.

THE ODD WALL

The English final wasn't so tough—Clara loved to read, and writing about something she'd read was almost a pleasure—but History was exactly as bad as she'd feared.

The assignment was a single sentence: "Describe your understanding of the causes and drivers of the American Revolutionary War." *Rich guys didn't want to pay taxes?* she thought. But she had three hours, and Mr. Brant would likely be expecting something more. The problem was... who *cared?* The war had happened over two hundred years ago, on the other side of the continent, and—like a lot of History, in Clara's opinion—was mainly about a bunch of middle-aged white guys. Why couldn't she write something about local history instead? She'd at least managed to pick some of that up, thanks to the many informative plaques scattered about the town's historic sites.

So she set in, her pen joining the soft *skritching* of the two dozen others in the room as she guided it across the lined sheets of paper they'd been provided. More than once she had to stop, to try to recollect the facts and stories they'd been told, and, before long, the end of her pen was thoroughly chewed. She finished with scant minutes to spare, took one last look at the paper she'd written—her handwriting had become pretty bad toward the end—and then trudged up to Mr. Brant's desk. She stood in line behind four other students to hand in her paper. Unlike Math, which was an easily scanned multiple-choice test, History would take a day or two to grade.

As she passed her paper to the teacher, he looked over his horn-rimmed glasses at her, one eyebrow raised in question. She shrugged, and his lips tightened a bit. "At least you're a good writer," he said with a small shake of his head. "That'll be worth something."

Clara left school feeling not at all reassured.

The afternoon ritual was almost exactly as she'd imagined it the day before: Danica teased her about probably flunking the History final (not impossible); Thomas commented how, poor as she was, college was out of the question for certain now (college had never been on her mind in the first place—how would Mom and Dad afford it?); and Sam's coterie critiqued her backpack, which just this morning had given up the ghost and separated from its shoulder straps. She'd been forced to carry it by the top handle, leaving Mom to lug her canvas tote full of pine-scented cleaning fluids. Daria, at least, was nowhere to be seen;

she'd stomped out angrily halfway through the English final and hadn't shown up for History.

Clara put her head down and plowed through Sam's chattering flock, who, as usual, abandoned her once she reached the street corner. *They* were turn-lefters, and they'd never dream of following her into the unattractive, bustling commercial district. She lifted her head long enough to check the crossing light, hustled across the street, and breathed a sigh of relief. She liked the commercial area this time of day: the brunch-and-lunch place would just be shutting down, with the last lingering smells of bacon wafting through its open windows. The barbershop was on its final few customers. The container park—a small shopping area built entirely from reclaimed steel shipping containers—was getting the first trickle of customers to its bars and shops. The neighborhood Irish pub was changing over to its dinner service, taking a much-needed break after—

KAW!

Clara stopped, whirling toward the harsh sound. There it was, perched atop a metal-tube bike rack that was bolted into the sidewalk, waving its odd wing at her. "What are you—"

Wait, was that the triplets?

Clara forgot the bird as she watched the three girls walking quickly past the neighborhood sushi place, past the smoothie shop, and past the windowless building that housed the telephone equipment for the entire area. They they ducked into the Art Alley.

She blinked, her mind failing to grasp the reality it had seen.

The triplets *never* walked. They certainly didn't turn right out of the school. And they absolutely never, ever, ever were the type to wind up in an *alley*, regardless of how many murals had been painted along its walls.

Clara's curiosity was overwhelming. She checked the light,

quickly crossed the street, waved to the sushi chef through the window, and looked into the alley.

It was empty.

The Art Alley was actually two distinct alleys that intersected to form a T. One ran east and west, connecting Sixth and Las Vegas Boulevard. The other ran north and south, from about the middle point of the east-west alley, all the way to Carson. Clara's parents had told her the city had created the alley in part to discourage homeless people from sleeping in it: it was well-lit at night, and numerous local graffiti artists had been invited to paint murals on the sides of the buildings.

Clara stepped slowly off Sixth and into the east-west alley, leaning left and right to see if the triplets had maybe ducked into one of the little niches that sat between the tightly spaced buildings.

Nothing.

A couple of the Fremont businesses had space back here, open patios that they'd recovered from former loading docks and such. But those were mostly walled-in, and the one gate— Clara tugged gently on it to be sure—was locked.

So where had the triplets gone?

She hadn't taken her eyes off of the alley entrance since they'd stepped into it, and they certainly hadn't had time to run all the way to the other end. She walked to the middle and looked down the north-south alley.

Still nothing.

There was no way the triplets could have moved that quickly, but all that was here was—

She whirled as something darted through her peripheral vision.

One of the most memorable elements in the alley was a statue of a woman. She sat on a sculpted rock, raised a few feet off the ground on a sturdy concrete pedestal. Her legs crossed at the ankles, and long hair flowed down over one shoulder. She was painted a brilliant metallic purple, and in her mind, Clara knew her as the Purple Lady.

But it was the mural behind the Purple Lady that had caught Clara's attention. It was an abstract blend of blues, teals, and purples, and Clara thought the painting most resembled a fantastic galaxy of some kind. White and red geometric shapes overlaid portions of it, making a striking backdrop for the statue.

But something on the wall had *moved*.

Clara took a step closer.

Was the wall... *wet?*

Another step took her within arm's reach, and the wall did indeed look... moist. She leaned in, and saw what seemed to be a glossy film covering the wall. But it wasn't running down from the top; it seemed to be staying in place. Wouldn't oil... drip, or something?

Another half step forward, and she leaned in, sniffing at the wall. Nothing.

She leaned back and regarded the wall again. It still seemed to—

There!

Another shadow zipped past, directly in front of her. It looked like a series of numbers, almost. She looked over her shoulder, back at the alley entrance, and again saw nothing that could have caused the shade.

She slowly turned her head back to the wall, waiting for another shadow to float by. Moments passed, and eventually one did. It was *definitely* numbers. Was this some kind of fancy art installation? Using a... screen, of some kind? Clara looked behind her, expecting to find a projector, but saw just another painted concrete wall. There was no telltale spot of light that would give away a concealed projector lens.

But where had the triplets gone?

Clara slowly extended one index finger toward the wall, intending to just brush the slightly gleaming surface. Slowly... slowly... slowly...

Her finger pushed through the wall.

Or rather, *into* it.

She yanked her hand back, clutching her finger in her other hand. It was complete dry, with—wait, was it *cooler?* She couldn't tell, as the sensation faded quickly in the afternoon heat.

The sounds of downtown Vegas faded away: the cars and trucks passing by outside, the clanking of nearby kitchen equipment, the *thup-thup-thup* of tourists in a helicopter overhead. All that was left was a *susshing* sound, a whispering of water twisting lazily through a brook. But there were no brooks here.

Clenching her jaw, Clara reach out toward the wall again, all five fingers on her right hand extended. Slowly... slowly... she watched her fingertips sink into the wall. She felt *nothing*, no sensation whatsoever. She pushed a bit further, almost to her wrist, and finally sensed something: a springy resistance of sorts, almost as if she'd contacted a sheet of rubber stretched across— what? The *inside* of the wall?

She took a half step forward and kept pushing. Wrist. Middle of her forearm. Almost to the elbow, and now the resistance was firmer, as if she'd stretched the sheet to its limit. Her fingertips were warm now, wherever they were on the other side of the wall.

Push, she thought.

Just as her elbow was vanishing inside the wall, the resistance *snapped.* She fell forward, through the wall, stumbling ahead and barely catching herself before she fell to her hands and knees. When she recovered her balance, she looked around...

...and found herself someplace else.

It was dimmer. The sun seemed well along its journey across the sky, settling into the deep, lazy orange of evening. The colors around her demanded attention, gleaming in intense, saturated colors: a deep emerald for the grass, a chocolatey brown for the dirt on the path. The tree trunks looked almost velvety in texture, and the leaves gleamed in a thousand intense shades of green. Color names from a long-past art class darted through her mind: olive. Viridian. Forest green. Sage. Olive. Persian. Reseda. Dartmouth. Lincoln. Kelly. Bottle. They were all there, mingled amongst the branches of the trees. And the *trees!* Each was a work of art, with sinuous, twisting trunks and branches that managed to jut out at wild, improbable angles and yet form an impossibly symmetric whole. High overhead, their branches wove together over the path, forming a long, gently winding tunnel.

Beyond the trees, glimpses of sky suggested heavens of the purest cerulean Clara had ever imagined, let alone seen. It was a blue so intense that it wanted to make her cry for its perfection.

She snatched her eyes away from that intense color when she heard a sound: a girl's voice, ahead of her on the path but too far for her to make out the words. The triplets! She hurried along. The air slid past her as she moved, offering the slightest hint of resistance, perhaps, but parting easily. She quickly came to the end of the tree tunnel, the beautiful wood thinning into a meadow. The road widened, and Clara saw the triplets off to one side, sitting in the long-bladed, brilliant grass. She backed into the tunnel, darted to one side of the path and behind a tree, and peeked out to watch the girls.

"I don't understand how we could have done so poorly in History," one of the girls was saying. Harriett, Clara suspected: the girls always wore a slightly different shade of hair ribbon each day, and she suspected those were how you were meant to tell them apart. Harriett—she thought—wore the darkest, Idalia the next-lightest, and Johanna the lightest. Today's ribbons had been red, but here—wherever *here* was—the colors had taken on a new vibrancy. Harriett was now the deep maroon, Idalia the cardinal, and Johanna the bright crimson.

"Because Brant is boring and we stopped caring after the second week," Idalia (perhaps?) grumbled.

"Mother and Father will *not* be pleased," Johanna (probably) pointed out.

The wind picked up a bit, blowing directly toward Clara and carrying the scent of cinnamon.

"Did you see Clara? She kept at it even longer than we did," Idalia said. That much was true: the triplets had stood as one and turned in their papers almost ten minutes before Clara had finally called it quits.

"I didn't see her on the way out," Johanna mused. "Usually she's out the door as fast as possible."

"With Dariel on her all the time, I'm not surprised," Idalia pointed out. "Remember when Dariel thought she could bully us?"

"Bound or not, we can at least stop *that* from happening," Harriett said with some satisfaction. "But I still think Clara is... *off*, somehow."

"Your eyes slide off her unless you focus," Idalia agreed.

"And even then, something just kind of... bores into you," Johanna said. "Is the wind picking up?"

It was, Clara realized. The gentle, cinnamon-perfumed breeze had shifted to a clove-scented bluster, whipping her unruly hair. She stood to move toward the triplets and found that the air seemed to have thickened as well. She could still breathe easily, but moving forward was like walking through syrup. She took a step backward and found herself not only unimpeded but *encouraged*, the air seeming to take her up on the offer to retreat and almost leaning on her to help make it happen.

A burst of blue-white light flashed and the triplets started, scrambling to their feet. "Professor Mycroft!" Harriett said.

Clara blinked hard, for there was indeed a fourth person on the side of the road. An older woman, with gray hair done up in a tight bun. She wore a long dress of deep gray, buttoned right up to her chin and almost brushing the ground at her feet, and she looked at the triplets with glinting eyes. Clara ducked further down behind the tree, hoping to remain out of sight.

"Girls!" the professor said, her voice cutting and urgent. "There's been a breach at the Border. Have you seen anything? Anyone?"

The girls, their attention focused on the older woman, shook their heads in unison. "We only just came through a few minutes ago," Idalia said. "We haven't seen anyone. They'd have passed us."

"If they stayed on the trail, yes," the professor said, rising on her toes a bit to look further down the road.

The wind had redoubled its efforts, now carrying a scent of rotting fruit and working itself up to a serious gale. The professor turned, looking down the road toward where Clara had come from, her eyes squinting against the waning sunlight.

"Professor!" Harriett shouted, and Clara's eyes snapped to where the girl was pointing. A shaggy dog of some kind was standing on the road past the girls, its head down and teeth bared, its eyes pointed toward the tree tunnel where Clara still hid. It growled ferociously.

"That's a kleinerwolf," Mycroft said evenly. "Get behind me, girls; I've got it."

The professor held her hands in front of her. She positioned herself between Clara and the creature, so Clara couldn't see exactly what happened, but a moment later, there was a flash of green light and a *yip-yip-yip* sound as the doglike animal bounded off the road and into the neighboring trees.

The wind was *really* working it now, and the air seemed to want to squeeze around Clara, pushing her back. She found herself sliding along the grass and back onto the path, her worn sneakers unable to find sufficient purchase to resist the driving wind.

"Professor!" a male voice shouted from behind her.

Clara turned, the wind still pushing her inch by inch along the road, and saw an older boy standing there. He was wearing a school uniform, like the kind she'd seen in movies, with a burgundy vest over a white shirt, gray trousers, and a lazily knotted gray necktie that streamed out behind him in the increasingly aggressive wind.

"Professor!" he shouted again. "Over here!"

Another growl managed to cut through the windstorm, this time from the side of the road and *much* closer to Clara. She turned, the wind almost fetching her up against the boy's legs, and saw another kleinerwolf hunched down. Its teeth were bared, its eyes glowed a sallow green—and it was looking directly at her.

"Christopher, *reicio!* Quickly!" Mycroft called. She sounded closer, but Clara was too terrified to turn toward her voice. "Girls, who is that?"

"It's Clara!" Johanna shouted over the howling wind.

The wind finally shoved Clara, still crouching, against the older boy's legs. She looked up and saw his hands stretched toward the snarling creature, his fingers twitching in a strange pattern. She blinked her eyes, which were so filled with tears and grit that she thought she saw glowing numbers flickering around Christopher's arms and hands. Then there was a flash, again like a bright-green strobe light, followed by a yelp from the wolf-creature.

"Not doing it, Professor!" Christopher called, his fingers again beginning to twitch in unison. Clara turned and saw the monster picking itself up. A matted line of grass showed where something had shoved it back, but it was once again focused on Clara and snarling fiercely.

"There's another!" Clara said, pointing. In fact there were two more, each stalking out of the tree line, heads low to the ground and teeth exposed.

"*Distineo!*" Mycroft shouted. Clara turned; the professor was suddenly just an arm's length away, one index finger pointing at the animals. Her fingertip was... glowing yellow? "That will only hold them for a moment, Christopher. It's the girl. She's not meant to be here." The professor turned her attention to Clara then, the fingers on her free hand flicking through a complex pattern. "*Perspeculor...* powers above and below, no, not meant to be here at all. You don't belong. Not yet, child. You'll need... well, a bit of work, but we've no time now. The land itself is against you. Christopher, get her back through the Border!"

With that, the older woman turned back to the wolf-creatures and shouted, "*Proturbo!*" Another flash of green light. "Christopher, go!"

Clara felt the boy grab her shirt collar and heave her halfway off the ground. "Sorry about this," he said, his voice remarkably calm. "*Iactus!*" he shouted as he hurled her back down the path. He must have been incredibly strong, because she found herself sliding rapidly along the dirt, directly toward a shimmering ring of light that she hadn't previously noticed. *This must be when I wake up,* a part of her mind calmly surmised.

But she didn't. She crashed into the circle of light—*Ouch!*—but didn't slide through.

Christopher cursed loudly.

Clara twisted on the ground. He charged toward her.

Professor Mycroft was still holding her ground, and Clara stared in horror at the half dozen kleinerwolves now stalking toward where the tree tunnel began. The animals seemed frozen to the spot, held in place by deep-gold halos, but their heads were unerringly tracking Clara. Six pairs of glowing eyes bored into her, and she could see their muscles tensed, ready to move the moment they were released.

"It'll be the membrane," the professor shouted. "You'll have to put her through yourself!"

"On it!" the boy hollered in reply. He skidded to a stop just next to Clara and knelt down. "Again, sorry." He offered her a quick smile, picked her up and shoved her through the glowing circle.

"Christopher!" Clara heard Mycroft shout, and then she was through.

She rolled onto the filthy asphalt of the alley and lay there for several minutes, breathing heavily. Her hands were shaking, her mind spinning. What had just happened? She focused on slowing her breathing, and as her heart slowed her mind followed.

Eventually, she pulled herself to her feet, staring at the colorful mural on the concrete wall. It still glistened as if it was wet, but she refused to touch it again.

What had just happened?

And what had that professor meant by... "Not yet?"